sifted

A RECIPE FOR LOVE SERIES

LANE MARTIN

SIFTED

By: Lane Martin

Cover design by Rebecca Pau, The Final Wrap

Editing & Formatting by Wendi Temporado, Ready, Set, Edit

Bash & June Bug drawn by Micheal Velasquez

ISBN-13: 978-1537783345

ISBN-10: 1537783343

For Ruby, you were a remarkable woman who I was blessed to have in my life. You will be forever in our hearts, Grandma Ru.

Ruby Loree Naylor

April 15, 1937 – January 9, 2016

Table of Contents

PROLOGUE

I had no destination in mind when I left the apartment.

"Where to, buddy?" the cabbie asked me as I slid into the back seat of the dirty cab. *Christ, what died in here?*

"I don't really know."

I just walked away from the best thing that has ever happened to me because my parents, or should I say, the people I thought were my parents, have been lying to me my entire life.

"OK. Well, I'm going to need an address because I don't think that will come up on my GPS."

Great, just what I need, a smartass cab driver.

"JFK," I said with a sigh. I knew I had to get away from her or I would never leave, and more than I needed her, I needed the truth. I was praying it would "set me free" so that we could begin our life together. I fingered the ring that hung around my neck. Until that night, getting it had been the surprise of my life.

"This was just delivered for you, boss," Monica said as she waddled into my office two days after Christmas. I couldn't help but imagine Emily round with our baby growing inside of her, and I rather liked the idea. I never thought I would want kids of my own. Let's face it, I didn't have the best childhood, but I knew with her things would be different. I knew without a doubt that our children would always know that they were loved. "It's from Cheryl Barnes, and it came registered." I had no idea what Emily's mom would be sending me, probably an unneeded thank you gift. Seeing her and my gorgeous girl together for Christmas was the best thank you I could have ever received.

Inside the box was an envelope and a small jewelry box. The envelope was addressed to "The One" in elegant cursive. Attached to the envelope was a Post-It note that said, "Declan, I was given this to hold when my mother passed away. I was told that I would know who to give it to. As usual, my mother was right. I knew the second I saw you with Emily that this was meant for you – Cheryl." I carefully opened the sealed envelope and pulled out a neatly-folded letter and began to read.

My Dear Boy –

I will never have the pleasure of knowing you, but I know that you exist and that you must be very special to have won the heart of our Emily.

Some may ask why I decided to leave this family heirloom with a stranger, hell they may even call me crazy, and secondly, they may wonder why it was meant for Emily's great love and not Libby's. I don't owe an answer to anyone but you. You see, Libby is a free spirit, she will love many, her heart will be broken, but she will love again, and when she finds the right man, she will love him with everything that she has. Now, our Emily is a swan. If she's yours it will be for a lifetime. Her loyalty knows no bounds. A swan is white, pure, a symbol of light, like my granddaughter. She is graceful and good. As a water bird, she is connected with emotions. She will see your inner beauty, maybe even when you don't. Love her and she will love you like no other. Like her, since you are reading this, I was lucky enough to find my "one". Henry gave me this ring as a symbol of our never ending love and now I'm giving it to you. Together again, Henry and I will be watching and smiling down on you both from above. Never forget to live every moment, laugh every day, and love beyond words.

Forever,
Grandma Rose

Holy crap, can this be happening? *With trembling hands, I put down the letter and opened the box. The ring was truly stunning and unique. Without a doubt, Emily would recognize it the moment she saw it. It should have scared the cac out of me that I was actually envisioning giving it to her.*

Live every moment.

I let out the breath that I'd been holding in.

Laugh every day.

I could see myself, down on one knee, fireworks lighting up the night sky. Finally telling her the words "I love you" and asking her to be my wife as I slipped her grandmother's ring onto her finger.

Love beyond words.

She would either think I was a complete header or brilliant. Why should we take things slow? It's not how I do things in business. Why should I in my personal life? *Emily was "the one" for me just as much as I was "the one" for her; I had no doubt of that. Nothing about our relationship has been slow but who gives a crap? We were doing it at our speed.* Fuck it! *I was going to propose to Emily at midnight on New Year's Eve.*

"The meter is still running, and I'm going to have to drive around the terminal again if you don't get out of the car, buddy." *Buddy?* I hated being called that.

"Sorry," I said as I tossed some bills at him and got out of the car. That night was supposed to be the start of something new for us. A new year, a new beginning with Emily as my wife. I never imagined that was how this night would end. *How could they do this to me?* Talk about a sick twist of fate. *Fuck my life.*

4

"Can I help you, sir?" the attendant at the counter asked. I must have looked confused. "Are you checking in for a flight?" she tried again, speaking louder and slower. I had no idea what I was doing or where I was going. I looked behind her at a list of flights, and like a beacon calling me home, the first thing I saw was a flight that was boarding in a few hours to Dublin.

"Do you have any seats available on flight 180 to Dublin?" She began typing into her computer. "One-way," I added before she could ask me.

"Only first-class, and it's going to be expensive this late of notice." It didn't matter how much it cost; I needed to get out of there, and since I couldn't be with Emily, Ireland was the only other place that felt anything like home. I tossed my AmEx black card down and she happily clicked away. I checked my small bag and made my way toward security.

"If I'm with you at the airport with this bag, sales will go through the roof." She was adorable on Christmas morning when she said that about her new luggage. I never thought I would be going anywhere without her.

Click.

"Where are you off to, Mr. Hayes?" I didn't know what about me or my life made me newsworthy; I was just a businessman. I ignored the annoying paparazzi and continued walking toward the security line. "Where's that hot little brunette you've been seen all over town with? Trouble in paradise?" It took everything in me not to deck the guy. Luckily for him, airport security was nearby and seemed to be out of patience with him. I needed to get away, but jail had no appeal to me.

I made it through security without incident and headed to the first bar that I saw in the terminal. "What will you have?" the bartender asked moments after I sat down. At least he didn't call me buddy.

"An Irish Car Bomb."

I figured if that was what they were going to call me, I had a reputation to uphold.

Emily

Hundreds of "friends" came to mourn the loss of Abigail Hayes, but I only cared about the one that didn't.

Declan.

It's been a week since I returned to the apartment to find his note and flowers, and I still can't believe he left. I've given up on calling him. His voicemail is full, and I know that his e-mails are being forwarded to his assistant, Monica. She called me to tell me that she hadn't read my messages but wanted to let me know they were coming to her so that I wouldn't think that he was ignoring me. She also gushed about how excited she was for me to meet with her husband, Nate, about my cookbook. Honestly, that was the last thing on my mind.

Luckily, the graveside service was private. It gave me time to accept the fact that he wasn't coming and time away from the crowd. I also learned some things about the Hayes family. Things Declan should know. *At least at the wake, I'll be able to drink.* I don't think I'd ever needed a glass of wine more. If I had to hear one more story about how "kind" Abigail was without the assistance of alcohol, I might have just killed someone. I wasn't there for her. I was there for Kian. I'd gotten to know him in the last week. He wasn't the man I thought he was at all.

I wished Declan knew this man. This broken man cried in my arms when I walked into his hospital room and just kept saying over and over again that he had "ruined everything good in his life". Yes, he had messed up, but, without *her*, I could see something clearly for the first time. *Kian Hayes loves his son.*

I had so many questions when I arrived, but those were all pushed aside the moment I learned that Abigail hadn't made it out of surgery. "Does Declan know?" I had asked. With his hands buried in his face, he shook his head no.

As much as I wanted to just go back to the apartment and drown myself in a tub of Ben and Jerry's, I couldn't. Kian was released from the hospital. He was alone and hurting. His wife was dead, and his son was gone. I was alone and hurting too, so I did what I had to do. I took him back to his apartment, a place that holds so many special memories of my time with Declan, and began planning the funeral for Abigail Hayes.

It nearly killed me walking back into that place. The beautiful winter wonderland that Declan had created for me was surprisingly still in place. It took me back a little. In my mind, I was sure that she demanded all traces of us and our happy time there were gone as soon as we left the apartment.

We'd stood under the mistletoe, and Kian kissed my tear-stained cheek. "I'll have it taken down today."

"Not yet," I pleaded. I needed to remember the good times we shared together there. Every single room of the apartment held memories of us falling in love. He nodded in silent agreement.

"I'm so sorry, Mr. Hayes," Maggie had said as she greeted us.

"Maggie, you clean my underwear for Christ's sake. Call me Kian," he snapped and Maggie's face fell further. You could instantly see the regret in his eyes. "I'm sorry, Maggie."

"You don't have to …" she started, but he didn't let her finish.

"Yes, I do. You've always been so good to us. It's just you and me now. Please, just call me Kian and lose the uniform." Laughter bubbled up from nowhere in him. Maggie and I couldn't help but laugh too. The timing sucked, but it felt nice to laugh, if only for a minute. "That didn't come out right. I didn't mean for you to go naked." He shook his head like even he couldn't believe what he was saying. "Just wear what you are comfortable in," he paused, "and thank you both for being here."

Where else would we be?

"Sir?" I knew that Mrs. Hayes had always expected a high level of professionalism from her help. Maggie once told me that she was even expected to wear her "maid" clothes even when they were out of town. *I mean, really?*

"Kian," he reiterated before telling us that he was going to try to get some rest before he had to start making phone calls. I think Kian and I were both in the same stage of grief—denial.

"Any word from him?" Maggie asked the moment we were alone. I had frantically called her before I left the apartment for the hospital. At that point, I was in a state of shock. More than anything, I wanted to call my best friends, but the last thing I was about to do was ruin their honeymoon before it even got started.

"Nothing, I just don't understand why he left. I'm here for him." In his letter, he said more than once that he no longer felt like he knew who he was. Maybe things would be different if he knew that I loved him.

If I had only told him.

"This isn't your fault. He knows that you are here for him." She offered me a cup of coffee. *What the hell?* It wasn't like I was going to be able to ever get any sleep anyway.

"But if I had just gone to the hospital …"

She stopped me. "He just found out the woman who raised him as her child isn't. I always knew something wasn't right with her. He'll be back. I know he will." If only I were as confident, but that was not the time to have such a conversation. The evil woman was dead, and Declan, the love of my life, was gone, and he had taken my heart with him.

CHAPTER
one

March

The bell chimed, announcing my arrival—much like the door at Mama M's. Jasmine looked like she was seeing a ghost when she looked at me. I'd never forget the first time I met her in person. It was the day after I met Emily. The moment I saw her dancing around my parents' kitchen practically naked, I knew she was special. Something about her called to me. I wouldn't have called it love at first sight, not then, anyway. I called down to the front desk to ask where my mother bought her flowers and Billy answered with an amused tone to his voice. He was lucky I thought the world of him. I did sign his paychecks, after all. I had no doubt that good old Maggie had told him all about her matchmaking plan for Emily and me. Hell, I probably

11

should have been sending *her* the flowers. I guess I should have listened to her a long time ago. Emily was everything she described and more.

"I thought you were only staying for a few minutes," he teased like I was his friend or maybe his nephew and not the son of the building owner, which was one of the reasons why I liked him so much.

"Do you know who I am?"

"Oh, I know exactly who you are. The little shit who used to love playing doorbell ditch at all hours of the night." His laugh was as robust as he was. Billy had been a part of my life for as long as I could remember. In many ways, he was more like family to me than my own. "What can I do for you, Mr. Hayes?"

"Ha ha. Only you, Billy, could get away with calling me a little shit and Mr. Hayes in the same sentence. Where do the flowers in the apartment come from?" I asked quietly so that Emily wouldn't overhear me.

Billy laughed again. "The same florist that's been doing it for the last fifteen years, boy, maybe more. Do you tie your own shoes?" It had been a long-standing joke since Billy was the one that actually taught me how to do that very thing. He'd done so much for me over the years. I really was a little shit, because I'd never truly thanked him.

"The name, Billy, just give me the name," I pleaded. This was all new to me. I'd never had an overwhelming need to do something like this for someone, but I had to do something for Emily, and it had to be special. I couldn't explain it, but it had to mean something.

"Jasmine's Garden on eighty-sixth," he said before I thanked him and got off the phone. I could have easily just asked Monica, my secretary, to do it for me in the morning, but I wanted to, no, needed

to do it myself. I wasn't the kid that couldn't tie his own laces anymore, and trust me when I say, my thoughts on that sexy brunette were far from childlike.

I set up my computer where I could watch her while she worked in the kitchen. It smelled amazing, but honestly, nothing smelled as good as her when she came closer to me to wipe up the egg. I couldn't really describe it, but one whiff and I was addicted to it, to her. After doing some research online, I sent my request to the florist. She must have been online because her reply came almost instantly. She said she could make it happen if I told her why it was so important that it be done so quickly. I liked that about her—it was about more than just the extra money she could charge me to make my request a reality. I didn't know the woman, but for some reason, I wanted to tell her why it mattered. Maybe I just wanted someone, anyone, *to tell me that I wasn't completely out of my mind.*

I typed in a direct message "I could have any woman in this city." I wasn't trying to come off as an ass, but it was true. Women threw themselves at me all the time. "Except maybe this one." But it wasn't about just the chase. She was surprised when I called her beautiful and attempted to cover her gorgeous body when she realized how little she was wearing. "She's beautiful and smart, she owns her business, and she couldn't care less who I am." That was obvious when she schooled me on how to correctly wipe up a mess off the floor—the hottest thing I'd ever seen in my life, might I just add. Hell, I had to even convince her to stay in the apartment with me and make up a reason for staying myself, just so that I could be close to her. She wasn't interested in my money, that was evident when she said, "Hey, that just cost me two dollars," when I popped a hot muffin in my mouth and when she called me "buddy" and gave me a Marketing 101 lecture.

Just thinking about it again took everything in me not to throw her over my shoulder and take her to my bed right then. "I guess you could say, I think this woman is worth the effort." I don't know how I knew that after only knowing her for a few minutes, but I did. "Please let me know if you are willing to help." I pushed send and nearly held my breath as I waited for her reply. I found myself feeling another new emotion: I was freakin' nervous.

"I anticipate watching this relationship bloom." The woman certainly knew her flowers.

"You're not the only one. I'll be in in the morning to personally sign the card. Thank you for your assistance." As I laid in bed in a room I once loathed, I found myself grateful for Maggie for being so persistent, for Billy who was the uncle I never had, for Jasmine who was had just confirmed that my request could be met, and most importantly, for the woman who slept down the hall, who had just turned my world upside down without even trying.

"It's so nice to see you. I suppose now I can stop sending the forget-me-nots every week. You do know that she won't allow me to deliver them to the apartment or the bakery any longer, right?" I did, but hearing it straight from Jasmine's mouth hurt more than reading it in Eric's e-mail had.

"Yes, I know, but please keep sending them anyway." I knew it was silly since she would never see them herself, but if sending them to the Brookdale, the nursing facility for people with Alzheimer's, was what she wanted, then that was OK by me. "I'm actually here for flowers for someone else and would appreciate it if you didn't mention to anyone else that I was here." My words must have shocked her because her mouth fell open and she dropped the small bouquet that she held in her hands. "It's not what you think." I didn't owe Jasmine any explanation, but I offered it anyway, "I'm going to meet my biological grandmother for the first time. I'd like Emily to find out about this visit from me when the time comes." And I hoped with everything that I had that it would lead me to my mother, and ultimately, back to Emily, the love of my life.

"That's wonderful, Declan." Her demeanor instantly changed back to that of the happy and helpful florist that I was used to. We agreed on a mixed bouquet. Unlike the flowers that I always picked for Emily because of what they represented, these just had to say, "Hi, you don't know me, but I'm your grandson."

CHAPTER
two

June

Jasmine was still sending Lemon Drop's forget-me-nots to Brookdale, but now she would no longer need to send them. The flowers I gave to Lurena Scott, my grandmother, were long since dead and gone, along with any relationship I thought we might have or any hope that she might have any information she could give me about my birth mother, Brianna Bailey. Now the only thing I had was the woman I left behind in Ireland, and the hope that I could still fix things with Emily and the rest of our friends. The bell above the door chimed, and a young family entered the shop.

"Happy Father's Day!" Jasmine offered in greeting, and it almost knocked me flat on my arse. *Father's Day? I swear this shit only happens to me.* I didn't even realize what the day was. Could I have picked a worse day to come back? I paced the shop as Jasmine helped the couple. Maybe the holiday or the family in the shop was a sign, a sign of things to come. That was, if Lemon Drop would still have me.

I paused for a moment at the door and considered knocking for a millisecond. Maybe she would be singing and dancing around or sticking out her tongue while she was concentrating on whatever she was doing. If I knocked, I would miss that. I'd already missed enough. I didn't plan on missing anything else. It was time.

The door didn't budge when I pushed on it. Locked. Good, the idea of a stranger sneaking up on her—scaring her, hurting her—made my heart beat faster. Why? Because that's exactly what I had done to her myself. Would the door to her heart be locked too? I said a silent prayer I wasn't too late, that if the door was locked at least a window would be open. I entered the first code I thought she might use—her birthday. Nothing. I held my breath as I tried my next guess—*my* birthday. No go. They were the same locks I had at HIP. I knew if I tried three wrong codes I was screwed.

Think, Declan, what date would be important to Emily?

I entered 1-1-2-4, the first day we met, and the red light turned to green. With a smile on my face, I hit the latch and pushed the door open. Knowing the date we first met still meant something to her gave me hope. The smell hit me first—it was even better than I remembered. The space looked much unchanged, except for the addition of some kind of shipping area. Large boxes lined the wall behind it. *What on Earth could she be using those for?* Eric assured me that he told me everything I needed to know. That seemed like something he should have told me about.

I think I need to have a word with my valued employee.

Another new addition to the area was a small table, and sitting at it was a wee Molly, who hadn't stopped working on her brightly-colored creation since I walked in the door. Her long hair was a mess of dark curls.

"I'm almost done, Mr. H," she said with a sing-song voice. Who was Mr. H., and who was this little ray of sunshine? None of our friends had kids. Oh, shit, maybe she met someone with a child. *Fuck!*

I buried my face in my empty hand, completely overwhelmed, and I hadn't even seen her yet. The child was looking right at me when I looked back up. She was a beautiful child with dark skin and eyes to match.

"You're not Mr. H., but you look kind of like him only younger," said the small voice whose attention was now completely on me. *Mr. H? Could she be talking about my father?* Nobody even calls him by his first name. "Come here." The little girl motioned with her finger as she got up and stood on her tiny chair. For some unexplainable reason, I did exactly as she said and moved closer. She put her hands on her hips and tilted her head as she examined me.

"Is that Mr. H. you're talking to, Fay?" a voice I didn't recognize called from the kitchen area. Her name suited her.

Relief flooded me. With her mother, I assumed, nearby, chances were that she didn't belong to a boyfriend. I'd probably deserve it if a guy was in the picture, but I held on to hope that Emily was still mine and that Eric would have told me about a new man in her life.

Sunshine Fay put her finger to her lips to tell me to hush, and I gave her a firm nod. "Yes, Mom." *Shit, does that mean they were expecting my father?* I really wasn't ready to see him. I wasn't sure I ever would be.

"Perfect. I'll be right out, Kian." So, Mr. H. was definitely my father. Her mother actually sounded happy to know my father was there and certainly didn't seem concerned about leaving her child alone with him. I never thought my father liked children. Hell, I was his child and he never seemed to like me.

"I know who you are. I've seen your picture." It seemed to me the child was wise beyond her years. Maybe if I had more time, she could tell more about Emily. "Those are pretty," she said as she looked at the bouquet in my hand.

They didn't have "I'm an arse flowers," so I went with a combination of yellow and red tulips. Red were meant as a declaration of love, and the yellow signified being hopelessly in love. They would be a start, but if I knew Emily the way I thought, I knew she would need to feel my love with all of her senses, and if she gave me the chance, I would do exactly that.

"She has sad eyes too," the little girl told me as she looked at me, and her statement almost brought me to my knees. Knowing I did that. I hurt the woman I loved, and it killed me.

"Where is she?" I asked in a voice I almost didn't recognize as my own.

"It's baby time!" Fay said excitedly as she jumped off her chair and began to do a dance around the room. *Baby? It couldn't be*. I haven't been gone that long. Emily was taking her smarties. She couldn't be. *Could she?* Without thought, I dropped the tulips and ran out of the building. Nothing was going to stop me from getting to her. Nothing.

I didn't stop at the main level of the hospital like the signs directed me to. Instead, I ran up the twelve flights of stairs to the maternity floor. "Emily Barnes!" I blurted out as I tried to catch my breath. Surely, I wasn't the first man to show up there in a panic. The nurse told me to relax and began typing into her computer. She shook her head like she hadn't heard me correctly the first time. She typed again and continued shaking her head.

"She has to be here. Check again. Emily Barnes." I didn't care that I was starting to draw more attention to myself than necessary. Someone had to be able to tell me where she was. She was there, I knew it. I could *feel* it.

"Declan?" I heard from behind me. Wheeler stood behind me with one of those plastic water jugs in his hand.

At first, I was overcome with joy, because I knew that he would be able to tell me where she was and then that changed to anger. He liked her. I knew it. Hell, we all knew it, but this? Did he swoop up to rescue her the second I left? *He wouldn't have been able to if you had stayed.* I thought he was a sham. Some friend. He must have seen something in my face because his smile at seeing me again suddenly dropped.

"Where is she?" I growled at him.

"Sir, is there a problem?" a nervous guard asked Logan as he looked back and forth between us. *Fuck that, he shouldn't even be here.*

"Maybe this isn't the best time for this, Dec." *Dec?* Emily was the only one that called me that. How could he be so calm and so casual when he was at the hospital with my girl and my baby?

My baby? Fuck! I've been such a muppet. Why the hell did I ever leave her? Them? Fuck!

"Where is she?" I asked again as I ignored the guard who separated us and began to approach him.

"Sir, we are going to insist that you leave," the guard interjected as he reached out to stop me."

"Logan," a strained voiced yelled from behind the closed door he was standing in front of. It sounded like her, yet different. Maybe it was because of the pain. The cry of agony was enough to have him rushing through the door with me hot on his tail. Nothing would keep me from my family any longer.

"Oh, for fuck's sake, what the hell is Dicklan doing here?" My confused gaze traveled around the room. I'd heard that women giving birth were prone to say awful things that they couldn't be held accountable for saying, but I completely deserved that one. However, the woman in the bed wasn't my Lemon Drop at all—it was her sister, Libby.

"Declan?" Emily asked from her sister's bedside. She was as surprised to see me as I was to see her not in the bed. Relief flooded me as Logan took Libby's hand in his and kissed it. She was naturally the one having the baby. OK, so maybe he wasn't a snake, but I was still an eejit for ever leaving. "What are you doing here?"

Her voice was void of emotion, which only made things worse. Anger I had expected. Joy would have been more than I ever deserved. But indifference scared the hell out of me. She looked different—her hair was shorter and lighter and she looked a little thinner, but she was still the most beautiful woman I had ever seen

"I told you I would come back." It was pathetic, but what else could I say?

"Ooooh," Libby groaned from her bed. Wheeler lovingly stroked her face with the back of his hand. Evidently, I had missed a lot. *Why didn't Eric think I needed to know about this?*

"It's almost over," Emily confirmed as she looked at a monitor beside her.

"I need to push," she told us all just as the doctor came in to check on her. It goes without saying, my timing was for shit. I stood in the corner, my eyes firmly locked on the only woman in the world who would ever have my heart. She tried to remain focused on her sister, but I caught her glancing at me more than once and noticed the blush in her cheeks. When the doctor confirmed that it was indeed time to push, I knew it was well past time for me to leave.

"Where are you going?" Emily asked as several nurses moved about the room in preparation for the birth. Logan stayed firmly at Libby's side. His face showed both joy for what was about to happen and concern for the woman whose hand he lovingly held. Suddenly, a bit a jealousy for what they were about to share overcame me.

"I'll just be outside. I'm not going anywhere. I promise." Not that my promises still meant anything to her, but in time, I hoped that she would remember what we had. At least, what I hoped we had. Like me, she had never said those three little words out loud, but I felt them. I know I did.

"Oh, for fuck's sake, just stay. I need my sister, and if you're out of her sight, she won't be any good to me. Good damn mother*fucker* this hurts; you are so fucking lucky you aren't the one that did this to me, Logan." From the look on his face, she was squeezing the hell out of the hand she was holding, and I had no intention of further pissing off the sister of the woman that I loved, so I sat my arse back down and tried to focus on Emily and Logan instead of Libby's lady bits . I couldn't help but wonder if I looked at Emily the way my friend looked at Libby. I hoped I did. I wanted them to able to remember the moment forever, so

I did the one thing I knew I could and began taking pictures with the camera that was sitting on top of the bag next to me.

"What is this beauty's name?" the doctor asked as she placed her on Libby's bare chest. As much as I didn't want to see any more of her naked body as I had to, it was a stunning sight. To my surprise, Libby looked up at Wheeler.

"What is your daughter's name, Daddy?" she asked as he tenderly wiped a tear from her cheek. Earlier, Libby had yelled about the dick that had done this to her, and I knew she wasn't talking about Wheeler. Plus, Libby and Logan hadn't even met when I left. He wasn't the baby's father by birth, but it seemed to all of them that it didn't matter. It nearly gutted me when he kissed them both and named his daughter Aria. Love oozed off of them.

My father had never once looked at me the way Logan did when he held the tiny bundle in his arms for the first time and I was his biological child. Abigail Hayes had certainly never loved me that unconditionally. I was so wrapped up in the moment, I hadn't even noticed Emily by my side. I was overwhelmed by emotions; I had to get out of there.

"I'm sorry," I said to Emily just barely above a whisper before fleeing the room. As I rushed toward the elevator doors, several familiar people stood from the waiting area. Gabe, Nat, Eric, Suzie, the little girl Fay, a woman I assumed was her mother because she was a mini version of her, Brit, Sadie, Maggie, and my fucking father. If looks alone could kill, Nat and Gabe would have had me dead. It was probably a good thing that Hope and Matt were missing from the group. Eric had said they were spending time in Nashville. If he had been present, I would have been in the morgue for sure. Thankfully, Brit had been around me enough to know that right then was not the time for a reunion.

"I told you," Fay proudly announced to the group. Before my father had the decency to look away from me, something flashed in his eyes. I didn't know exactly what it was, but I knew for certain that I had never seen that look on his face before. It was then that I realized she was standing behind me. Did she think I was leaving her again? Because I wouldn't, I couldn't. It just about killed me the first time—I wouldn't survive it again. I just had to get out of that room. It was too much. The way that Wheeler looked at that baby that wasn't biologically his with so much love completely overwhelmed me. Nat nearly bulldozed me to get to Emily. *Shit, I get it, Nat; I'm pissed at me too.*

I had to get out of there, so I rushed toward the elevator. As I turned in the car, I couldn't help but lift my hand to my chest, to the place where her engagement ring lay hidden. Nat held her as she watched me leave with tears streaming down her beautiful face. "A Chori," I mouthed, and she gasped. She had to know that she still had my heart. No matter what happened, she always would.

Gabe blocked my view of her as the doors began to close. "O'Mary's in one hour, Declan." I nodded, message received loud and clear. I knew it wouldn't be a simple walk in the park, but the best things in life were worth fighting for, and Emily was nothing but the best.

Eric offered to join me at the bar; I told him to stay with his wife. Gabe slid into the seat beside me exactly one hour later as I thumbed the glass of Tullamore Dew that I hadn't taken a sip of. I don't even know why I ordered it. I haven't had so much of a drop of alcohol since shortly after my arrival in the Emerald Isle. For two solid weeks, I drowned myself in my sorrow and then I realized that I was wasting time, time I should have been using to find my birth mother, time I would have rather been spending with my Lemon Drop.

"So you're back." Gabe motioned toward the bartender who, without question, began to pour him a beer. "Thanks." Gabe lifted his glass in a salute before offering up a toast, "To Emily." Well, I had to drink to that. The "water of life" burned on its way down, but I had to say that it did give me the extra dose of courage I felt I needed in order to withstand the chilly reception I was receiving despite the hotter than the average temperature outside. "I'm not her father, but I feel like I should ask." He looked me right in the eye, which I had to admire. "What are your intentions, Declan? Because, honestly, if you hurt her again, they'll never find all your body parts." His wife probably would have been first in a very long line of people ready to murder me.

I wanted Gabe to know how serious I was. That my intentions were indeed honorable and that if she would have me, I would spend the rest of our lives making it up to her. Words weren't enough, so I decided to show him. I removed the chain from around my neck for the first time since I had put it there on New Year's Eve.

"Holy crap," Gabe said as he began to examine the ring that he held in his hand. "Why did you show me that? You do remember who I'm married to, don't you? Nat already threatened me with sleeping on the sofa if I don't tell her everything about this little meeting. I can't tell her this. She'll tell Emily, and honestly, I think it's about time Emily started hearing things directly from you. For fuck's sake, Declan, the first time you told her that you loved her was just before you passed out drunk, and the second time was in a goddamn letter."

"Christ, it must have been Christmas Eve, I was fluthered because my parents came over, but I wanted to tell her so much. How could I be such a gowl?"

"Will you speak English?" he asked as he took another drink of his beer.

"I said that I was very drunk and that I'm an annoying stupid person." He nodded his head in agreement. For the first time, I began to worry that maybe I wouldn't be able to get her back. No woman wants to be told she is loved like that and then why would she believe it for even a second when that wanker just up and leaves her for almost seven months? I had waited too long and was a complete arse to boot. With my elbows raised on the bar, I buried my face in my hands in defeat.

"For what it's worth, she's still in love with you. But, let's just keep that I told you that between the two of us. Now, what are you going to do to get her back?" I really hadn't given it much thought other than the tulips that I abandoned earlier at the bakery. Other than her grandmother's ring, I had nothing else to offer her, and really, what would I tell her when she asked me if I had found what I was looking for when I left? "Oh, shit, man, I thought you knew what the hell you were doing. You better figure it out or you'll never hear the end of it. M's not frilly but every woman wants to be wooed. My parents have been married thirty-five years, and Mom is still complaining about what a shitty job Dad did proposing. You need to get this right, and I need to go before Nat comes barreling in here with guns blazing. You should surprise her at Columbus Circle at seven in the morning and wear your running shoes, but if anyone asks, you didn't hear that from me, either." With that, Gabe tossed some bills on the bar and left. Gabe was a good guy. A true friend.

Then, my phone buzzed.

Brit: Meet me at our spot 6:00 am

I knew it was serious for Brit to voluntarily get up so early in the morning. I was kind of glad little miss Fay already spilled the beans to everyone that I was back before they saw me. I could just imagine the looks I would have received had she not. I was expecting anger, but what I wasn't expecting was the hurt that shone in several eyes. Most of all, my father's.

I thought for sure I would have to wait for her, and I didn't have a lot of time since I was going to follow Gabe's advice and surprise Emily on her run. Surprisingly, I was wrong. Brit sat at the dingy Formica counter of Johnnies Luncheonette when I walked in the door. We'd been coming to this hole-in-the-wall since we suffered our first hangovers together. At some point, it just became "our spot".

"I'm mad at you." She sighed without looking up from her chipped mug of thick coffee. We'd never been able to tell what they put in the stuff, but what you would think of as sludge was surprisingly delicious, just like everything else there. Brit was my oldest friend, my first crush, and the first girl I ever kissed. As soon as I did it, she pushed me away and told me to never do it again. We were five or six at the time. Brit had always known exactly who she was. It was one of the many things I admired about her. That, and her ability to forgive me. *I hope.*

"I know." I flipped over the empty cup that sat before me and it was instantly filled. It seemed that everyone was mad at me and for good reason. At the time, it seemed like I didn't have any other choice but to leave. Now I could see how foolish I was. You know what they say about hindsight? Well, it's true.

"You didn't just leave Emily, you know." *Ouch*. No bullshit, that's another thing about Brit. She always called it like she saw it, but I'm not going to lie, the truth hurts.

"I know, and I'm sorry. Breakfast is on me." That was a longstanding joke between us. It was only for a second, but I caught the way her lips curled up in a smile that she tried to hide. I ordered Brit her regular order while I opted for yogurt and granola with a slice of peanut butter toast. It was then that she took in my attire.

"You're going after her?" Our order arrived and Brit didn't hesitate to dig into her banana pancakes. *And they say the way to a man's heart is through his stomach*. Obviously, they didn't know Brit.

"I am."

"About damn time" I could barely make it out because she had a mouth full of food. Sometimes it was hard to believe that we were raised attending the same cotillions and prep-schools. She swallowed before turning her complete attention to me. "She's got a date tonight." Brit must have registered the look of horror on my face because she instantly started laughing. "Oh, this is going to be so good." If she was a guy, I would have punched her, and that's when I realized—Brit and I were going to be just fine.

"Fuuuuck," I said below my breath when I caught a glimpse of her stretching out. She was wearing little black shorts that made her ass look fantastic. I really had to get control of myself because one, I looked like a perv with a boner in athletic shorts, and two, because running with a stiff dick was never a good idea. I closed my eyes and tried to think about what I had seen in the delivery room the day before. Just thinking about Libby's giblets seemed to do the trick. Before I could join her, Emily started down the path toward the main loop. Her form was impressive, as was the pace and route she took. I must say, I was enjoying the view, but if I stayed there much longer, I would have had to start thinking about Libby giving birth again.

"I was wondering if you were going to just stalk me again," she teased when I began to run alongside her. We fell into a natural matching cadence.

"Stalk?" I asked with a curious tone.

"Well, you did show up at the hospital unannounced yesterday. You should have seen the look on your face when you came in the room." She giggled as she came to a stop for a water break at the top of Cat Hill. God, I missed that sound. Even dripping with sweat she was gorgeous. Before I could tell her just how beautiful she looked, she took off running again. I followed her. "What exactly did you think you were going to see when you came in the room?" she asked after some time had passed with us running side by side.

I had to be honest; it was the only way I would ever have a chance with her. "I was afraid that I had lost you to Wheeler and freaked out that you were having my baby—our baby." Just the thought of it knocked the wind out of me. I stopped running right in the middle of the bridle path

31

and doubled over which was a surefire way to hear it from the other runners. I had almost forgotten how colorful the city was.

When I stood to my full height, Emily was standing before me with a new look in her eyes. Anger. "You asked me not to leave. I didn't. You told me to talk to you yet you didn't talk to me." She turned away from me and began to run again. This time, I stayed behind her. She was right, and I knew it. I knew it months before when I told myself to come back but I couldn't figure out how to justify my actions. Hell, I still couldn't.

Let your faith be bigger than your fear. That was what brought me home. I had to have enough faith for both of us. I didn't say anything else as Emily finished her run and stretched before she walked out of the park and straight into a familiar apartment building; the place where it all began between us. She said a friendly hello to Billy before she got in the elevator—our elevator. I'm not sure if it was tears or sweat that she wiped away from her face while I stood frozen in the lobby as the doors closed. Either way, it nearly dropped me to my knees. Stumbling over to a chair, I sat down.

"You look like you could use this," Billy said as he tossed me a cold water bottle. My father was coming to the bakery. My father was in the waiting room at the hospital. Emily was at my father's apartment. *Why?* The question must have been written all over my face. "She comes here every day after her run. They're close."

That stung. He was my father and we had never been close. Hell, he spent my entire life ignoring me. I still didn't understand why he always seemed to distance himself from me; *I am, after all, his biological child.* "She's been here for him since the accident. Since we lost your mother." I couldn't help but cringe. I could hear it in the tone of his voice— Billy was disappointed in the fact that I wasn't there.

I could understand, but at the time, the anger I had over the betrayal outweighed everything else. Abigail and Kian lied to me my entire life. Not only that, but they had denied me of the only thing I ever wanted: unconditional love. Was that too much to ask for? Parents that loved you for no other reason that because you were theirs? Now that I had loved Emily, I knew how easy loving someone could be. True, I fucked it up, but it wasn't because I didn't love her. My love for her was bigger than anything else. It wasn't until I met Emily that I even realized that I did have it. I had it in her, Maggie, Logan, Brit, Sadie, Eric, and even Billy, the gentle giant standing before me. It had even been given freely to me by the Medinas, Chapmans, and Sutherlands because they loved Emily.

"Why do you think they have become so close?" I asked hesitantly, unsure if I was prepared to hear the answer.

"For a smart man, you sure are pretty stupid, Declan." He snickered before adding, "Because they both love you. Holding onto each other is how they held on to you. I sure hope you have a plan to fix what you've done." Shit, he was the second man to tell me that. It was time for me to come up with something. Anything.

I didn't know how long I sat in the lobby trying to come up with ideas on how to fix things with Emily. How could I prove to Emily that I was there to stay? *You told me to talk to you. I love you. She deserves to hear the words from you.*

Before I left Ireland, Anastasia Flemming, the great grandmother I just recently found out I had, told me that in the end we only regret the chances that we don't take. She was right. I didn't want to live my life with regret. Faith, hope, trust, and love—they were enough, and I would do anything to prove to my lovely Lemon Drop that we had them in spades.

"Do me a favor, Billy, and tell M that I will catch up with her later." I had plans to make, and she was already pissed at me, so how much more trouble could I really get in?

CHAPTER
three

"Hey, come on in," Logan said in a whisper when he opened the door. He was holding a bundle that was covered in a thin pink blanket against his bare chest. After I took a shower and changed at the hotel, I went to the hospital. Apparently, they don't keep women in very long after giving birth, so I went to their home. "Lib says that skin on skin contact is important for babies. Helps with brain development, calms them down, and will help her sleep better, or some shit like that."

I put down the enormous pink gift basket that I felt foolish bringing. Maybe a trust fund or savings bond would have been a smarter choice. I'd have to look into that too. Wheeler's place was small in the first place and everywhere I looked I saw nothing but baby stuff. I had no idea why something so small needed so much. The one thing I didn't see was Emily's sister or mother who I expected would be coming to see her first grandchild. I knew it was a risk coming there. For all I knew, Emily could have been there too. With Libby calling me "Dicklan" the day before, it was obvious she wasn't a fan of mine.

"Where's Libby?" I asked as he settled down into a rocking chair. The baby stirred, and he began patting her on the bum and humming. She settled right back down; he made it seem so easy. He pressed his lips against her head before he answered me.

"She didn't get much sleep last night. You know how hospitals are, and this one seems to have her days and nights mixed up. Don't tell Lib, but I hope she doesn't figure it out soon so that she'll be awake at night when I get home from the restaurant."

Not many people know that I owned Swayed where he was the head chef; it's independent of my family's company, Hayes Investment Properties. Well, I should say that Logan and I owned it. I didn't know shit about restaurants, but I did know that Swayed wouldn't be anything without Logan and his genius in the kitchen, so I gave him a stake in ownership. Logan and I had been what most people would call unlikely friends for a while. While I came from money and privilege, Logan came from destitution and disadvantage. Wheeler used to say that we were always "destined to be friends". *I wonder if he still feels that way. I hope he does, he means a lot to me.*

"I'm sorry."

"For what exactly? For ditching us all? For worrying everyone that cares about you? For thinking that I stole your girl?" So yeah, I guess he caught that but he continued before I could apologize for being a fuck face again. "For screwing up so bad that Libby rode a bus all the way from Memphis to be with her sister? For leading her and my daughter straight to my front door?" His tone changed when he talked about Libby and Aria. Maybe it was hard to be mad when you held such perfection in your arms. Maybe Emily needed to be holding her niece when I talked to her next. Once again, he pressed his lips to Aria's head. "I'm not going to pretend to understand what you did for a second. I've wanted to just take off plenty of times in my own life, but I never did." *I really am an arse. Wheeler has been through more shit in his life than I will ever know and he never ran away from any of it.* He always believed that with hard work and determination anything was possible. Fuck, he even proved it was true by making Swayed one of the most sought-after restaurants in the city. The baby began to stir on his chest again, but unlike me, he didn't seem to panic.

"I don't think I've got what she's looking for," he said in amusement as he rose from his chair. "M's got a date tonight." I stiffened even though Brit had already told me and I was already implementing a preemptive strike. "Cheryl will be here soon and she tried to get out of it. She doesn't want to go but Lib and Nat wouldn't let her get out of it." I should have known those two were behind the date. I think he saw the flash of anger in my eyes. "They just want to see her happy." With his back to me, he added, "I just want you both to be happy." He didn't say it, but I got that feeling he was saying that he thought were meant to do that for each other.

"Grandma Rose said that when Libby found the right man she would love him with everything that she has. I'm glad she found you, Logan." And I was; if anyone deserved the love of a Barnes woman, it was Logan, and now he had two. He slipped into his room with an unhappy baby in his arms but a smile on his face.

Eric was waiting for me outside. He was more than a driver, but that was between us. It allowed him to be close to me while he did his job. That day, I was relying on his expertise. Keeping tabs on Emily wasn't a part of his duties, per se, but he did it anyway, and I was grateful for that, especially when I had been away. Like everyone, he cared for her. Did she have any idea how many protectors she had? One of the things that I loved the most about her was that she seemed so unaware of how truly amazing she was. She gave herself without even thinking "What's in it for me?". She had a truly amazing heart, and I knew if any other man got a glimpse of how positively wonderful she was that I would have a fight on my hands. I fight that I wouldn't lose. Ever.

"Who is he?" I shot out as soon as we were both in the car. Without a word, Eric handed me a dossier on her date that included when and where they were meeting. That was exactly what I needed. Seemingly, the guy had no idea who he was dating. It was perfect.

Thank you, Eric. It appeared that whatever diversion he had come up with to delay Emily's "date" had worked, but I had no idea how long I had. She played with her napkin as she sat at the bar waiting. She looked amazing. Most of the women in the club were scantily clad, but not mine. I couldn't believe that once upon a time that did something for me. Emily was a one of a kind woman, *my* woman, and she certainly didn't belong in a place like that. She was wearing a white short-sleeve dress with some sort of green design. *Was she wearing green because it reminded her of me?* She always had a thing for my eyes. She had her hair pinned up on one side with some kind of feather flower thing. When she tilted her head to the side, I could no longer hold in the groan I let out. With her head tilted and her hair back, her neck was on full display. I wanted to smell her sweet scent before sinking my teeth into that beautiful skin.

"Can I get you something?" the bartender asked as he wiped down the bar with a rag in front of me.

"Can you deliver this and a lemon drop to the feek brunette?" I motioned toward her with my head, and he grinned like he was in on some kind of inside joke.

"Dude, I don't think even you've got a chance with that one." He shook his head as he took the note and the twenty I handed him before heading over to Emily. I slipped out of my seat and began to make my way toward her. The bartender placed the martini glass in front of her as he slid the folded piece of paper toward her. She opened it up and read it and then she looked at him. I couldn't hear the exchange between them, but he motioned toward where I had been sitting. He shrugged his shoulders when he realized I was no longer there and turned away to help another patron. The music changed, and I knew it was my chance.

I repeated the words that were written on the note, "Dance with me." It wasn't a question. She needed to be in my arms. It was where she belonged. She stiffened at the sound of my voice over the loud music. I moved closer to her and a swell of people leaving the dance floor because of the change in music surged me even closer. I couldn't help myself; I lowered my head and breathed in. Her scent was intoxicating. The only space that remained between us as more bodies approached the bar was the invisible wall that I had caused her to put back up when I left. She lifted her glass and drank the sweet concoction like it was a shot.

"You're still sweet with a little sucker punch, Lemon Drop." She swung around faster on her barstool than I knew was possible. It caught us both off-guard, but luckily, I caught her before she fell. I put my arms around her, and I swear she was trembling.

"Don't call me that," she demanded as I lowered my forehead to hers. Suddenly, it was as if we were the only two people in the crowded club. Even though she was upset, she closed her eyes as I began to sway back and forth in time to the music.

"And we found love right where we are," I sang as the song ended before I placed my lips upon her forehead. Somewhere along the way, she stopped resisting me and her arms were wrapped around my neck. With my lips, I traced the familiar path down her nose before placing a kiss on the tip of it. I murmured her nickname before I placed my lips upon hers, but she pushed me away and ran out before I could stop her. "Lemon Drop," I yelled as I tried to follow her. It was pointless—she was gone.

Damn, that girl was fast.

CHAPTER
four

She was wearing ear buds when I began stretching out beside her. OK, I guess we weren't going to be talking about what happened the previous night. I racked my brain but I couldn't figure out what that even was. What had I done? *This time.* One second she was in my arms, and the next minute she was gone. Sleep evaded me. I was exhausted, but not running with her never even crossed my mind. I had to see her, and no it had nothing to do with the tight black little running shorts and athletic tank that showed off every curve of her amazing body. It was her, my lovely Lemon Drop. Fuck, that was it. *I'm an eejit.* She asked me not to call her that right after she spun around in her chair, and I did it right before I kissed her. That was when she pushed me away.

"Why?" I asked out loud, but I knew she couldn't hear me. We ran, side by side. Even with our height difference, our stride was well matched. Running beside her felt natural—next to her was exactly where I was meant to be. At the end of the same route we ran the day before, she turned to me and finally removed her headphones. I didn't know what I was expecting, but it surely wasn't the words she said.

"I'll be out of your apartment by the end of the day." She knocked the wind out of me. It wasn't my apartment anymore, it was her home, and I hoped with everything that I had in me that she could find it in her heart to let me back in. That it could once again be ours. I didn't want it without her. Any of it. I had been warned that it might not be as easy as I thought it would be to pick things up right where I had left them. I should have heeded that warning.

"Tell me about Fay and her mother," I asked Eric as I held the heavy bag in place for him. I didn't want to talk about Emily right that minute because I was still reeling from her announcement that she was moving out. I had wrongly assumed that her still being in the apartment after all that time was a good sign. He raised his brow at me asking without words if this was what I really wanted to talk about. I nodded.

"Willow is her name. They are good people. Your fath—Kian loves her. Fay, I mean, not Willow," he

43

clarified. The idea of my father loving anyone besides himself was laughable. "No really. You should have seen him when she fell off her bike when he was teaching her how to ride it." The thought of him doing that with her nearly sliced me in half. *I know it's ridiculous; I'm a grown ass man.*

"Da." He had barely made it inside the door of the apartment when I came rushing toward him. It was the first day since my birthday that it was dry outside and he promised me that he would teach me to ride. My mother scolded me to keep my voice down from behind her large desk. Why did the woman need such a big desk? She never worked a day in her life. "It's not raining," I reminded him as he looked up at my mother.

"Your father doesn't have time for silly games, Declan. We have an engagement tonight at the club." Silly? Bikes weren't silly, and I knew that everyone would laugh at me if I didn't learn to ride soon. Brit told me she would teach me, so did Billy, and my nanny, but I wanted him to do it. He promised. Besides, they always had an engagement. They never had time for me.

"Shit, boss." I guess I got lost in the memory. The blow to the bag knocked me flat on my arse.

"Sorry, I wasn't paying attention." I hadn't thought about that day in a long time. Needless to say, my father never taught me how to ride a bike. But a new memory surfaced—it was the look on his face when they left that night. He was holding a paper or something in his hand. He looked at it and then he looked up at me before tucking whatever it was in his jacket pocket. He put his hand over it, over his heart, and gave it a pat. What is that emotion?

Sad? What had he been looking at? Why did he pat his chest when he looked at me that way?

"What were you saying?"

"I was saying that you should talk to Emily. Tell her what your intentions are. I probably shouldn't be telling you this, but she called Suzie last night. She was pretty upset, and she asked me if I would help her move her stuff out of the apartment tonight." He hesitated, and I knew he didn't want to tell me what was coming next. "She's moving in with Kian until she finds a place of her own." *My father?*

I swear I saw red. None of it made any sense to me. He and Abigail were the reason I left in the first place, and now she was seeking refuge with him. Didn't she understand what that did to me? Fuck, until I met her, I never truly understood what it felt like to be loved unconditionally. He was the one that betrayed me. His lies were the reason we weren't together. *Was I wrong about her?* She never said it. Maybe she never loved me. Eric must have read something on my face.

"Don't! Just talk to her, Declan," he implored me as I paced back and forth like a caged animal.

"Why? She evidently doesn't care about what he did to me. Every time I turn around he shows up or she goes straight to him. He lied to me. How can she trust him?" Even as I said the words, I thought about what Billy said.

Eric tore off his gloves and marched toward me. He stuck his finger into my chest. "You don't get to judge her when you're the one that left her." He jabbed at me again.

45

"She was ruined. Your father is the one that told her not to give up on you. You shit for brains." His admission nearly knocked me on my arse again. "You need to fucking talk to her, and for God's sake, listen too. You might just learn that your father isn't the monster you've made him out to be. Unless you don't want her back." Not having Emily in my life wasn't an option. It never would be. He was right; it was past time for us to really talk.

"What time are you supposed to pick her up?" I asked, and his glare instantly softened.

"Five."

"Don't bother showing up." He knew exactly why without asking.

"It's about fucking time." *Yes, it is.*

You could tell she wasn't expecting me when she answered the door. She looked beautiful with her hair up in a messy bun on the top of her head, cut-off denim shorts that made her legs look longer than I ever thought possible, and one of my t-shirts. She had it knotted in the back, and a sliver of her creamy skin peeked out between the shirt and her shorts. Fuck, even though she was fully clothed, I couldn't help but think of that first time I ever saw her. I didn't think it was possible for me to be more attracted to her than I was the first night, but I was, because I knew what her face looked like when she came, the sounds she made when she was about to climax, the taste of her skin, the places on her that body that made her writhe when I touched them. But with Emily, it wasn't just about the heat. Hell, we could probably bake her muffins without ever turning on the oven. No, with her, it was about much more than that. It was the way she fit. The way our hands laced together. How I'd never slept more soundly than when she was curled up beside me. The way our hearts beat in tandem with each other. The way she looked at me when she didn't think I was watching.

I knew I sounded like I gowl, but what could I say? She made me a better man. She made me feel like maybe, someday, I could deserve the love of someone like her. No, not someone. Her. She was the only one I wanted, and it was past time that I told her.

"What are you doing here?" She didn't seem angry, just surprised.

"Eric said that he was going to be late and that you could use some help." *That's great, tool, keep lying to her. That's sure to get you far.*

Why didn't I just say that we needed to talk?

"Um, OK, let me just finish getting my stuff. I could just call Gabe or Uber it. You don't have to help me."

Didn't she know that I would do anything for her?

"It's really not a big deal." I slipped my hands into my pockets to keep myself from reaching out and touching her.

"I'll just grab a few more of my things." She practically ran into the bedroom. I looked around the apartment. The red and yellow tulips that I had dropped when I rushed out to the hospital were in a vase on the dining table. I moved closer thinking it was a good sign that she hadn't just tossed them when I noticed the photos on the wall. I stood in front of the wall and looked at the images. I had to put my hand against the wall to keep myself upright. My head fell forward against my arm as I struggled to gather myself.

I heard her gasp when she entered the room, but I didn't move. "You took them down," I stated. It hurt beyond anything I could have imagined to see that the pictures she had printed of us and our time together were no longer hanging on the wall where I had placed them Christmas morning. They were gone; in their place were the original photos that hung there. It nearly broke me to see those again. When I thought about my life and what I wanted, that wasn't it anymore. I wasn't a boy who wanted his father's attention. I wasn't a kid who needed his mother's arms to guide him, and I wasn't a boy who longed for a loving family. Well, maybe I did still long for a family, but I was certainly no longer a child, and being with Emily had proven to me that family isn't always blood. I think that was what I struggled with most about Kian and Abigail. They could have loved me, *should* have loved me, but for whatever reason, they didn't. I think that was what hurt so much to see the other photos gone, plain as day—they had shown me that with Emily I had everything I was ever looking for.

Love.

"I couldn't look at them. I thought that we were happy." Oh, God, how could she doubt that? My time with her was the happiest that I had ever been. My heart nearly broke in two when I saw her wipe away the tears from her eyes in the reflection of the glass. "I called a car so that you don't have to worry about driving me. I'll just get out of your hair. Goodbye, Dec." She was gone before I could get my feet to move. I crumbled to the ground. I didn't know how long I sat in the spot before I peeled myself off the floor, resigned that I was going to do whatever it took to get my Lemon Drop back.

Is that what she really thinks? It was impossible anyway. She was under my skin. Even more so, she was embedded in my heart. Call me pussy whipped, I don't care. She was the one for me. I looked around the apartment; it seemed so empty without her, so lifeless. My office looked just the way it had when I left. It nearly crushed me when I saw her toothbrush was no longer in its place. The sheets were freshly changed, but thankfully, her pillow still smelled like her. It crushed me to know that she probably felt exactly like I did at that moment when I left. I thought I had to leave to figure out who I really was, turns out I left the best part of me behind.

She deserved better, but I'm a selfish prick, so I was getting her back and I was going to prove to her without a doubt that I was the man for her.

Just when I was beginning to think that I was too late, I saw it out the corner of my eye. On the counter in the kitchen was her prized cherry-red mixer. She would never have left it behind, and maybe, just maybe it meant that she wasn't ready to leave us behind, either.

I didn't join Emily on her run the next morning. It was a part of my new plan. I wanted her thinking of me; wondering with each stride that she took where I was and why I hadn't joined her. She would know soon enough that I was thinking about her. My strategy was simple—remind her that we were happy and to prove to her that we could be happy again. I might have gone a little bit crazy, but they say go big or go home, so that was exactly what I did. I was expecting a text so I was a little surprised when my phone began to ring with her ringtone. The sound made me laugh.

Brit set it when we had breakfast. After I told her I was going to get Emily back she demanded my phone and entered "You're The One That I Want" as Lemon Drop's ringtone. She was the only thing I wanted. I didn't need to get to know her better to know that. Sometimes I thought I knew her better than I knew myself.

I could just picture her in the guest room she first used at Kian's apartment. Yes, at first I was a little sad to hear from my spy Maggie that she wasn't using my room, *our* room, but then I realized that being in the original room might help her to remember what she had felt for me the first time. In my mind, she was surrounded by bachelor buttons in a variety of colors ranging from white, pink, lavender, to dark maroon and she held my hand signed card in her hand. I had struggled with what I should write. I almost wrote the same words as the first time, "I look forward to getting to know you, Miss Barnes – Dec", but it didn't seem right. Anticipation, that's what they signified. Her in my arms, her in my bed, her in my life forever. I anticipated so many things with her, but one thing I knew for sure about my brilliant, beautiful, loving Lemon Drop was that she was probably terrified that I would hurt her again. Not to mention Libby was probably calling me "Dicklan" every chance she got and Nat was probably researching things like "how to make Voodoo dolls" or binge watching that television show *How to Get Away with Murder* while planning my demise. On the card, I simply wrote:

Will you go out on a date with me? – Dec

I'd never asked her that question before. I told her to get dressed and that we were going to Swayed. I didn't give her a choice. This time she wasn't only holding my heart in her hands but all the cards too. That didn't matter because I was going all in.

"Dec," she said quietly into the phone. God, I missed hearing her call me that. It was another good sign. I knew if she was pissed or upset she would call me Declan or even worse, drop the dreaded full Declan Kieran Hayes.

"Hi." I wanted to say so much more. To thank her for giving me confidence, but she had been the one to call me, so I wanted to let her do the talking. Suzie, Brit, and Sadie came over the night before and gave me some pointers. I prayed they were right—they told me to go her speed. To let her drive. I just hoped we didn't crash and burn.

"Hi, thank you for the flowers. They are just as special the second time around. You didn't have to do that."

"I know. I wanted to. I'm so sorry Lem—Emily." As much as it killed me, she asked me not to call her Lemon Drop, and I wouldn't until she told me that I could.

In a rush of words that I could barely understand, I think I heard, "Oh, Declan. I don't blame you for leaving. I was a complete wreck." *What? Did she? Could she really blame herself for me leaving? No. No way, it couldn't be.* This was all on me. Hands down, leaving her was the dumbest thing I'd ever done. Well, that, and then staying away for so long. *Son-of-a-bitch.*

"Stad!" I yelled in an effort to get her to stop and listen to me. She stopped talking but all I heard was her crying. I wished we were together. I would hold her in my arms and kiss away all of her tears.

"Please don't cry, sweetheart. How could you ever think that this is your fault? I'm the one that screwed everything up by taking off like that."

"Because I was a crazy woman. I was like a roller coaster. I was up and down, all over the place. I'm surprised you didn't get whiplash. I'm supposed to be this smart, strong-willed person who can stand on her own two feet, and then you came along and I just let you hand me my bakery on a silver platter. Who agrees to a rent agreement for eighty-eight ninety a year? And then I've been living in your apartment since December and not once has a single bill come. It's like winning the Powerball, and I let myself get carried away. Christ, the first time we went out I acted like I had some right to you. I told a perfect stranger that camel toe wasn't a good look on her, and I don't even what to think about the way I acted when I saw you and Brit together."

"Emily," I tried to interrupt her but she wasn't stopping.

"She's one of your best friends, and instead of talking to you, I assumed you were a lying, cheating, bastard like my father." I couldn't help but laugh. It was amusing now that I thought about it. Hell, I liked it that my girl had some claws. They were especially fun when she raked them down my back while I was buried deep inside of her. Yes, communication was something that we needed to work on and before I took off, we had been doing better. We were learning to work together as a couple. It was new to both of us.

"It's not funny, Declan. Shit, Brit, Marissa, your mother, the bakery, the book deal, I handled them all wrong. That's not who I am. That's not me." *Is that really what she thinks?* I let her continue to spew—she needed to get everything out of her head so that we could move forward. The phone went quiet after several more minutes passed.

"Are you done?" I asked, and she squeaked in response, clearly taken by surprise by my question. I patiently waited for her answer.

"Yes," she finally whispered.

"I don't ever want to hear this crap again." I didn't stop to let her get a word in. "You are one of the smartest people that I know. You saved me millions of dollars and hundreds of jobs with one deal, so technically, you paid for your bakery. Yes, I might have called in a few favors to get your permits in order, but you would have done exactly the same for me. I know you, Emily, you have the most giving heart of anyone I've ever met, so don't bother to tell me that's not true. As for your protectiveness of me—and yes, that's what it was, not petty jealousy—besides being insanely hot, it made me feel important to you. The way you stood up to Abigail for me, nobody has ever done that for me. Yes, meeting was you was like a roller coaster ride, but not for the reasons you think. Being with you was exciting and fun. You are worth that long wait in line. Those ups and downs. I don't want them with anyone else but you. Hell, for you, I would put my hands in the air, close my eyes, and decide to just enjoy the ride. You make my heart race. You put a smile on my face. You are the scariest yet best thing that has ever happened to me, and more than anything I've ever wanted, I want to prove that to you. Please say yes." She was softly crying again. I was hoping that a single yes was more than just an answer to my question about a date, but right then, I needed to take things one step at a time. "Emily, will you please go on a date with me?"

She didn't hesitate with her answer. "Yes, Dec, I'll go out with you." *Thank fuck.*

I have a date with my girlfriend, and now after talking with her, I know exactly what we are doing.

CHAPTER
five

"I don't think I've ever seen you like this." Eric was enjoying the hell out of me freaking out. Business was one thing, but this was another. This was my Lemon Drop, and I only had one chance to get things right.

Our first date. I knew it sounded idiotic because I knew every inch of that woman's body, but we were starting over. A fresh start, I hoped. We hadn't really talked about the time we spent apart. I didn't know who was more nervous about that conversation, her or me. I wasn't afraid of anything that she might need to tell me. Although I was almost five thousand miles away from her, I always had a heartbeat on what she was doing. I knew she'd be pissed off if she found out that Eric and I were in constant communication with each other. No, he didn't tell me specifics. Surely, I didn't even know that Libby was here, having a baby, and shacked up with Logan. He didn't even tell me that Matt and Hope were gone until I returned. He certainly didn't tell me that my girl and father were best buddies.

"Are you trying to take the piss out of me?" We were almost to the apartment, and I couldn't wait to see Emily after our conversation. Unfortunately, it ended shortly after she agreed to go out with me because Libby needed help with baby Aria. We'd shared a few text messages, but they were more for details about the date. I hadn't told Emily where we were going or what we were doing. I just told her when to be ready and to wear something comfortable and casual.

"Me? No, never. Fuck, you need to get laid." *Don't I know it.*

"You're a gas."

"And you're in big trouble, boss," Eric said as we came to a stop outside of the apartment. I followed his gaze to just inside the building. Christ. She was talking to Billy, her back turned to us. She was wearing faded jean shorts that showed off her muscular calves and her hair was pulled up into a high ponytail exposing the curve of her neck. Billy motioned toward the car and she turned toward us.

"Totally fucked," Eric added once we could see her from the front. She was just wearing a simple white t-shirt but it was a V-neck and her tits looked amazing. No doubt about it, I was fucked. Eric was enjoying this way too much.

"Asshole." I scowled as I hurried to get out of the car before she reached it. As much as I knew she was all about gender equality, I knew that Emily loved it when I opened doors for her. She flashed me a smile before she slid on a pair of black sunglasses; I thought maybe she was checking me out too. Not that I liked to spend a lot of time on what I wore, but I did pick out my green t-shirt with her in mind. I knew Emily loved my eyes and she told me in the past that when I wore green it brought out the color. I paired it with khaki shorts and leather docksiders. Sadly, as of this morning, her engagement ring was no longer hanging on her chain around my neck. I didn't want to take the chance of her seeing it before the time was right and if the past repeated itself, it wouldn't be long before we were tearing each other's clothes off. Fingers crossed.

I paused before sliding into the car after her trying to get the thought of her naked beneath me out of my head. I knew I had broken her trust and that as difficult as it would be, I would have to go slow with her. I would need to prove myself to her. Needless to say, I wasn't thinking straight the night I left. I was tempted on more than one occasion to just go to her; I knew that in her arms I would feel better, whole. Only in that moment, I didn't want to feel better. I wanted to understand why I had been lied to my entire life. I wanted to know why my father could barely look at me and why my biological mother had given me away. After a lifetime of lies, I thought that my birth mother was the one person who might just tell me the truth. I also wanted to know why he cheated on Abigail. I'd always thought my father was a man of his word. Thinking back now, I'm not sure why I ever thought that. He never kept his word to me.

I was pleased to see that when Emily got in the car, she hadn't moved completely to the other side. She wanted to be close to me, and as hard, pun intended, as that would be, it was another welcome sign of hope.

"Do you trust me?" I asked once I was seated beside her. Sadly, she looked up and met Eric's eyes in the rearview window. He nodded before she answered that she did. *Baby steps*, I reminded myself as I removed her sunglasses and placed a mask over her eyes. Once we began to move, she surprised me once again by placing her hand palm side up, an invitation I wasn't expecting but gladly accepted as I laced our fingers together. As much as we both knew we needed to talk, we didn't. We held hands and listened to music as Eric navigated us toward our destination.

"We're here," I whispered in her ear once the car came to a complete stop. Her breath hitched, and I noticed goose bumps had suddenly broken out on her arms when I moved away to open the door. It was nice to know that I still had that kind of effect on her, but I wasn't above using our off-the-charts chemistry to help get her back.

Even though she was still blindfolded, I'm sure she knew exactly where we were the moment the door opened. You could hear music, machinery, people, and even screams and the smell was a mix of ocean, deep fried foods, and sweets. I stepped closer to her and untied the silk that covered her deep chocolate-brown eyes. She blinked several times to try to adjust to the bright light before I placed her sunglasses back on her face.

I took her small hands in both of mine. "I know it was just a metaphor when you said it, but I wanted to bring you here to show you that life can be good even with the ups and downs." I paused because I wanted this date to be fun, but I needed her to know this one thing more than anything. "I never wanted to hurt you, Emily." I begged her with my eyes to believe me.

"OK," was all she said as she smiled at me brightly. *OK?* I had no idea what that meant, but at that moment, it was enough. Eric silently handed me the keys, giving me an approving head nod before leaving us.

"Do you have on sunscreen?" I asked as we passed by one of the many tacky souvenir shops that lined the boardwalk.

"No, I forgot." I reluctantly let go of her hand and told her I'd be right back before dodging in the shop to buy a bottle of lotion. On an impulse, I also bought her one of those cheap mood rings that were on display at the counter. Yes, I had noticed she was no longer wearing my grandmother Hayes Claddagh ring that I had given her for Christmas. Also missing has the heart pendant that she had worn around her neck, another gift from me. It made me sad to know that she no longer wore them, but at the same time, I knew that my sentimental girl would still have them and that if I could prove to her that I was deserving of her heart, she would wear them once again.

"Will you hold this for a second?" I asked as I handed her the bottle of sunscreen. With a smirk, she took it because she knew I was up to something. She held the bottle in her right hand so I took her left in mine. As I slid the simple silver band on her finger, I imagined it was a different ring and that I was down on one knee asking her to be mine forever. The aqua color instantly changed to a dark shade of blue. "You're happy," I stated, as if I actually knew what the change in color signified. She didn't question me but she did surprise me by leaning forward and kissing me on the cheek.

"Wait here," she told me before she rushed into the store I had just exited. Moments later, she returned with a wide smile on her face. "Give me your hand," she told me, and for some reason, I offered her my left. Moments later, she slipped a matching band on my finger. We both laughed as she struggled to push it on. It reminded me that the sound of her laughter was my second favorite sound ever, my favorite being the sound she made when she was about to come. And just like that, I was hard again. "Looks like someone is happy," she teased, and I wasn't sure if she was talking about the giant bulge in my pants or because my ring had turned that same color of blue as hers.

Originally, I had planned to offer to help her with her sunscreen, but touching her would have done nothing to help me with the problem in my pants. After we were both lathered up, we walked hand and hand along the boardwalk. Several times we stopped to take selfies with our phones, and we even asked someone to take a picture of us when we put our heads through one of those ridiculous face hole cut-out boards. I was a giant muscle man showing off my massive guns while wearing a banana hammock, and Emily's character was a scantily-clad woman hanging off said muscles. This time around, I wanted to be in every picture with her. If she would have me, I would fill the apartment with photos of us together.

We acted like children. We laughed so hard we almost puked on The Scrambler. We both nearly suffered from whiplash on the bumper cars, and together, we screamed our heads off on the rickety wooden roller coaster.

"Are you hungry?" I asked as we walked holding hands on the boardwalk.

"I could eat," was all I needed to hear before leading her toward our late lunch. I think she was surprised when I ordered for her without asking what she wanted. I knew what she would order; I didn't have to ask. Somehow, it seemed important to me for her to know that I did really know her. What she liked, what she didn't. I didn't want Emily to use our lack of time together as an excuse. I knew everything I needed to know. She was "it" for me.

"Can I ask you a question?" she asked after popping one of the hot crinkle cut fries in her mouth.

"Anything." And I meant it. She could have asked me to rob a bank and I would have done it for her.

"Did you find her?" I'd wondered how long it would take her to ask me that.

"No." I didn't mean to sound so curt. It still hurt to know my mother seemed to have vanished off the face of the Earth, but I hadn't given up hope on finding her. I didn't really want to talk about that. I had things to tell Emily that I knew would upset her when it came to my quest to find my biological mother. If I wasn't careful, she might not give me a second chance.

"One more question." She took several nervous sips of her lemonade. I could tell whatever it was was hard for her to ask. I held her hand and patiently awaited her question. "Why are you here now?

That was easy. "Because this is where I am supposed to be." I was trying not to scare her away, which was ironic since I was the one that ran before, not her. In my letter, I told her that I loved the way she "loved the unlovable me". That was still true. I also promised "to be worthy of that love" when I returned. I still wasn't sure that I was worthy of her, but I also knew that if I had any chance with her that I had to come back. I had already lost so much time. Our first Valentine's was spent apart. Emily didn't get to make me my favorite cake for my birthday. We didn't get to spend the long Memorial Day weekend at the beach. I wasn't about to miss her birthday too.

"New York?" she asked.

I moved from my seat across from her to her side. I leaned forward and kissed her forehead before trailing my lips down her nose. Like so many times before, I rubbed my nose against hers before moving my lips to her mouth. The kiss was soft and tender. It was me telling her without words how much I loved her. With our foreheads pressed together, I whispered, "With you."

You know how sometimes a second feels like a lifetime? That was how the moment felt.

"OK." For the second time today, that was her only reply. As frustrating as it was that she hadn't given me more, it was enough for now. We were running a marathon, not a sprint, after all.

The mood had certainly changed between us. My girl seemed to have a lot on her mind, but she still held my hand as we walked off our lunch.

"Can we go in here?" she asked as we stood at the entrance to the historic sideshow.

"Of course." I paid the woman at the ticket booth. Part of me wondered if she was the first performer in the show. Her hair was shockingly blue and ink covered every inch of her exposed arms and chest. One side of her face boasted a variety of tattooed stars and she had more piercings than I could count. I wondered how she ever made it through a metal detector. Emily sat beside me on the bench-style seating. I watched as she was entranced by the fire eater and the sword swallower. She fascinated me more than anything on the stage. I could have watched her forever. When the snake charmer appeared on stage, Emily practically climbed into my lap.

"Not of fan of snakes?" I teased as we exited the historic building.

"Just one," she answered playfully before running ahead of me. For fuck's sake, she was trying to kill me. My balls were probably as blue as my mood ring. I caught up with her at the line for the Ferris wheel. The sun had set while we were watching the freak show. I reveled in the fact that she took my hand the second I was next to her. The wheel had two types of cars. Cars that swung and cars that didn't. I'd wondered if she was trying to tell me something when she picked the rocking cars. Was our relationship a little rocky or was it a little exciting on an otherwise safe and longstanding wheel of wonder? Like in the car, we sat much closer than was necessary. Her smooth, bare legs were flush against mine and our hands remained twisted together. Every time that car swung, she seemed to inch closer than I thought was even possible. She buried her head in my shoulder when we stopped at the top of the wheel.

"I'm scared, Declan." She said it so quietly, like she was afraid to say the words out loud. I kissed the top of her head.

"Me too," was my only response. I was scared too, and it had nothing to do with the ride. If things with Lemon Drop weren't "OK" then nothing else ever would be.

"Oh, I need to win that for Fay," Emily said as she pulled me to the carnival game. I think we were both still reeling from our ride on the Ferris wheel. We shared a funnel cake, and it reminded me of the night that we shared a crème brûlée on the street and she welcomed me to her world. I didn't want that night to end just like I didn't want this one to.

"Is that a dog or a bear?" I asked, and she giggled. I wanted to hear that sound again and again. Whatever it was, it was giant and pink, and if my girl wanted it, she was going to have it, even if it wasn't for her. I placed a five-dollar bill down and was handed two darts. I'd played my fair share of darts and was confident that I could break one of the balloons easily. Forty dollars later, and I was pissed. Not only was the carni eyeing my girl, but he had also just shown me again how "easy" it was. Fucker. Emily had urged me several times to just walk away, but no way in hell were we leaving without the ugliest stuffed monstrosity ever known to man.

"You're acting the maggot, Declan." Emily scowled when I placed another twenty down. *Have I mentioned that I love it when she uses Irish slang?*

"I'm not being a jerk, M; I'm giving you what you want." That's what I thought, anyway.

"Really?" She stopped me from tossing the last dart I had left in my hand. She took it and turned her attention toward the pimple-faced jerk that was running the show. "I'd like to use one of those," she said as she pointed my dart at the ones that were in his shirt pocket. Something passed between them and his face changed the instant he handed over the requested dart. Emily took her stance and the balloon popped easily when it hit its mark. That took the piss right out of me. I was scammed by a fucking kid.

Within seconds, Emily was trudging the stuffed animal in the direction of the car. I wasn't trying to be a maggot, but I was sure doing a good job being a muppet—a fool.

It was past time for me to smarten up. It was the only way I was ever going to get her back.

CHAPTER
six

To the promise of more to come.
I'm sorry for being a tool - M'fhíorghrá – Dec

I signed the card that would accompany the apple blossoms, and Jasmine smiled at me. She had told me many times that she was impressed by my choices—if only Emily was as enchanted. I had never used the term M'fhíorghrá before, but in my heart, I had no doubt that Emily was my true love. To say that last night didn't end well was the understatement of the year. Emily was pissed, but I wasn't sure if she was madder at me or herself. She told me that she hated the way she acted when we were together. I knew how important it was for her to stand on her own two feet. I should have known that when I went all caveman on her that it only made her feel weak. Nothing could have been further from the truth; she was the strongest person that I knew.

"I'm not a damsel in distress, Declan. I don't need you to save me, and I certainly don't need you to waste your money on a stupid stuffed animal just because you have something to prove. I'm surprised you didn't challenge that punk to a dick swinging fight." *Ouch, that hurt.*

That hadn't been my intention at all. Honestly, I'd just wanted to make her happy. I would do anything for her. At least she kissed me on the cheek before rushing inside the bakery. I watched from the window as a very large man that I didn't recognize came out of the kitchen. Despite what she had just told me, I almost rushed out of the car to rescue her, but before I could move, he put his arms around her, and from the way her body was shaking, it looked like she was crying. *Who was this guy? Why the fuck was he holding my woman? Why didn't I know about him?* Eric had some explaining to do. Again.

"*I don't need you to save me.*" Her words ran through my head on a loop. If I ran in, it would have just made things worse, so, instead, I hit my Bluetooth.

"Who the fuck is Popeye?" I cursed out before Eric could even utter a hello.

"So, you've met Tank?" he asked with an amused tone.

"Who the hell is he, and why the fuck didn't you mention him before, Eric? She practically ran straight into his arms."

68

"You asked me to keep an eye out for her and to tell you anything important. He works for her and you damn well know that anyone that she knows becomes a friend, Declan. She cares about him … like a brother."

A brother? I didn't even know he existed. How could so much change in the time that I was gone? Does he think of her as a sister? Probably not. Fuck! He's a man and she's the most incredible woman on this planet. Of course, he's attracted to her. Who wouldn't be? Maybe he's gay. He better be.

"And you didn't think telling me she had someone named 'Tank' working at the bakery was important? Maybe we need to re-define important." I didn't even realize that I was still driving. It had taken everything in me not to go rushing in after her, and I couldn't go up to the empty apartment when she was downstairs crying in the arms of another man.

"God, did you and Emily talk about anything? Tank is a friend of Willow's husband and part of a work program for wounded veterans. Emily needed to replace Kenzie."

"Who?" I bellowed into the phone before I heard a scuffle and then Suzie was suddenly on the phone.

"Declan, you and Emily seriously need to figure this shit out, but here are the Cliff Notes. Kenzie is Hope. She and Matt are together in Nashville. Lord, don't they have television in Ireland? Tank is a big, harmless Teddy Bear, but if you mess with his girls, and by his girls, I mean, Emily, Willow, and Fay, you'll be sorry. PTSD is a bitch, and the job at the bakery saved him. Now, if you need any other info, call four-one-one, or better yet, ask Emily. If you don't mind, I'll be hanging up now because, frankly, I'm sick of your cock blocking. Eric will call you tomorrow. Good night." Eric was laughing his ass off in the background because I swear Suzie said all of that without taking a single breath. Ha, at least I wasn't the only one not getting any action. Somewhat relieved that he was only an employee and friend, I slowed down and headed back to the apartment. I struggled not to go inside and to apologize for acting like an arse, but, instead, I went upstairs and worked on my plan to get my girl back. Obviously, it needed work. The ugly bear/dog came with me.

After leaving the flower shop, I went to Logan's apartment. I needed allies and knew that Libby was at the top of the list. They were wombmates, after all.

"Logan isn't here." Libby looked a lot like her twin sister but now looking at her I could see subtle differences in them. She was beautiful, but she wasn't Emily. Her hair was in a messy bun, and she looked like she hadn't slept in days; the baby was crying, and you could tell that it bothered her because she left me just standing at the open door, so I let myself in. She picked up Aria and tried to sooth her.

"Shhhh," she pleaded and patted her back. "Mom made it look so easy. I can't even imagine having two of us at once. I've tried everything. She's been fed, burped, changed, and rocked, but she still won't stop. I just want five minutes to take a shower." She sounded so defeated but the look she gave her newborn daughter was one of nothing but pure love.

"I'll watch her," I volunteered without hesitation. I'm not going to lie, the idea of being responsible for the tiny human scared the piss right out of me, but if it earned me points with Libby, I would do it.

"Are you sure?" she asked skeptically.

"Positive," I said as I reached out to take the baby from her. Careful to support her head, I brought her close to my body and began to rock and pat while I hummed a lullaby. It must have been one that one of my many nannies had sung to me when I was a lad. Whatever I was doing seemed to be working because Aria quieted. That seemed to appease the nervous mother.

"Five minutes, and I'll be back."

"Take your time." I always wondered why people said that babies smelled so good, so I brought her higher up my chest and then buried my nose in her neck. Damn, she did smell good.

"You did good, Dicklan." Aria had fallen asleep on my shoulder, and I had sat down on the couch, but I didn't even try to put her down. One, because I didn't want her to wake up, and two, because holding her was almost as good as holding Emily in my arms. Almost.

"What would it take to get you to stop calling me that?" She shook her head in amusement as she went to the kitchen and poured two tall glasses of ice water before joining me.

"But Dicklan seems so fitting." *Ouch. Would I ever be able to get her on my side?*

"I know I hurt your sister and I'm glad you've got her back, but I'm back now and I don't plan on leaving unless Emily tells me herself that she doesn't want me in her life." I didn't want to even consider that as a possibility "Haven't you ever screwed up royally?" I asked her as she looked down at her beautiful daughter before returning her gaze to me. From what Emily had told me about Libby, I knew in her past she had made a lot of questionable choices. Maybe she would grant me a second chance. Doesn't everyone warrant at least one?

"Mom said she gave you Gram's ring. She wouldn't have done that unless she thought you deserved it. What did the letter say?" I could do better than just tell her. I shifted Aria and carefully removed my wallet from my pocket. The letter was beginning to wear. I had folded and re-folded it so many times since I got it. At least once a day I read it as I held the ring against my heart. Grandma Rose said in her letter, "If she's yours it will be for a lifetime" and I wanted that to be true more than anything. Cautiously, Libby took the letter from me. After several minutes, she swiped at the tears that fell from her eyes.

"Hormones," she said as she carefully refolded her grandmother's words and handed it back to me. Did that mean I had her blessing?

CHAPTER
seven

A text alert startled me awake.

Mo Eala: We need to talk

I changed her contact name from Lemon Drop to "my swan" after she asked me not to call her that. It hurt, because to me, she would always by my lovely Lemon Drop, but I wanted to respect her wishes—for now. Her grandmother had said that she was a swan, and I had to agree with her. She was sophisticated, gentle, noble, and from above the waterline, she made everything look effortless while in reality her constant paddling was taking a lot of her emotional stamina. I wanted her to know that I saw her from below the water's surface, and I still thought she was the most beautiful thing I had ever seen.

The day before was a busy day. When I left Logan and Libby's apartment, she actually said the words, "Thank you,

Declan", so I took that as confirmation that I had her support in getting her sister back.

Natalie was a little harder to convince, but Gabe had given me some guidance in the name of her favorite coffee joint. Like Libby, Natalie didn't seem happy to see me when she opened the door, but the second she eyed the large white cup with the blue lid, her eyes lit up, and when I extended my hand and offered my "peace offering", she almost did a little jig.

I opened my mouth to speak once we were both seated on the sofa but she put her hand up for me to stop while she enjoyed several pulls off her drink. The sounds of pleasure she made reminded me of the nickname Matt had once given her—screaming orgasm. *Note to self: when traveling with Nat and Gabe, do not get adjoining rooms.* I remained silent while she had her moment with her coffee.

"When M gave her toast at our wedding, she said that Gabe and I have the recipe for a perfect marriage: romance, humor, joy, trust, respect, tenderness, friendship, and patience. I hope she's right, but I think she left one out. Forgiveness." Nat's gaze shifted out the windows, and for a moment, she seemed to struggle with what she was about to tell me. I waited with bated breath. "Emily doesn't know this, but I cheated on Gabe." *Oh, fuck.* "It's the one secret I've ever kept from her, and I hope that you will keep it that way." Tears sprang to her eyes; it was clear that it was very hard for her to tell me. I also understood why she would think that keeping it from Emily was for the best, not that I agreed, but I did understand it. She finished her drink and put the empty cup down on the coffee table. Wow, this wasn't how I was expecting this conversation to go at all.

"No relationship is perfect," I said as I took the hands that she had fisted together in mine. "Gabe loves you, and as far as I'm concerned, this is between the two of you." I paused. "I think she might be more forgiving than you're giving her credit for." Yes, Emily would be hurt by Nat's betrayal of Gabe, but like with me, I believed she would forgive. She had the biggest heart I had ever known.

"Thank you. You know, I told her that I thought the two of you had it too, a winning recipe, that is. You hurt her, Declan, but I don't think you would be here trying to bribe me with the nectar of the Gods unless you were serious about getting her back." That was true. "How much of a hypocrite would I be if I didn't believe that you deserved a second chance like I got? I won't stand in your way, and if she asks me, I'll tell her that I think she should at least let you try to make this up to her." Thank God. "That being said, I think you know what you'll be facing if you screw up again." Yeah, I was painfully aware. Honestly, I would rather kill myself than hurt Emily again.

All in all, it was a good day. After talking with both Libby and Natalie, I felt better about them supporting a relationship between Emily and myself. Not that I would have let them stop me, but their support certainly did make things easier. I also got the pink beast to its rightful owner. I swear that dog/bear was watching me sleep at night. It creeped me out. Fay loved it. Willow, not so much. I told her it was all my idea so that she wasn't upset with Emily. I could take the heat for my woman.

Me: Yes, is gá dúinn a labhairt

I knew she didn't understand Gaelic, but I also knew she thought it was sexy as hell, and let's face it; I needed all the help that I could get. Speaking of sex, it was morning so I was already sporting morning wood, but now that my mind was on Emily, I was painfully hard. I hadn't choked the chicken this much since I was a pubescent teen myself. In those days, I would need my magazine stash from under my bed. I would lie on my stomach with my face inches from the centerfold as I rubbed myself against my sheets. When I got a little older, I got pretty good at being ambidextrous, clicking my mouse with my left hand while pumping the python. The housekeeper could never seem to figure out why I was always missing socks. Yeah, right, it's the dryer monster. You know, the age-old question of how one sock always seems to go missing in the wash.

What can I say? I was trying to be considerate and save her from having to wash my sheets on a daily basis. Too bad I wasn't smart enough to put a password on my computer or to clear my browser history. For whatever reason, Abigail decided she needed to be "parental" and check what I was up to online. That got me a quick trip back to boarding school. She said a deviant like me didn't need privacy, so I roomed in a barrack-style dormitory. Holy shit, you should have heard the nightly whipping of the willies concerto we performed. No amount of air freshener could change the smell of that dorm. I'll just say that we used a lot of toilet tissue and a large portion of it wasn't on our arses. Nowadays, I like to clean my rifle in the shower. No mess on the sheets, no tossing my cum-filled socks in the trash, and my room doesn't smell like a splooge factory.

"Yes, Sister Mary, we know the windows are open, we like it cool in here." Yeah, right.

I didn't need any visual aids anymore. All I needed to do was think of my Lemon Drop, my swan.

She's on her knees and wet inside and out from both the hot water and from the sight of me stroking myself. I know she likes what she sees because she licks her luscious lips and leans forward. She's reluctant at first. Licking the head of my dick like it's a lolly. I stroke harder, and she rewards me by circling my ridge with her tongue. I can't help but moan when she licks the pre-cum from the tip. Feeling brazen, she reaches one hand up and begins to massage my balls while her free hand travels down her body to touch her bare mound. The combination of touch, sight, and sound are intoxicating. I'm not going to last at this rate, so I release my cock. She immediately licks the area my hand just left. One of my hands goes to the back of her head and the other I use to support myself against the wall of the shower. She opens her mouth and engulfs me; this elicits a deep moan of appreciation from me. A finger from the hand on my balls easily finds that magical spot on the underside of my cock. I have to remind myself to loosen the firm grip I have on her silky brown hair. She looks up at me, and it is almost my undoing. If her eyes are the window to her soul, right now I know with every fiber of my being that she loves me. And I ... oh, fuck. Her adept fingers roll my balls before she pushes that button, and I go off like a rocket. Houston, we have liftoff, and she takes everything that I give her. Incredible, and I think it's only fair that I show her how appreciative I am, so once she releases my cock I lift her and fall at her feet. She's the sweetest thing I ever tasted, and what can I say? I'm starving, so I place her trembling legs on my shoulders and eat.

F-U-C-K. I curse as I coat the shower wall with my release. What could be better? *Oh, yeah, how about her really being here with me?*

Lemon Drop would be there any minute. She'd asked for no distractions, so I suggested that she come to me. She'd agreed. After ordering her favorite pie and making sure that the beers were cold, I decided to jump in the shower for another yank. It's the only way I'd be able to be in the same room alone with her and not attack her, not that I didn't want to because I did, but this wasn't about sex. I was also a sneaky bastard, so I put on the jeans that I knew she loved to ogle me in and tossed my shirt on the back of the couch. Her knock was timid.

It's show time.

I clicked the remote and familiar music filled the air. They do say that all is fair in love and war, and this was the fight of my life.

I answered the door with my towel hanging from around my neck, my hair still wet from the shower. I read some shit about women swooning for glistening men.

"Oh, hi, I didn't realize it was so late." *Yeah, right.*

I moved aside from the door and began to towel dry my hair. She seemed to forget that I could see her reflection in the mirror that hung on the wall. Her skin was flush and she darted out her tongue like she did in the morning when I imagined her sucking on my dick. My cock was already starting to get hard; it was a good thing I just choked the chicken again, but that shit was getting old really fast.

"Thanks for coming." She looked stunning in a long black sundress. It was tied at her shoulders and my jeans tightened at the thought of how easily her dress would come off with just the tug of the two small bows. I wondered if she was wearing any of the sexy underwear I got her for Christmas underneath it. Her gaze lowered to the small bakery box tied with string that hung from her finger. I couldn't help but notice that we both were still wearing our tacky mood rings. I loved the fact that they were both practically identical in color. Purple. Passion.

"Let's dance," I said as I took the box from her with one hand and quickly wrapped my other arm around her. I'd never been this much of a dancer, but I'd use any excuse I could to touch her. I probably should have put my shirt on first, but we'd already established that I didn't fight fair, not when it came to getting my Lemon Drop back where she belonged. She was stiff in my arms again. "The pizza will be here any minute and then we can talk." That seemed to put her at ease. I pulled her closer. *Damn, she smells so good.* "This was the song we danced to at Eric and Suzie's wedding."

"I remember, Declan. You also had them play it at the club when I had my date. I don't even want to guess how you knew about that." But she wasn't angry. She melted into me as we moved in time to the music. I knew she felt it, and I'm pretty sure she saw it when I showed her the file of photos I had taken of her. I should have just said it. I should have yelled it from the rooftops. I just couldn't be sure. What did I know about love? Looking back now, I think I probably loved her the second I laid eyes on her. How could I not? I didn't loosen my hold on her as we swayed back and forth, the rapid beating of both our hearts nearly drowned out the beautiful lyrics, but I know she heard me when I mouthed, "maybe it's all part of a plan" against the soft skin of her shoulder.

"Em." I was so lost in the song, in her scent, in her being in my arms that I was on the brink of telling her everything I was feeling. Just then, the intercom buzzed announcing the arrival of our dinner. Reluctantly, I let go of her and tossed my shirt on. I couldn't help but delight at the instant frown my addition of more clothing caused. While I went to the door to get the pizza, she went into the kitchen. It made me giddy when I realized she had kicked off her shoes and grabbed us each a beer. She was making herself at home again. Maybe she'd never leave.

"Lombardi's?" Like she had to ask. Maybe history would repeat itself and she would attack me after she attacked the pie, but sadly, she sat on the floor on the opposite side of the coffee table from me. She had a serious look on her face. "No more stalling, Dec, we need to talk." *Mutts Nutts, time to pay the piper.*

I knew Emily probably had just as many questions as I did. In all fairness, I should have just let her ask me what she wanted, but a thought crossed my mind. In a partnership, we would both have equal opportunity to ask questions and give answers. "I've got an idea." She raised a brow. I reached out for the deck of playing cards that sat on the table. "High card on each turn gets to ask one question." I could tell that she liked the idea. I shuffled the deck and motioned for her to cut it before dealing us each a card. Hers was the three of diamonds. I had the ten of clubs.

"How did you meet Willow and Fay?" She smiled as she swallowed the bite of pizza she had just taken. Before she answered, she took a long swig of her cold beer.

"Willow saw the article about me in the paper. Her husband, Dillon, is deployed. It's his third tour and she sends over care packages to his battalion. She wanted to know if I would donate any baked goods. They love getting treats from home. Fay called them hugs from home." She had a huge smile on her face as she continued to tell me about it. "That first month we made like thirty boxes filled with anything we could get our hands on. Nat wanted to put something about it on the Mama M's site; she needed a name so we called it 'Hugs from Home' and the next month we sent one hundred and fifty boxes. After that, it all kind of went crazy. The red tape is a nightmare, but the e-mails, tweets, and posts that we get from the men and women that serve our country who receive our boxes make it all so worth it. Plus, Willow does all the hard work." That explained all the boxes that were along the wall in the bakery. "Have you ever heard of those monthly subscription boxes? They have them for everything; books, make-up, razors, snacks, and well, now they have one for our military. We're having a packing party this weekend. You'll have to come. We get volunteers from all over. It's amazing. Even your father volunteers and he has donated so much." While my father had always been generous sharing his fortune, I had never once seen him offer a second of his own time. Yes, I had seen him at plenty of black tie fundraisers, but the thought of him actually rolling up his sleeves and helping was laughable. She must have noticed the smile had dropped from my face when she started talking about Kian.

"Declan, he's not the same man. Maybe if you just gave him a chance, talked to him, you would see it for yourself."

Fat chance.

"In due time," I told her flatly. I didn't want to talk about my father. Kian Hayes could wait. Not that I had given up hope on finding my mother, but Emily was my priority. It took a while, but I had come to realize that it didn't really matter who I was if I didn't have her by my side. She nodded in understanding and smiled broadly when I added, "I'd love to help with 'Hugs from Home' in any way that I can. Put me to work."

"I will." She picked up the deck and dealt us each a new card. Luck was on my side when I drew the high card a second time. I was tempted to ask about Tank, but I didn't want to come off as a jealous boyfriend. *Boyfriend? Was I even that?* I decided to go with the safe route and hoped that it would actually get me answers to two questions I had.

"What are Matt and Hope doing in Nashville?" Every single time I had asked anything about them I had been treated like I was a complete idiot for not already knowing. Lemon Drop actually fell back on the floor and laughed at me. I couldn't just sit on the sofa and watch as she practically rolled around on the floor, so I quickly joined her and began tickling her.

"Stop, stop. I give, I give." I stopped, and it was then I realized that I was straddling her with her hands pinned above her head in one of my hands. We were so close, the air around us stilled. I traced my free hand up her side from her waist. She bit down on her lower lip. I palmed her breast and she released her lip with a low moan just as I leaned forward and kissed her. I fought the urge to ravage her because I wanted this to last. Very slowly and gently, I kissed her face, her eyes, her nose, her forehead, her cheeks, and even her chin. Then I moved to her mouth. She wanted my tongue, but I didn't give it to her yet. It was driving her crazy. Hell, it was driving me crazy.

I almost lost all control when she pressed her hips up and tried to grind against my cock. In a complete frenzy, she groaned when I sucked her bottom lip into my mouth and sucked hard, giving her a good reminder of the way I could suck other parts of her body. As badly as I wanted to keep going, I knew it was time to stop. While I wanted

Emily in my bed, I wanted in her heart even more. *This isn't about sex.* Not that I wouldn't like anything more this very second.

When I sat back up, she was definitely disappointed that I had pulled away and she had that glazed over look in her eyes. Good, she needed the reminder of how good we are together.

"Alainn. You're beautiful." I didn't think it was possible for her to blush further, but she did. I let go of the grasp I had on her hands and painfully got off of her, but instead of returning to my original spot, I joined her on the floor.

"Matt and Hope, I mean, Kenzie, are in Nashville because that is where she's from. He's helping her deal with some stuff with her family." I knew Matt had a thing for that girl, I also knew she was hiding something. Emily must have seen my fury because she quickly came to Hope, I mean, Kenzie's defense. "She had her reasons for keeping who she was from us, Declan." That just made me angrier.

"She—"

"What? Lied to me? Kept the truth from me? Hurt me?" Damn. She was pissed. She got up from the floor and began to pace the room. It was no longer about Kenzie. Son-of-a-bitch, and I thought that I had asked the easy question.

She fisted her hands in her hair. "I need to go." She moved toward the pair of sandals that she had kicked off.

"Wait, "I pleaded as I quickly picked up the deck of cards and began to flip through them as quickly as I could until I found the card that I was looking for. Her hand was on the door when I reached her. "Here," I said as I handed her the queen of hearts. No, it wasn't the highest card in the deck, but I hoped it told her something.

She took the card in her trembling hands, closed her eyes, and raised it to her lips.

"Ask me anything," I implored. I was desperate. She couldn't leave like that. She choked up as I fell to my knees before her. "Please."

Our eyes were locked on each other, and she took a deep breath before asking, "Was any of it true?" It was a good thing I was already down on my knees because that question surely would have knocked me flat on my arse. Did she really not know the answer? A single tear fell from her eye, and she whisked it away, but she didn't need to hide her tears or her pain from me because they were mine as much as they were hers.

"Every single word," I told her without hesitation while I looked straight into her sad, brown eyes.

After several minutes, her lips turned up slightly before she simply said, "okay." Then she leaned forward and rubbed her nose against mine like we had done so many times before, and then she was gone.

Most would have been frustrated with her reply of "OK", but with Emily, it gave me dóchas. Hope for our future. All I had to do was make-up for everything that I had missed while I was gone. Piece of cake. After she left, I decided it was time to figure out why everyone thought I should know more about Matt and Kenzie, so I decided to ask my good friend Google.

Holy shit! I must have been living under a rock the last six months. Damn Eric.

CHAPTER
eight

"What do you think of this?" I asked my assistant enthusiastically.

"It's pretty, but you are going to be in trouble with Mommy." Willow was in the kitchen.

"Why?" I asked Fay. Willow hadn't been that thrilled when I arrived, but when I explained what I was there for, she seemed to soften. Of course, it might have had something to do with Fay being so excited to be my helper. Emily was at Bristol working on her book. I didn't know if I'd ever known anyone that worked as hard as she did. She was truly amazing, and I waited for her new "friend" Tank to leave for the day before coming in.

"You are making a mess with the glitter." I scratched the end of my nose while I looked around the room to inspect the damage and the little cutie began laughing. Her laughter was infectious so I couldn't help but pick her up and begin to spin around the room with her. First baby Aria and now little Fay had both easily wrapped me around their fingers without even lifting them.

"What's going on here?" Emily asked with a smile from her spot just inside the door. Fay and I had been having so much fun that neither one of us had heard the door chime when she came it.

"Mr. Dec has glitter on the end of his nose, Miss M," Fay announced as I set her back down on the floor. Her mother, Willow, was a stickler when it came to her daughter showing adults respect. It was commendable of her, but Mr. H. was my father to Fay and it seemed silly for her to call me Mr. Hayes when we were sitting on the floor coloring together, so I told her to just call me Mr. Dec. I tried to wipe away the offending specs as Emily approached us both with a bemused look in her eyes.

"What are you doing here?" she asked me, but before I could answer, my helper chimed in.

"Happy Valentine's Day!" she cheered as she pulled me out of the way so that Emily could see our handiwork.

White, pink, and red hearts in varying shapes and sizes adorned the walls of the front area of the bakery, and a large glittery sign read, "Will you be my Valentine?"

"It's June," Emily stated in utter disbelief as she took it all in. All the embarrassment I had felt that morning when I explained to the clerk at the craft store what I needed was instantly gone because her reaction was more than I ever could have hoped for. Suzie had offered her assistance, but I didn't want Emily to doubt for one second that I had done it for her. Yes, I could afford to have the room filled with twinkle lights and hundreds of flowers, but that wasn't what Emily would want. She wanted my heart, so that's what I gave her. She was happy, and I did that, for her. Now if she would just grant me my wish.

Fay cleared her throat and she pushed the box in my direction. "You're not very good at this. You need to stop looking at her all funny and give her this." Honestly, I think Fay just wanted to have some of the candy. She had been eyeing the box since I arrived with it and the overabundance of art supplies earlier. Emily covered her mouth as the pipsqueak schooled me on how to romance my Lemon Drop.

"Fay Veronica Hill, get your bottom in here," Willow called from the kitchen door. I took the box of chocolates from her and she skipped over to her mother. Fay winked at me, and once we were alone, Emily let out the burst of laughter she had been holding in.

"Wow, she told you, Mr. Dec." I loved the way her smile lit up the room and the way she mimicked the way Fay said the name she had given me. I took a step in her direction with the chocolates still in my hand. "Really, Declan, what are you doing here?" It was then that I noticed how tired she looked. Beautiful still the same, but in much need of the pampering I had planned for her.

"I meant what I said last night, Emily. I know I've missed a lot, but if you'll let me, I'd like to try and make it up to you. Will you be my Valentine?" I asked as I presented her with the giant heart-shaped box.

She didn't hesitate in answering me with a grinning yes which was quickly followed by a loud cheer from a very excited five-year-old girl. "Sorry," Willow said as she shooed Fay away from the kitchen door.

"Let's get out of here," I said as I took the box from Emily and put it on the table. I wondered briefly it would be safe there with little Miss Fay.

"Where are we going? I still have work to do." Her strong work ethic was one of the things I admired most about her. I knew she wouldn't just drop her commitments, so I made arrangements with Maggie and Greta to do her baking that night. Maggie and Greta were the only ones that didn't threaten me with bodily harm if I didn't make things right with Emily. I think they knew they didn't have to,

"I hope you don't mind, but I've got it all taken care of," I assured her as I laced my left with her right hand together while opening the door for her with my other hand. The last thing I wanted was for her to be mad at me again for taking liberties with her business. I learned my lesson on that the hard way. I raised our joined hands to my lips and pressed a kiss to the top of her hand and she blushed. She didn't say anything, so I took that as an "OK".

The last time she was there, it was to meet Abigail for tea. She needed new memories. Good memories.

"What are we going here? We aren't dressed for this place; let's just go back to the apartment." I was wearing shorts and a basic t-shirt while Emily was wearing a Mama M's "best muffin tops in the city" t-shirt and a short flowy skirt. As always, she looked beautiful. According to Monica, her meeting at Bristol had just been to go over some page layouts and photo edits, so she was dressed pretty casually. Emily could have been wearing a brown paper sack and I wouldn't have cared one bit, but I planned for that as well. In fact, I had asked Nat to help me, which I thought might have scored me some points with her BFF.

With a squeeze of her hand, I asked, "Do you trust me?" She simply nodded in reply.

While I knew her trust in me was not what it once had been, I believed that she did still have confidence in me, and, more importantly, I wanted her to trust herself. If she didn't do that, she would never fully be able to forgive me for my mistake. That was what we needed to be able to move forward. I knew she still had a ton of questions, and I would answer every one of them. No matter how difficult they might be. I had to have faith that our love was strong enough to get us through anything. Even the things that I was afraid to tell her.

We bypassed the lobby and entered the elevator. We were joined by several others before the door closed and I asked for the sixteenth-floor button to be pushed for us. Emily said nothing, but from the flush in her cheeks and the way she was breathing, I knew she was nervous, but despite that, she didn't ask any questions. The idea that she would follow me, even though she was terrified, thrilled me to no end. The car began to empty as we went higher. I put my arm around her and pulled her closer to my side.

"It will be OK," I whispered into her ear, and she trembled in response. It was funny what one simple word could do to both of us. OK. O. K. An adjective, adverb, interjection, noun, and a verb. One little word, with so many different meanings.

She sighed in relief and placed her head against me. The doors opened on our floor, but I paused to place a kiss on the top of her head before moving, my hand still around her showing her the way to the room. I swiped the card, and I opened the door for her but remained in the hall as I motioned for her to go in. *Note to self: she'll still go to a hotel room with your gimp ass.*

"You aren't coming in?" she asked, noticeably confused by what my intentions were. I would have liked nothing more than to take her inside and make sweet love to her all night like we probably would have done on the real Valentine's Day if I had stuck around, but now I needed to prove to her that we still had that perfect combination she talked about at Gabe and Nat's wedding. Nat showed me the video, and I could see why Nat thought she wasn't just talking about them in her speech. Lemon Drop and I had all the things she mentioned: romance, humor, joy, trust, respect, tenderness, friendship, and patience. Emily had said that it didn't matter about the ingredients, that it was about the way you mixed them together. She toasted to the sweet life, and that was exactly what I wanted for the two of us. I knew it wouldn't always be sweet, and I'd take the sour as long as I had her.

"I'll be waiting for you downstairs." I quickly kissed her and left before my little brain started to do the thinking for my big brain since that was where all my blood was flowing.

"Bloody hell, Hayes, ye plonker," I cursed at myself as the elevator descended to the lobby. I used the time to try and calm myself down. The ride wasn't long enough. Hell, the ride from One World Trade wouldn't have been long enough.

The concierge directed me to where I could change. The heat of late June didn't bode well for a full suit, so instead, I put on a pair of black slacks, a fresh white dress shirt, and a textured waistcoat. I decided to forego the tie because Nat said that Emily's knickers would melt off when she saw me like that. Nothing was wrong with a bare box in my book, especially if it belonged to mo eala, my swan. Before going to the place I instructed her to meet me, I entered the Pembroke Room and ordered a neat Connemara. The barkeep poured the drink and raised an eyebrow at the box that I placed on the bar top.

"They aren't mine," I said as I raised my glass. He probably didn't believe me, but I was sure it was not the strangest thing he'd ever seen in the hotel bar, so I ignored his amused smile. The peaty aroma of the whiskey reminded me of Anastasia's cozy cottage and I looked at my watch noting that it was probably a little late to dial her up. I would definitely call her tomorrow. I placed a twenty on the granite bar and left with a smile on my face as I imagined the stunned looks of all the snotty women there for tea when she asked for a doggie bag like it was an everyday occurrence. *That's my girl.*

"You must be Mr. Hayes," the elegant woman, whom I knew was Madame Angela by the way she carried herself the moment I saw her, said in greeting.

We shook hands, and I had the distinct feeling that Nat was right about the melting undergarments, but I was only interested in one woman's knickers. A door closed, and it startled me, not because I was doing anything wrong but Madame Angela still had my hand in hers. Emily had not reacted favorably to the way other women threw themselves at me in the past. I wanted to leave no doubt in either woman's mind that I only had eyes for one, so I pulled my hand away and nearly ran to Emily. She looked stunning, as always. It amazed me how she could look so beautiful so quickly when other women took hours to achieve the same results. She truly was spectacular in every way. I dropped the box in my hand at her feet and pulled her into my arms. She had no choice but to rise up on her tippy toes because of the way I held her. The snog was possessive, or maybe I should say submissive. With everything I had I wanted her to know that I belonged to her. Only her. *Take me; I'm yours, my love.* At the end of the kiss, I fell to my knees before her.

Without thinking I said, "Tá tú álainn." She didn't understand, so I repeated it in English. "You are beautiful." I kissed the tops of both of her hands.

"And barefoot," she giggled. She looked amazing in the maxi dress that was the color of red wine with the flowing skirt that was perfect for what we were about to do. Her hair was up, showing off her amazing bare shoulders. She was sheer perfection. I would have drank her if I could because she was certainly intoxicating to me.

"Yes, sorry about that, but I wanted the pleasure of helping you slip these on." I picked up the box as I stood and took her hand in mine.

Either she was oblivious to Madame Angela's presence in the room or she just didn't care. That was fine by me. I pulled out a chair for her and she sat as I once again went down on bended knee before her. After opening the box, I slowly lifted the billowing skirt of her dress. She pointed her polished toes as I held her behind the calf and slipped on the black, patent-leather, platform pump. Nat assured me that some people had orgasms simply from wearing the red-soled shoes. Fuck, they were sexy. Was Nat talking about the women that wore them or the men they wore them for? I couldn't stop myself from leaning forward and kissing the top of her foot before repeating the same action on her other foot.

"You kissed my feet."

I pulled her up from her seat, and with the addition of the heels, she was at the perfect height, so I kissed her again.

Madame Angela cleared her throat from behind us. "You two are just lovely." I could see in her eyes that the hunter was gone; thankfully, I was no longer her prey. Emily dropped a kiss on my cheek. I took it as a sign of thanks.

For the dress, for the shoes, the compliment from the other woman, for what? I didn't know. "I'm Madame Angela, and I'm here to teach you how to dance," she said as she reached out to shake Emily's hand. When she stepped forward, I couldn't help but notice the back of her dress, or should I say the lack thereof. With the exception of the spaghetti straps that crisscrossed, her back was completely bare. *Yer like a blue-arsed fly*, I scolded myself internally. Dancing with a stiff wab wasn't going to be fun at all. I took several deep breaths in an effort to get myself under control. *Fat chance.*

"It's nice to meet you. I'm Emily Barnes, and I can't dance to save my life." I knew the way the woman could move her body, and I had no doubt that she was completely wrong about her dancing abilities.

"Well, that's why I'm here. Mr. Hayes, if you'll be so kind as to take your partner and show me where we are starting from." Madame Angela was all business as she walked toward her sound system. "All of Me" by John Legend filled the room. It was the perfect song for us, and believe it or not, I took that moment to silently thank Abigail Hayes for all those forced years of cotillion and black-tie events.

Undoubtedly, Emily was out of her element because she lifted both of her arms up as if to put them around my neck at the same time I lifted my left arm and attempted to put my right on her shoulder blade.

"Oh, my God." She giggled as we both dropped our arms. "I told you I have no idea what I'm doing, Declan. I do a mean running man and I can twerk like nobody's business, but I can't waltz." She lowered her head and shook it.

"Hey—" I put my thumb under her chin and tilted her head back up "—you can do anything you put your mind to. Just follow my lead. I've got you." More than anything, I wanted her to understand that I wasn't just talking about dancing. I lowered my forehead to hers. That always seemed to ground her. I trailed my lips down her nose before placing a kiss on the end of it and silently willed her to believe that she was safe in my arms. Then I rubbed her nose against mine and let out a small laugh when she smiled again like all was right in the world. I kissed her chastely on the lips and then took a step back. I was confident that together, we could do it. Together, we could do anything. I placed her right hand in position and then took her left in mine.

Legend crooned about his head being under water. I knew that feeling. "Right-side-close," I told her with a smile as we began to move. "One-two-three. Good." We were doing it. Just like I knew we could.

The song ended and Emily jumped into my arms. "We did it! You are amazing," she gushed as she peppered my face with kisses. Our instructor began clapping. I had almost forgotten about her. We probably didn't really need her, but I wanted Emily to know that I was taking this seriously. I think Emily had forgotten about her too because she buried her face in my neck in an effort to hide from Angela.

"You two are so natural together," she praised. While I didn't want to let go of Emily, I did so Angela could give me a few pointers on my hold. Then she pulled Emily aside and the two women spoke in hushed tones. They acted like they had known each other for years. It was a relief and I was intrigued at what they could possibly be talking about. Emily hugged Angela and then returned to my side. Music filled the room again. The only other thing I heard was the door closing behind Madame Angela. We were alone.

"May I have this dance?" I asked as I held out my arms to her. Her cheeks were pink and her breathing was shallow as I took her in my arms. I felt dizzy, and it wasn't because of the circular motions we were making on the dance floor in our private room. The tune changed, it was a song I hadn't heard before.

Although I had seen the Northern Lights and the Eiffel Tower at night, I felt the words were meant just for us.

I wished that I knew the lyrics so that I could sing them to her. She was everything that he described, more than I could ever dream of. If I had nothing but her in my life I would certainly die a happy man. As the song came to an end, I dipped her back. Her eyes were shining and her smile was bright, I almost told her right then that I loved her more than anything, but I was terrified that just when I felt she was coming back to me that I would scare her off, so when I brought her back upright, I crushed my lips against hers and hoped that she would feel it in my kiss.

Her stomach growled so loud that we both heard it. She covered her face in embarrassment, but we both laughed out loud. "Come, mo eala, it's time to feed you." I took her hand in mine and led her over to the table that was set for us at the edge of the dance floor. As requested, our settings had been placed next to each other instead of across from each other. The moment I filled our champagne glasses, our first course was served.

"Have you ever done this before?" I asked as she hesitantly skewered a piece of bread and carefully dipped it. I, on the other hand, went for something a little more unusual, a slice of avocado. It was buttery and sweet and completely delicious.

She stared at me as I swallowed down the scrumptious bite. She still hadn't answered my question. "They say that avocado is an aphrodisiac," she blurted out before she licked her lips and stared at mine. Fuck, I was going to have to have all of my pants altered to give me more room in the crotch at this rate.

"You don't say," I said as I loaded my dipper with another piece of avocado. I hoped I sounded much calmer than I was. She feigned innocence and tried to escape my stare by looking for her long forgotten utensil. "I've been told that if you misplace your dipping fork in the fondue that you need to kiss your sweetheart. Open," I demanded as I lifted my fork to her mouth with the other hand raised beneath it so that nothing dripped on her dress. She did as I asked, and I carefully placed the bubbly blend of Gruyere, Raclette, and Fontina cheeses in her mouth. She moaned as she savored my offering. I lowered the empty fork and placed my other hand on her chin as I wiped the tiniest bit of cheese away from her lips with my thumb. She caught my hand as I began to move away from her, opened her mouth, and placed my thumb in her mouth and sucked. For Christ's sake.

I'm not even sure how I made it through the salads and our entrees. Hell, I couldn't even tell you what I ate. All rational thought had left my body the moment Emily's lips were wrapped around my thumb sucking. Did I mention that I could die a happy man if all I had was her hand? In my hand, in my mouth, on my thigh, where she had placed it every chance she got, or any other place on my body she wanted to put it. Or her mouth, or her breast—anyway, you get the picture. Neither one of us had talked much during the meal. I couldn't. I got the feeling that she was just as affected as I was. Our waiter brought out the pot of melted chocolate, and I had no idea how I was going to survive the rest of the meal. A variety of fresh fruits were accompanied by cookies, marshmallows, brownies, and pound cake. I just wanted to dip Emily. I didn't know if it was an accident or intentional but we only had one of the dipping forks with our dessert, so we took turns feeding each other. It would have been so easy, too easy. Emily was worth everything to me and the only way that she would know that, that she would trust in what we had, was if I proved it to her. Erasing all her doubts.

I took her hand and escorted her back to her room. Thanks to the waiter, the timing was perfect. I opened her door for her but again did not step into the room. Kissing her goodnight at the door was the most bittersweet thing ever.

"You aren't coming in?" she asked as I reluctantly kissed her one last time.

"Not tonight, mo eala." She looked so disappointed. "Your bath is drawn and waiting for you. Don't let it get cold. Thank you for an evening I will never forget." I traced the side of her face with the back of my hand and she leaned into it.

"What does that mean, and why are you calling me that?" I couldn't very well tell her that her grandmother had called her a swan. Not yet; it would give too much away. She wasn't ready, but we were heading in the right direction.

"Because you won't let me call you Lemon Drop." It hurt to say those words out loud. I kissed her chastely on her lips and whispered, "Goodnight, my swan. Happy Valentine's Day."

"Yet," she said so faintly that I almost thought it was my imagination.

"Good morning," she opened the door to the hotel room looking refreshed, radiant even, and then she saw what I was wearing and started laughing. I couldn't help but laugh too. We looked like twins, dressed in the same exact outfit.

"I swear, I didn't know what Maggie packed you." Last night when Emily returned to the suite after our dance lesson and dinner besides her bath being drawn, she found candles lit, an arrangement of freesias, the latest release from her favorite author, an overnight bag packed by my favorite partner in crime, and a note from me.

Grow with me - Dec

It was good to see her so relaxed and happy. She even snapped a selfie of us and texted it to Maggie, who I'm told was rather pleased with herself.

After securing her favorite doughnuts and coffee, we got on the road. I loved how she hadn't asked a million questions and was just going along with whatever I had planned.

"Are we going where I think we're going?" I decided to drive myself because I wanted to be alone with Emily but driving also meant I had to keep my hands on the wheel and my eyes on the road. We were headed in the direction of Stuart's tree farm, and I did plan on stopping to see them after we finished our main excursion.

"Later," I promised as we arrived at our destination. I'd never been there myself, but I had sent teams from HIP; I'd heard nothing but good things. At the least, it would be fun, and if we were lucky we would leave there stronger than we were before.

Now my girl was usually game for just about anything, but when I turned off the engine, I noticed she was no longer chatting about random subjects like she had been for the rest of the trip. I looked over at her, and I swear she was green. "What's wrong? Are you sick?"

She shook her head before finally answering shakily, "We're doing that?" She pointed to the course that could be seen from where we were parked.

"Yeah," I said as I unbuckled her seatbelt for her.

"I'm not a big fan of heights." She was fine on the roller coaster and the Ferris wheel. She could do this. She wouldn't be alone. We would work up to the tallest obstacle that she seemed to be focused on.

"We'll start out on the ground." I kissed her cheek before getting out of the car. I opened her door for her and squatted down in the opening. "Do you trust me?" That was the million-dollar question. It wasn't the first time I had asked.

With my question, her fear faded and was replaced with something new.

What? I don't know. Determination? Maybe. Whatever it was, I was up for it.

"Welcome to Challenger, are you Declan and Emily?" a guide who looked like an extra from Bill and Ted's Excellent Adventure asked as he held up two helmets and harnesses.

As promised, we started out on the low ropes first. The course certainly lived up to its name. Our harnesses were clipped together with only about an arm's length span separating us. We must have fallen off the Mohawk Walk five times before we started really communicating and working together.

"You guys make a good team," Jake, our guide praised as we finished the last of the lower obstacles.

"We are," Emily agreed.

"Ready for the fun stuff?" Jake asked, oblivious to Lemon Drop's fear.

"We can do this," I encouraged her. Together, we could face all of our fears and beat them.

"I'm ready," she answered. We both were. I believed that together we could do anything, face anything, and overcome whatever challenges came our way. Before free falling, off the highest platform, I realized something. I had always believed in her. It was me I didn't believe in, but she gave me the strength I needed to believe in me too.

"That was amazing." She rushed to me as soon as my feet hit the ground. "Thank you." She kissed me. It was me who should have been thanking her. She'd given me so much. She faced her fear and jumped. I hoped it was a metaphor for our relationship too.

After our adventure at Challenger, we headed to see the Stuarts.

"Where are Buck and Bruce?" Mrs. Stuart asked very seriously after she finished hugging us both. Would they ever let us live down the lie we had told them about having twins at home?

"I'm kidding, Declan, lighten up." The three of them laughed at my expense. I deserved it.

While the "women" talked recipes, Alex and I went out to the barn. I feared that I was about to get another talking to about hurting my girl. I was prepared for it.

"You wouldn't be here if you weren't trying to make things right."

"No, sir."

"She'll forgive you." How could he be so certain? "That's what you do when you love someone." Could it really be that simple?

CHAPTER
nine

Mo Eala: Thank you again for yesterday

She told me to just come down whenever I wanted to. I knew she usually took a nap after working her early morning hours and her jog, so I took my time. I called Anastasia and answered e-mails from my home office. HIP had done surprisingly well without me. Monica e-mailed me any questions she had and any contracts that I had to review. It had been difficult at first with her maternity leave and me being gone, but once she returned, we figured it out. Once she stopped asking about Emily, that is.

My plan was to go and get bagels for the packing party she had invited me to, but when I got to the street level, I couldn't help but notice the hustle and bustle happening at Mama M's. The room was crowded with people, boxes, and tables. I couldn't see Emily in the crowd but Libby sat at a small table just inside the door, and she looked better than the last time I saw her. Possibly, my suggestion to my father via e-mail that Maggie help Libby with the baby a few hours a day had been a good one. He didn't need full-time help for himself. Aria was strapped snuggly to her chest in some kind of papoose-like carrier. A nametag was affixed to the back, and Libby wore one too.

"Name?" she asked with an amused look on her face while she held a marker to a new nametag, presumably for me.

"I'm kind of shocked you haven't already written Dicklan." She pressed the pen down and giggled as she began to write, but an "e" followed the "D" and then the rest of my name. Under that, she wrote, "AKA ICB". That had me smiling. Nobody had called me that in a long time. Maybe the return of it would also signal the return of the name Lemon Drop.

"Thanks," I said as stuck the tag to the front of my shirt. "This is crazy," I said under my breath, but she heard me.

"Yeah, I don't think they ever thought it would be this big." I had been on the web page for Hugs from Home that Natalie created and was impressed. The page was flooded with comments from soldiers who had received boxes, but what really stuck out to me the most was that little was mentioned about Emily or Willow. Anyone could see that it wasn't about them. It was about sending a stranger, who was protecting our country, a piece of home. It was about making them smile and thanking them for their service.

While at the site, I clicked the subscribe button and purchased one hundred boxes per month for one year. It was the most it would let me do.

Fay was sitting at a table surrounded by other children—they all looked to be working as hard as the adults who were filling boxes at the tables.

"Mr. Dec," she called out when she saw me and began waving her arms around for me to join her.

"You're being paged," Libby said as she waved me over toward the table full of kids who were now looking at me.

"Hey, kiddo," I said as I kneeled down next to her. "Whatcha doing?"

"We have the most important job," she told me in a very serious tone. The table was littered with colorful papers, markers, crayons, and even the glitter I had been reprimanded for making a mess with. It appeared the excess of art supplies I bought wouldn't be going to waste, and I made a mental note to go back and get even more. "We're in charge of the hugs."

All her counterparts eagerly agreed and began showing me their "hugs". The children ranged in age, so it wasn't a surprise that so did the complexity and style of the artwork, but one thing was abundantly clear—no matter the age of the artist, these children were proud of the work they were doing.

"Are you all right, Mr. Dec?" Fay asked as I silently admired their work. She could have been sad; she could have been selfish. Her daddy was somewhere far away from her. She probably wouldn't see him for months, if she was lucky. It made me sad to think of this little girl and her father, it made me think of my own. It made me wish things could be different. Dillon Hill was one lucky man. I couldn't help myself; I pressed my lips to her temple and told her that I was more than all right. When I pulled away, I noticed Emily and Willow were both watching the exchange and that both women wiped away tears from their eyes.

"Keep up the good work," I told all of the children before I stood upright and strode over to Emily. It didn't matter that we were in a packed room, most of them strangers, I had to kiss her, just like I "had" to kiss her on that cold sidewalk last November. I placed one hand on her hip and pulled her close, my other hand went to the back of her head, and I kissed her like we were alone in the room. It wasn't until the crowd began whistling and cheering that I broke the connection.

I bowed my head and placed it against her forehead. "This is incredible, *you* are incredible," I told her breathlessly. This woman had no idea how amazing she truly was, but if I had the chance, I would spend the rest of my life telling her just that.

Apparently, my anonymous purchase of one hundred boxes had both Emily and Willow in a bit of a tailspin. While they never complained about it, they clearly hadn't planned on it, but instead of just pushing the start date of the subscription out to next month, they were bound and determined to get the boxes out this month. I got the feeling that many of the volunteers were returning. One, because they seemed to work like a well-oiled machine, and two, because many of them had on t-shirts with the Hugs from Home logo on the front and the words "FREEdom is NOT Free, Hug a Hero" on the back that looked like they had been worn before. I talked to many of the volunteers as I tried to make myself useful. I needed to prove myself worthy to be hers.

"Where are you from?" I asked the woman who was stuffing boxes with bags of nuts.

"I'm from Palmer," she said as she happily continued to work.

"Massachusetts?" I inquired. "That's about a three-hour drive," I answered my own question, and she nodded in agreement. She was wearing one of those t-shirts, so I was fairly certain it wasn't her first time making the long trek.

"That's nothing, have you met Val yet? She and her daughter take the bus every month from Buffalo." That was crazy, the bus had to cost at least three hundred dollars for round-trip tickets for two. Why didn't she and her daughter just buy a couple of monthly subscription boxes instead of spending all that time and money every month?

"Her son is serving." Evidently, she must have read my mind. "Says if her baby can sleep in a tent with twelve other guys on a cot that is six inches shorter than he is tall, that she can ride the bus once a month so that he and his brothers can have a little piece of home."

What was truly incredible was that the boxes were sent to military all over the world and to all the different service branches. Emily explained to me earlier that the names and addresses for the boxes were randomly generated from a database that was shared amongst several different organizations. Soldiers had to apply to be part of the program and had strict rules that they had to follow, along with the rules that had to be followed by Hugs from Home when filling the boxes. Val had no way of knowing that her son or anyone in his brigade would ever receive one of the boxes, yet she came every month.

I was grateful that my father was nowhere to be seen; his presence would have been a damper on this otherwise perfect day. I tried to help wherever I could. Everyone was happy, that is, except for one person. Tank. If looks could kill, I'd be dead. I didn't give him a second thought when I decided to put myself to use by taking out the trash once lunch was finished. He was smoking a cigarette against the side of the building. When he saw me come out the back door with my full hands, he stubbed it out and lifted the lid to the dumpster for me.

"You can save your breath," I told him when I turned to face him. I didn't need him to give me the same lecture I had already heard from everyone else. None of them would have to kill me if I hurt my Lemon Drop because if I did anything to make her unhappy again, I would do it myself. "I know what you'll do to me if I hurt her." This caused him to chuckle.

The guy was massive and if the dreamy looks many of the ladies inside gave him were any indication, I guess I would say he's good looking. He walked with a limp, more than likely the result of an injury that landed him there in the first place. His hair was cut short, reminiscent of a military cut, and his eyes were a steely gray. His size was pretty intimidating. I had to remind myself, *Emily loves him like a brother.*

"It's probably not what you're thinking at all," he drawled out with a shake of his head and a smirk. That was when I realized exactly what he was thinking. He wanted me to fail. He wouldn't kick my ass at all. *Son-of-a-bitch.* It was clear; his feelings for my Lemon Drop weren't sisterly.

"I'll be the arms she turns to, and once I have her, I don't ever plan on letting her go." As much as I would have liked to, I wasn't in a position to do anything about Tank other than making sure I never gave him the opportunity to have her. That was one chance I never planned to give Zeke "Tank" Sherman. Not ever.

I carried a sleeping Fay to Willow's waiting cab. I told her that I would have had Eric drive her, but she insisted that she was fine in the cab. It was a long day, but a satisfying one. After Gabe came with a large company truck and loaded up all the boxes, Emily, Willow, and Fay agreed to join me upstairs for dinner. "Why don't you put muffins in the boxes?" I had asked while we were passing around cartons of Chinese food. Willow and Emily both started laughing uncontrollably like I was missing some kind of inside joke

"Dillion told me that he loved the crumbs." It was clear when Willow talked about her husband that she missed him, but that she was very proud of him. "When Emily agreed to help me, we worked on a recipe that would withstand a lot of abuse."

"The Monster Bars?" I had also seen a lot of comments about them online. Everyone wanted to know where they could buy them. Apparently, they couldn't, because they were exclusively available to the troops in the Hugs from Homes boxes.

"It took us a few tries," Emily said as affirmation. "They had to be yummy, but they had to be sturdy, and then we had to figure out a way to package them. You should have seen us actually throwing them against the wall." This memory caused both women to laugh again.

"Who came up with the name?" It didn't seem like something either one of them would have come up with.

"It's what Dillon calls Fay." I hoped when Emily talked about me she got the same look Willow had in her eyes when she talked about Dillon. "She's his little monster baby. She's the one that wanted to send her daddy and his team snacks in the first place, so it just seemed like the perfect name."

I'd tasted a Monster Bar. Not only were they healthy, but they were delicious. Those girls could have been making a mint, but that was not who they were. If only the world had more Emilys and Willows, but luckily for me and Dillon, they were ours. I didn't know about him, but I planned to never let Emily go. I had a feeling he didn't, either.

"We couldn't have done it without your dad." My entire body tightened when Willow began singing my father's praises. Great, another admirer. Emily put her hand on my thigh under the table and gave it a squeeze. "Uncle Sam won't let you send home baked goods unless you are a direct relative, which was fine when I was sending boxes to Dillon and his buddies, but when things went crazy and we decided that our boxes would go to soldiers everywhere, we had to package them commercially."

I didn't know what pissed me off more—that my father had helped, or that I hadn't been here to do it. It should have been me. I didn't know why I ever thought I deserved a second chance with her. I wasn't good enough. She deserved a man who wouldn't leave her, ever.

Emily squeezed my thigh again before leaning over and whispering, "I want you to stop." I told her that in my letter. I didn't want her to think the worst. She didn't want me to, either.

Willow became distracted by Fay who was struggling to use her chopsticks. Her words had helped, but I was still struggling when she did something that gave me hope—she pulled the heart necklace that I had given her out. My heart beat faster when I realized it had been hiding inside her shirt all day. Hope—she just gave it to me. Faith—they say it doesn't make things easy, it just makes them possible. I'd take possible because a life without her simply isn't. Trust— it was something we'd been building on even the smallest moments since my return. The ropes course had proven that. And love? I didn't think it was possible to love her more than I did before, but I did.

CHAPTER
ten

I looked like an idiot, but I didn't care. Emily was worth it. She looked beautiful in a pair of white capris paired with a pink flowy blouse, but she also looked a little tired again. As proud as I was of her, I was worried too. She was doing so much between the muffins, the specialty desserts, the cookbooks, Hugs from Home, and still volunteering at The Bowery. She couldn't possibly keep up the pace.

"Hi." I loved that despite all the things we had done together, she still flushed when she saw me. She had the same effect on me.

"Hi." I opened my arms for her, allowing her to see my "kiss me I'm Irish" t-shirt. With a smile, she stepped into my open arms and did just that, kissing me. Something had definitely shifted between us. She kissed me, and it wasn't a brief kiss because she was doing what my t-shirt instructed, either.

"Wow." She giggled as if her own words surprised her. "Did I say that out loud?"

I couldn't help but laugh too. She was simply adorable. "You kind of did, but you're right, that was wow.

She took a step back from me, and I instantly wish she hadn't. "Declan, you don't have to keep doing this."

"Doing what?" I asked coyly as if I didn't know exactly what she was talking about.

"You know what I mean." She had her hands on her hips. Oh, those sexy hips. *How I would love to have my hands gripping on them as she rides me hard.* Her tits would bounce in my face and her moans would fill the room as I rammed my cock up her tight wet pussy while I pushed her down by those sexy as fuck hips. I had to turn away from her to tame my raging hard-on. I laced my fingers on top of my head while I tried to think of anything else but fucking her silly. It was not a simple task.

"This is nice," she said as she sat across from me at a table in the restaurant we ate at before I surprised her with tickets to Radio City at Christmas. I had to put a loaner blazer on over my t-shirt, but it was worth it because not only did I want to make-up for the things that I missed but also wanted to remind her of the great times that we had shared together.

"It is," I agreed wholeheartedly.

"How did you learn to do that thing with the chopsticks last night?" While it was fun watching Willow try to teach Fay how to use them, the little cutie was getting frustrated, and so without thinking, I got up and pulled a rubber band out of a drawer in the kitchen. You know, that catchall drawer. Every kitchen has one. Maggie told me, so it had to be true. After wrapping the rubber band around the two sticks, I rolled up the paper wrapper and inserted it between them. Faye quickly mastered the skill as Willow and Emily watched in shocked amazement. Her question caused me to think, how did I know? And then it dawned on me.

"Abigail was out of town, and Mrs. Ford, the housekeeper was called away unexpectedly, so Kian ordered dinner." I couldn't help but smile at the memory. "I didn't think I had ever seen to-go containers in my life before, I must have been about Fay's age." Now she was smiling too. "Anyway, I guess he thought since we were already breaking all the rules that we would sit on the floor in the media room and eat out of the cartons with chopsticks while we watched the baseball game." She covered her mouth with both hands mimicking shocked horror. "It was the Subway series, I think, and I was worse than Fay when it came to using chopsticks." I can't believe I forgot all about that night. It was great, we even made plans to go to see the next series between the Yankees and the Mets. He promised me he would take me. He never did.

"Don't," she said as she grabbed my hand and pulled it across the table. "Whatever you just thought, just don't. It's OK to remember the good, Declan. He loves you." I didn't know about that. He lied to me my entire life.

"Tell me about your time away." I knew the conversation was coming. I was surprised she hadn't demanded to know more. I didn't think I could be as patient as she had been. "You were in Ireland," she stated, and I nodded but realized this was it, the time to tell her the truth, a truth that I feared would tear us apart.

"Most of the time," I said the words softly, trying to gauge her reaction to my confessions. She didn't give anything away in her face but squeezed both of my hands. I hoped it was a sign that she wasn't letting go. "I came back briefly and went to New Jersey."

Shock, hurt, anger—all three emotions flash in her eyes, but she said nothing, so I continued, "I found Brianna Bailey's mother." That caused her to gasp as if in pain.

"Why didn't you tell me? I would have come with you." I knew that, I also knew that the distance of the table between us was too much, so I pulled our joined hands so that she was forced to get up, and I pulled her into my lap. I didn't care if everyone in the restaurant was watching.

Even with her in my lap, it wasn't close enough, so I dropped my forehead to hers and brushed my nose back and forth against hers like I'd done so many times before. Apparently, it grounded me too. "I had to do this on my own," I admitted, not wanting her to think for a second that I didn't need her. She was all I needed.

119

"OK." There was that word again. I took a deep breath before I continued.

"Conor Bailey had a massive coronary about six months after I was born. My grandmother, Lurena Scott was remarried practically before his body was in the ground."

"You? What are you doing here?" she asked angrily. She had opened the door and had smiled when she saw the large bouquet of mixed flowers, but as soon as she saw my face, my eyes, she came out the door and shut it behind her. It was instantly clear that she didn't want me there.

"I'm—"

"I can see who you are. What are you doing here? Haven't you caused enough damage?" Me? I hadn't done anything. I didn't have to wait long for the answer. "You're the reason Conor is dead, his heart was broken into a million pieces when he lost his beloved Brianna because of you." What the hell? Wasn't I an innocent child? Did she really blame me in all of that? Did she even care about Conor? She remarried before his body was even cold, and it didn't look like she was doing too badly for herself. Sure, it was New Jersey, but it was nice.

"I have a half-aunt who's twenty-five," I blurted out. It was the first time I'd said the words out loud, and it was like a weight had been lifted off my shoulders. "And a great grandmother. Her name is Anastasia Flemming. She's who I've been with in Ireland. She's also the reason I had the courage to come back to you."

Her lips crashed down on me. I didn't know how long we kissed before a throat cleared beside us. Emily buried her head in my chest in embarrassment by our public display of affection. "Would you like dessert maybe, or possibly a room next door at the hotel?" the waiter asked impassively.

Emily attempted to scurry off my lap, but I wasn't ready to let her go. "We'll take one of everything," I said. Sadly, that time, I wouldn't have the pleasure of using her body as a plate.

"Tell me about Anastasia," she said as she lifted a fork to her mouth. I didn't even realize I was licking my lips. She raised a brow as she seductively pursed her lips around the fork. God, I wanted to be that fork.

"You're going to love her when you meet her." I had already told her that she was ninety and no longer traveled.

"Really?" *Don't look so shocked, Emily, of course, I want to take you to Ireland. Nothing would make me happier, except maybe finding my mother and having all three of you together.*

"Of course, maybe on our honeymoon." I was tired of taking things slow. Anastasia told me once that in the end we only regretted the chances that we didn't take. I wanted Emily to know without a doubt where I saw things going with us. We still hadn't said those three little words, but I was no longer afraid to say them. I was just waiting for the right time. "We better get going. Mass is about to start."

121

"Mass?" she asked as we left the restaurant hand in hand.

"Yes, it is Saint Patrick's Day." I flashed my t-shirt at her, and she rose up one her tiptoes and placed a kiss on my cheek.

"But I'm not wearing green. I wouldn't want anyone to pinch me." If I'd had it my way, I would have been the only person ever touching her again.

"Actually, I've got that covered." I reached inside my jacket and removed the envelope that was tied with a green ribbon, handed it to her, and she immediately tied it in her hair. She looked absolutely beautiful. "These are from the land of my ancestors. Here, hold this." I awkwardly pinned the shamrock on her shirt before she returned the action by pinning the other on mine.

Sitting next to her in the nearly empty church was magical, or maybe I should say Divine. I wouldn't call myself an overly religious man, but I did believe with everything that I was that Emily Barnes was a true gift from God who was brought into my life for a reason.

"A reading from the first book of Peter, chapter four, verses seven thru eleven, new international version." The reader cleared her throat before she began to read the ancient scripture. "7. The end of all things is near. Therefore, be alert and of sober mind so that you may pray. 8. Above all, love each other deeply, because love covers over a multitude of sins. 9. Offer hospitality to one another without grumbling. 10. Each of you should use whatever gift you have received to serve others, as faithful stewards of God's grace in its various forms.11. If anyone speaks, they should do so as one who speaks the very words of God. If anyone serves, they should do so with the strength God provides, so that in all things, God may be praised through Jesus Christ. To Him be the glory and the power forever and ever. Amen (1 Peter 4:7-11 NIV)"

We entered O'Mary's and were immediately greeted by a course of, "Happy Saint Patrick's Day" from our friends. The strange glances we got from others in the bar were priceless. Shots of whiskey were placed in front of us, but I stopped Emily before she could pick hers up. She watched me as I removed the shamrock from her shirt and dropped it in her glass and did the same with my own.

"It's called drowning the Shamrock," I explained as we raised our glasses. "Dóchas," I offered in a toast to my swan, my Lemon Drop.

"What does that mean?" she asked after downing the contents of her glass.

"It means hope." I shrugged and then added, "Bringing faith to the future." She nearly melted into my side. "Now toss that over your left shoulder and make a wish." We both fished our shamrocks out of the bottom of our glasses and did just that. I knew my wish, but I wondered what hers was.

"Why your left shoulder?" she asked, and honestly, I had no idea, but I didn't tell her that.

123

"Because that's the side that this is on." I placed my hand directly over her heart. "When you make a wish, you should want it with all of your heart." And I meant it.

"Hayes, did you know that a guy named Thomas Hayes was the first to die beer green on Saint Patrick's Day over one hundred years ago right here in New York?" Paul, the owner of the pub offered as he handed us each a glass of the green liquid in question. His timing sucked, but at least his beer was cold.

"Sounds about right," I offered as I drank. An epic rematch of boys versus girls flip cup ensued. That time, the girls weren't so lucky, and by the time it was time to leave, my girl was plastered.

"Where are we going?" she asked as she leaned heavily against me in the back seat of the car that was waiting for us.

"I'm taking you home." I gave the driver the address to my father's apartment, and Emily began shaking her head. I didn't like the idea of seeing him or her not having anyone to watch over her when she was this langered, but I didn't think I had another option.

"No, take me home. Our home." She begged with her eyes, and I shook my head. That wasn't a good idea. "Please," she asked again before I found myself redirecting the driver to our apartment. She could barely stand, so I lifted her into my arms. With her head resting on my chest, I heard her whimper, "Is breá liom tú". *She loves me.* Like me, the first time she said it, she was sloshed.

124

CHAPTER
eleven

She wasn't in bed beside me when I woke up. Unsurprisingly, it was the best night's sleep I'd had since the last time I slept with her curled up next to me. The water bottle I had left her and the acetaminophen tablets were gone, too. I hoped she wasn't mad because I undressed her after setting her down in our bed. I started with her shoes. I'd never really thought of myself as a toe guy before, but it took everything in me not to suck her brightly-painted piggies into my mouth. Then I worked on her pants, I swear I wasn't trying anything, but her panties came down with her tight capris. Fuck me, I nearly came in my pants when she moaned my name as I slowly pulled the lace back up her toned legs. Her shirt came next, and I began reciting Hail Mary's because her nipples nearly spilled out of her bra since she was lying flat on her back. I couldn't help myself as I traced the top fringe of the white lace.

She loved me, she said it. What was even more amazing was that she said it in perfect Gaelic in her intoxicated state. Had she been practicing? That must have been one lucky shamrock because hearing her say those words was exactly what I had wished for. I pulled at the back collar of my shirt and put my new favorite shirt on Emily before I unclasped her bra. If I had undone it before she was covered with my shirt I might not have been able to contain myself. After making sure she was tucked in for the night, I had to take an ice-cold shower. My lucky charms weren't happy, but I was—my girl was in our bed. Sure, passed out drunk wasn't how I wanted to get her, but I sure as shit would take her any way I could get her.

"Shite!" I cursed as I hoped she didn't think I had taken advantage of her when she was langered. How could I be such a tool? I should have slept on the sofa. I had to find her and let her know that nothing happened. Well, nothing sexual, anyway. I scrambled out of bed, and that was when I saw her note on my nightstand.

"Thank you for taking such good care of me and for my new shirt ;) - LD"

"LD? LD! Holy shit!" I realized I was talking to an otherwise empty room. Lemon Drop. She was my lovely Lemon Drop again. I had to see her and fast. Just as I was about to head into the bathroom, my phone rang. The smile that I wore because I thought it was Emily quickly fell when

I saw that it was my assistant, Monica, and not the girl of my dreams.

"I hope this is important," I said more gruffly than I had originally intended.

"Do you want me to quit again?" Monica threatened to do so frequently. I usually knew she was teasing, but that day I wasn't as sure. Before I could answer, she added, "Shit's about to hit the fan. You need to get down here A.S.A.P.."

It had been a hell of a day. While Monica had been rather overdramatic that morning on the phone, she had kept me very busy all day at HIP. So much so that I only had time to send one text to Emily thanking her for her note and wishing her a great day and time to call Jasmine to place an order for flowers to be delivered.

She wasn't downstairs when I left for the office. Tank seemed very satisfied when he announced, "She isn't here." *Arse.*

Something was different when I entered the apartment as I loosened my tie. I'll admit it, I was sulking. I hadn't heard anything from Emily all day; I even called Jasmine from the backseat of the town car to make sure she had successfully delivered the arrangement of white violets. She had. It didn't help when I discovered the lights were all out downstairs and the bakery door was locked. Where the hell

127

was Emily? Music was playing softly and candlelight lit the room.

She rose from her favorite seat near the window and said, "Lá breithe shona duit, Declan." *Happy birthday, Declan.* Christ, she was wearing my "kiss me, I'm Irish" t-shirt and the black fuck-me pumps I bought her for our dance lesson. *That's it. Yeah, I needed to thank Anastasia again for those magic shamrocks.*

"It's not my birthday," I said after tossing my jacket and tie over the back of the sofa without taking my eyes off her. Hell, I really couldn't care less where they landed. She bent in front of the coffee table; the too big for her shirt hung low, giving me a glimpse of her perfect tits that were not being constrained by a bra. She picked up a cake that I hadn't even noticed before and walked slowly, seductively in my direction.

"I thought we were making up for things that you missed while you were gone." Those were days I thought she missed, not the other way around. To me, my birthday was usually just another day in my life, although, that year I had spent the day missing Emily terribly. I wondered so many times how we would have spent it. Without a doubt, I knew for once in my life that I would have felt special, wanted. Something must have flashed in my face.

"Oh, Declan, you have no idea, do you?" she asked as she stood before me, but she quickly changed the mood by swiping her finger in the frosting and smearing it on my nose.

"Did you just butter me?" I asked in mock shock.

"Well, it is buttercream," she admitted. I didn't think she was expecting my retaliation of putting my hand in the cake and smearing it all over her face. "You did not just do that." Before I could move away or respond, she lifted the remainder of the cake to my face. The plate and remnants of the delicious confection fell to the floor. We both began to laugh, and then I hauled her into my arms.

She gasped when we finally separated from our kiss. "What? It's my birthday, and I want to eat my cake, Lemon Drop." Thankfully, her smile didn't fade at the once banished nickname. *Yeah, have my cake and eat it too if I had my wish.*

"It's your birthday; you can eat whatever you want." Hell, if that wasn't an invitation, I didn't know what one was. I picked her up bridal style and carried her to our bedroom. She kicked off her heels, and I deposited her gently on the bed. She looked absolutely beautiful covered in only my t-shirt and birthday cake. The only thing that would have looked better would have been her covered in me. I tried to unbuckle my belt as quickly as possible, but between the frosting and the idea of being with my Lemon Drop, I was fumbling like an awkward teenager. I guess my woman didn't appreciate the wait because she quickly sat up, swiped my t-shirt off her body, used it to wipe my hand and our faces off, and then proceeded to pull my dress shirt open. Buttons went flying everywhere. I somehow undid my cuffs while she went to work on my pants.

"Oh, God," I groaned as she wrapped her hand around my raging hard cock and began to stroke. Then she leaned down and kissed my Jap's eye gently before taking me in her mouth. "Holy shit, Emily, I'm never going to last if you keep that up, I haven't done this since I left." She hummed in appreciation. Did she not know that before? I couldn't have been with anyone else. She was the only woman in the world to me. Cheesy, but true. Don't get me wrong, I beat the meat, as they say. I'm a guy after all, and six months is a long God damn time, but I always thought of her when I did it. She ran her finger to the spot, for a moment I wondered if it was called a g-spot for men too, and then she did it again, and I lost all ability to think as I came. Hard.

"Best cake I've ever baked," she teased as she sat up on her knees in front of me on the bed.

"I thought I was going to get a taste," I said as I pushed her back on the bed and widened the space between her legs to accommodate me. I could tell she was wet and my limp pipe sprang instantly back to life.

She quivered when I touched her with my fingers, and with the first touch of my tongue to her clit, she arched off the bed and screamed my name. I wanted to hear it again, so I pulled back. She wasn't pleased when I stopped. I looked up at her and said, "I hope this is all you can eat." That time, she wrapped her fingers in my hair. *Yeah, baby, I get it. I don't plan on stopping again.*

Every time she said my name, I rewarded her. She was without a doubt the best dessert I ever ate. I plunged two fingers inside her soaking wet pussy and she came so hard I almost did too. I couldn't wait any longer. I kissed the inside of her thigh.

"Let go, Lemon Drop, I need to get inside of you." She reluctantly let go of my hair, and I moved up her body. She wrapped her legs around me, and I slid inside of her. I was home. "I. Love. You." I punctuated each word with a thrust, never taking my eyes off of her. It felt so good to finally say it, so I said it again. And again.

She placed her hands on the side of my face and said the sweetest words I had ever heard in my entire life, "I love you too, Declan. Is breá liom tú." And with that, we both fell apart.

I don't know how long we laid there. Sweaty and sticky, and perfectly content before I pulled her up and out of the bed.

"What are we doing?" She still had the happy "O" glow about her.

"I'd like some cake in the shower," I said with a smirk as I pulled her behind me and into the bathroom.

"Hey." I rubbed at the spot that smarted because my beautiful, meek swan smacked my arse.

She put her hands up in surrender. "Well, I couldn't very well hold you upside down and bump you on the head twenty-eight times, could I?" It was sweet that she had done her research on Irish birthday traditions.

I pulled her into the waiting water and against the wall and kissed her down her neck. I knew exactly what she wanted when she lifted her leg and wrapped it around me, and I was all too happy to comply. "Why don't we just bump like this twenty-eight times instead?" The tradition of the birthday head bump was overrated, but the birthday bumping fuzzies was something I was in full support of.

"Oh, shit," Emily said as she tensed up completely.

I kissed her neck again, but when she didn't instantly relax, I asked. "What? What's wrong, mo eala?" Something was really upsetting her, but I didn't pull out of her. Whatever it was, he would handle it together. It wasn't just our bodies that were connected, together we could face whatever had her upset.

"We didn't use a condom." The thought never even crossed my mind. We weren't using them before I left. She was on the pill. *Oh, fuck, could she possibly think I've been with anyone else?*

"I haven't been with anyone else." I had told her earlier, but maybe she hadn't understood. While she seemed happy to hear that, she still was not relieved.

"What's going on in that brilliant head of yours?" I tapped her temple with my index finger.

"You really haven't been with anyone in six months?" She seemed surprised. How could I be? Nobody else even held a candle to her.

"No." She needed to understand. I kissed the end of her nose. "You're the only woman in the world for me."

"I'm your fantasy?" *Oh, she's got jokes.* My cock twitched to life inside of her. *I'm telling you, just her giggle makes me hard.*

"You're my reality." Two can play at this game. I shift my hips, causing her to moan. *That's right.* She felt so good, but I could tell she wasn't telling me everything. "You're everything I need, so tell me why you're still upset." I leaned forward, every inch of our naked bodies touching.

She buried her head in my neck like she didn't want to tell me. I placed my finger under her chin and forced her to look at me. "I stopped taking my smarties months ago; I didn't see the point. I never planned on having sex again." She was so cute, I couldn't help myself; I pulled almost completely out of her before surging back in. She tried to get away, but I pressed further inside of her. I couldn't help but chuckle.

"Why are you laughing? This isn't funny. You do understand what I said, right? Smarties, it's your word, Declan. Are you listening to a word I'm saying? Birth. Control." She wouldn't stop talking so I did the only thing I could think of, I kissed her. At some point, she stopped caring about the wick pills too.

"What are you doing?" Her voice was a little horse, probably from screaming my name so many times. I was playing with her pussy while sucking on one of her gorgeous tits. I am a gentleman after all, so I decided not to put my cock inside of her until she was actually awake.

She was awake then, so I rolled on top of her. Emily had said that she would go to the pharmacy and get a morning after pill and a fresh supply of condoms. I let her think that was a good plan. Plans could change, and I've been told I can be very persuasive.

"Egg hunt," I said with a grunt as I lifted both of her legs and rested them on my shoulders before entering her. I was so deep that way. She felt so good.

"What?" She still wasn't fully awake or she was in a pre-orgasmic state of bliss.

"Happy Easter, Lemon Drop." And I fucked her like I was the Energizer Bunny.

CHAPTER
twelve

"I think you got the holiday wrong," she said as her hips began to move in time with mine.

"Oh, really?" I asked with a playful smirk after releasing her pebbled nipple from my mouth.

"Oh, God," she moaned as I pulled almost completely out of her before rocking back in. Her words were almost a pant. "Yes, I'm pretty sure it's April Fool's Day." She insisted the night before that we needed to wait to have more sex until we had things "covered." Having a baby with Emily would be the least foolish thing I had ever done. Just the thought of our baby growing inside of her ignited me. Fuck me, she felt so good. I needed to be deeper. I pulled completely out of her and flipped her over onto her stomach. She didn't hesitate in spreading her legs slightly and lifting her perfect ass to me. I sank back in, eliciting another pleasure-filled moan from her. *That's right, baby.*

I was buried deep inside of her. I loved the way she gripped her already tight pussy around my cock. I reached around her and started rubbing her clit. I was winded as I told her, "I'm no fool for putting all my eggs in one basket."

She was close, I could tell, and that was a good thing because I didn't know how much longer I could last, and as I said before, I'm a gentleman. Ladies first.

"And I wouldn't go counting your chickens before they're hatched." *We'll just see about that, Lemon Drop.* With a well-timed flick to her clit and a thrust of my flute, we both came gloriously together. *I think I might have a new favorite holiday.*

She tried to get out of bed to run to the pharmacy, but what could I say, I was still a great negotiator or maybe I was just good at distracting her. *Maybe we could just stay here forever.* Now that she was mine again, I never wanted to go without her. With her finger, she slowly traced a familiar symbol just over my heart. She'd done it before; the first time was the morning after I gave her the Celtic heart necklace she just started wearing again.

"Just like us," I said before pressing my lips to the top of her head.

"What?" she asked as she returned the kiss right over the place she was just tracing.

"Timeless. Do you remember what I told you the first time you traced an infinity symbol on my chest?"

"Yes, but tell me again." She needed to see my eyes when I told her, so I surprised her by quickly rolling over so that I was hovering over her.

"My life began when I met you, Emily Barnes." She sighed in pleasure as I eased inside of her. "My love for you has no beginning and no end. I love you. If I am your infinity, then you are my Trinity. My yesterday, my today, and my tomorrow. "

"Oh, Declan." Usually I would freak out if a woman cried while I was inside of her, but she wasn't just any woman. She was my woman, my Lemon Drop, and I knew her tears were of sheer joy, so I kissed them away and continued making love to her. "I love you too."

"I don't think I'll ever get tired of hearing that. Say it again."

She looked straight into my eyes and said the words I longed to not only hear but feel my entire life, "*Is breá liom tú*. I love you."

"Sometimes when I look in your eyes, they look so familiar to me. Like I've seen them before."

"It's probably because I was gone so long." I would always feel guilty for the way I left, but at the time, I thought I was doing what I needed to do, and part of the reason I stayed away was because I just didn't know how to come back especially since I never found my mother.

"Don't." She brushed her nose against mine and then kissed the end of it. "That's not what I meant. Libby said the same thing when she first saw pictures of you. Neither of us can put our finger on it, but something in your eyes is so overwhelmingly familiar."

"What do you have planned for today?" I asked. I would have remembered if I ever met Emily before November. She was unforgettable.

"Oh, shit." She tried to leave our bed, but I still wasn't ready to let her go, so I pulled her to my side. "I have to go. I'm going to be late. Let me go, Declan." The tone of her voice told me that she wasn't kidding, in fact, it seemed like she was starting to panic. Was she hiding something from me?

"Hey, what's going on? Where are you going?" For the first time, I noticed she actually had a bag with her. *Good, this is where she belongs, not with my father.*

She hesitated as she scrambled around the room trying to get ready. "I agreed to this before we, you know." She blushed. Yes, I knew, and half the neighbors probably did too. Agreed to what? A date with someone else? No way was I going to sit back and let her go out with another man. She must have sensed what I was thinking.

"It's not a date or anything," she assured me.

"Then tell me," I urged as she continued to look worried about whatever it was she had planned.

"I'm going somewhere with your father. Today is a very hard day for him and he asked me to join him. It's important. He needs me." *Oh, hell no.*

"Not without me you're not." As much as I didn't want to spend time with my father, I didn't want to spend time without Emily more. Sadly, a day in bed naked with Lemon Drop wasn't in the cards. *Not today, anyway.*

I called Eric, and we were waiting for him at the curb forty-five minutes later. Emily wore a simple navy dress, so I followed her lead and wore a pair of navy slacks and a white button-down without a tie.

"I agreed to this weeks ago," she tried to justify, "and it's important." It bothered me that she had become so close to my father during my absence, but part of me said I had no one to blame but myself. If I had been there, that never would have happened. "Are you sure you want to do this?" She bit her lip, a nervous habit as I opened the car door for her and told her that I was sure.

Eric looked pleased seeing us together. "Thanks for your help yesterday," Emily said as she leaned forward and kissed him on the cheek. *What the fuck?* It appeared that my friend/employee had more explaining to do.

"Don't be mad. I needed you out of the apartment so I could surprise you for your birthday." She squeezed my thigh, and when I turned my head toward her, she kissed me, and let me tell you, unlike the kiss she had given Eric, nothing about the one she gave me said "friend".

Eric cleared his throat and Emily buried her blushed face in my chest. "So I guess Monica was in on this too."

"Guilty as charged," he admitted as he pulled the car up in front of the Fifth Avenue apartment building that had only ever felt like home when I stayed there with the woman who sat beside me.

Billy offered to call up to the apartment to tell Kian we were there, but Emily said she had to get something from upstairs. If I'd had it my way, she would have been collecting all of her things as soon as possible. My father had his own car and driver, so Eric dropped us off at the apartment and left.

"I'll wait here." I still had no desire to go upstairs. I noticed, like mine, her mood ring had changed from orange to black. A fitting color for the mood I was in. It was amazing how in so many ways we were so in sync with each other. Why couldn't we just agree to just stay as far away as possible from my father?

"OK." This time, it didn't give me hope, like it had the other times she had said it. I didn't think things would ever be OK between me and my father.

"She's an amazing young lady," Billy said once we stood alone in the lobby.

"The very best," I agreed whole-heartedly. My eala was an amazing woman. Just thinking about her calmed me, and my ring changed to blue.

"He didn't just lose Abigail that day, he lost you too. So did she." Much like Brit, Billy always called it like he saw it. "So they held on to each other. You asked her not to forget you, she didn't, but if you want to move forward, you're going to need to let go of the past." At the ropes course, Jake had encouraged us to let go of our fears because they would just hold us back. Just then, the elevator doors dinged and my father and Emily stood arm in arm. I noticed something—for the first time in my life, my father looked happy to see me.

Emily sat between Kian and me as his driver navigated us to an unknown-to-me destination. Emily took my left hand in her right, and it was then that I noticed what she had gotten when she went upstairs. She was once again wearing my grandmother Hayes Claddagh ring that I had given her for Christmas. I lifted our joined hands and kissed the ring—she truly had captured my heart.

"You still have it," I said with a smile as I examined the heart, hands, and crown. Love, friendship, and loyalty. That was my Emily.

"You asked me to never give it back." I had been talking about my heart, and she knew it.

"Never." The car came to a stop. I looked out the window and noticed we were outside of Jasmine's flower shop.

"I'll be right back," Emily said as she climbed over me and out the door. It took everything in me not to smack her delectable ass. She quickly shut the door, leaving me and Kian alone, with the exception of his driver who couldn't hear us because the privacy screen was up.

"She's very special, son." Did he think he was telling me anything I didn't already know? "Don't ever let her go." Something about the way he said it made me think that he had done just that, let someone go.

"I don't plan on it, Da." And I didn't.

Emily quickly returned to the car with two bouquets of flowers and a small stuffed bear. We merged onto the FDR and then crossed the Brooklyn Bridge. Where the hell were we going? Nobody spoke, and at some point, Emily took ahold of my father's hand with her left, so she sat between us holding both of our hands. She looked pale like she was going to be sick. I let go of her hand and put my arm around her and pulled her as close to me as possible.

"Are you all right?"

"No." She shook her head and tears began to stream down her face. She undoubtedly knew where we were going and was very distressed about it. "I shouldn't have let you come with us, I just got you back." *She just got me back? I thought it was the other way around.* Was she really afraid that wherever we were going would cause me to leave again? Billy's words about letting go of the past rang true, to move forward I had to let go of the past. Emily's grandma Rose had said to "live every moment, laugh every day, and live beyond words" and my own great grandmother had told me "we only regret the chances that we don't take". They were all right. It was time to stop living in the past, nothing could change it, but I could certainly make sure that history didn't repeat itself.

"M'fhíorghrá," I said as I kissed away her tears. "It means true love, Emily, and that's what you are to me." I didn't want to give anything away but I knew her grandmother's words would comfort her. "Grandma Rose said that when you found yours that it would be for a lifetime. Remember what I told you, you are my Trinity. Yesterday. Today. Tomorrow," I kissed her between every word. I couldn't care less that my father sat right next to us. I fingered her heart necklace. "The knot has no beginning and no end just like my love for you." The car came to a stop, but I kept my eyes on her. It didn't matter where we were. Nothing was going to separate us again. I pleaded with my eyes as I held her beautiful face in my hands before dropping my forehead to hers. I rubbed my nose back and forth against hers before placing a kiss on the end of it.

"OK," she said. I had no doubt in my mind that together we would be just that.

"OK," I answered before kissing her soft lips.

I stepped out of the car and took the bouquets from her before taking her hand and helping her out of the car. I still hadn't taken in our surroundings. All my focus was on Emily.

"I love you, Declan Hayes," she said as I first noticed where we were.

The section of the cemetery where we were in held older graves. The end of June heat was rather unforgiving, and I was glad that Emily had suggested that I wear my sunglasses. My father led the way, and soon, we stood before two graves. It didn't surprise me that one belonged to Abigail Hayes, but what did was the grave that was beside her.

"Beloved son, Finnigan Thomas Hayes," read the headstone. According to the dates, he lived only three short days just ten months before I was born. "Until we meet again, may God hold you in the palm of his hand." It was the anniversary of his death. My father lovingly removed remnants of old flowers before placing the large bouquet of white roses on the grave. Pure love. I had a brother. Emily heaved as my father fell to his knees and began to speak like Finnigan was there with us.

I knew for a fact that she barely left my father's side when I first left. She was there when they buried Abigail. She knew I had a brother. I could have been mad, but I wasn't. I felt blessed to have this woman at my side, and for the first time, I felt sorrow for not being there when Abigail died.

"Your brother is here with me today. He would have loved you so much." I couldn't see his face from where we stood behind him, but it was obvious that he was crying. Emily was crying too, and she took a step toward my father, but for reasons I could not explain, I wanted to be the one to comfort him. I let go of her hand and kneeled beside him in front of the grave. I placed the bear that I was still holding in front of the stone, and my father continued to speak. "Like me, you would be so proud of the man that he is." Emily put her hand on my shoulder as soon as I too began to cry for the brother I never knew I had. I didn't know how long we stayed there. My father told Finn, as he called him, all about me. My father seemed to know more about me than I ever thought he cared to know. When he finally stood, my Da went to her grave. He placed the second bouquet of flowers on her marker before kissing his fingers, and then, touching her name, all he said was, "I'm sorry Abby," before turning toward the car to leave. *What did he have to be sorry for?*

CHAPTER
thirteen

The car ride was eerily quiet as we drove back toward Manhattan. Emily tried to comfort me by tracing the infinity symbol over and over again. I had rolled up my shirt sleeves and just the contact of her fingertip on the bare skin of my forearm soothed me. So many different emotions battled in my head, but the one that seemed to win was sorrow, for the brother I never knew and surprisingly for Kian and Abigail. I thought of Aria, and how much joy she had brought Libby and Logan in her short life so far, hell even mine for that matter. I thought about what it would do to me if Emily lost our baby. It would break me. Is that what it did to my parents? Had the loss of my brother broken them? It seemed that my father and I suddenly had a lot to talk about, so when we arrived back at the apartment, I didn't hesitate to go upstairs.

The apartment looked different—no, it felt different. Maggie greeted us in the foyer. She was wearing khaki shorts and a simple black t-shirt. It was so much better than seeing her in that stupid maid uniform that she used to wear. She greeted my father warmly by his first name and hugged me and welcomed me "home". While I had always loved Maggie's hugs, she would never have given me one like that before in the presence of the lord or lady of the manor, but my father didn't seem to mind; in fact, he seemed pretty pleased.

"You must be starved. I have dinner ready for you in the kitchen." Abigail Hayes never ate in the kitchen. *Yes, things certainly had changed around here.*

"I need a moment alone with Emily," I said as I took her hand and began down the hall toward the bedrooms. I stopped at the threshold of the room where we had stayed together. We had a lot of good times in that room. I couldn't help but chuckle when remembering how Emily said she felt like Goldilocks when she was picking her room when she arrived there the first time. I asked her if that made me the Big Bad Wolf, and then she reminded me that would make her Little Red Riding Hood. Who knew children's bedtime stories were a turn on, but we certainly proved the line "the better to eat you with" that night.

I pushed her against the closed door as soon as we were inside the room that was entirely too girly for my taste with its flowers and birds in varying shades of pink and green and pressed the length of my body against hers. She opened her mouth with a moan, and I took full advantage of it. She wrapped her legs around me while she fisted my hair. I was desperate for more.

"I need you," I told her, although, from the way I ground against her, I knew she was fully aware of my need. She fumbled with my belt and zipper.

"It's going to have to be quick," she said. She squealed in surprise when I ripped off her lacey black cacks, and buried myself deep inside of her. She still hadn't made it to the pharmacy, but I didn't care. She was mine and nothing was ever going to come between us again, not even latex.

"Oh, God," she moaned as I rocked into her. She began to tremble, and I knew she was close by the way she clamped down on me. Fuck yes, I was right with her. I covered her mouth with mine but if Da or Maggie were anywhere near her room, they would without a doubt still hear us pounding against the door. With one more thrust, she came apart in my arms which pushed me right over the edge of oblivion. I didn't know how long we stood there before she put her feet down on the floor which caused me to slip out of her.

She looked at me shyly. "I can't believe we just did that. They are going to know what we were in here doing." I loved the way her cheeks flushed. Of all the looks my Lemon Drop had, I think I loved the freshly-fucked looked the best.

"Who cares if they know I just flattened you? You have no idea how many times, I've pictured this very moment." It was true.

"Flattened? Charming." But she was amused, not angry. "You've thought about 'flattening' me against the door?"

"Since that first time I brought you back to this room after our date at Swayed." She attempted to fix my hair by running her fingers through it.

"You kissed me goodnight and wished me sweet dreams." By the look on her face, I knew she was remembering that night fondly.

"And you welcomed me to your world. I was a neddy for leaving it behind." She put her finger over my lips to silence me.

"None of us can change the past." I got the distinct feeling she wasn't just talking about me. It was the same thing so many others told me.

"We better get back before they send out a search party for us."

The meal Maggie prepared was simple but delicious. I loved the fact that she joined us. I'd always thought of her like family, and I knew Emily did too. I'm not going to lie, I liked seeing my father so comfortable in his own home. Before, it always felt like a mausoleum. None of us spoke about the elephant in the room; instead, we talked about safe topics. Emily's cookbook project, Hugs from Home, and Aria. I couldn't help but notice Emily's eyes lit up every time her niece was mentioned.

After the meal was complete, my father asked us to join him in the family room. That was also something new. Over the course of my life, I had been summoned to his office to "talk" many times but before, his massive desk was always between us. It was symbolic of our entire relationship up to that point. Emily sat between us like she had in the car; I think she was trying to offer us both comfort. It was obvious they both cared deeply for one another. And her being between us didn't seem like an obstacle to keep us apart; instead, she felt like a bridge to bring us together.

Once we were seated, my father didn't waste any more time.

"Abby's mother was a total bitch." All right, that wasn't how I was expecting this conversation to begin. I didn't remember her. "She was so proud of her when she landed me. It was as if her daughter had just won a prize, not a husband. She could care less that we loved each other. All she saw were dollar signs. She told her over and over again that she had to get pregnant, and the sooner the better. I told her I didn't care about an heir, that I just wanted her, but we decided to just leave it up to fate. She had three miscarriages before Finn was born." Emily patted his knee, urging him to continue. "The entire time she was pregnant with him, I think we both held our breath, so when she made it to full term, we were both so relieved. When I held him in my arms the first time, it changed my life. I wish time could have just stood still." My father leaned forward and covered his eyes with his palms. Emily squeezed my hand before moving away so that she could comfort him by rubbing his back. "Three days later, he was gone, and I swear, my Abby died right along with him."

After wiping away the tears that fell down his cheek, he told us about Leigh's disease. We learned it only affects about one in every forty thousand people and is carried by the mitochondria in the mother. More than likely it was the reason she had lost the other babies. It affects the central nervous system and was what caused my brother to die from cardiomyopathy. "His heart just wasn't strong enough. Holding your baby in your arms as he takes his last breath changes you forever, and Abby blamed herself."

"Oh, Kian," Emily said as she hugged my father with one arm while she reached out for me with the other.

"And her bitch of a mother just kept going on about trying again. We put our son in the ground and she bought her daughter new lingerie to entice me to get her pregnant again. I was so lost. Abby didn't want me around, so I did the only thing I could: I went to work." I looked at my father and he looked so broken. I stood from my spot and moved to the other side of him and placed my hand on his back. The look of sheer pride on Emily's face as I offered him my silent support knocked the wind out of me.

"Brianna was working for us that summer. She was so young. I was grieving the loss of my son and my wife, I know she wasn't dead, but it felt like I had lost her. What I was doing certainly wasn't living, but being around her was like having faith again."

"If you have faith as small as a mustard seed," Emily stated, and my father looked up and smiled at her.

"Nothing is impossible," I finished. My father nodded in agreement.

151

"I never planned on falling in love with Brianna. I did love Abby. I would never leave her, and Brie knew it. I don't know, maybe she thought if she gave us a healthy child that things would be better." *Wow*.

I didn't know what to say, so I blurted out, "My great grandmother says that I have her eyes." I'd seen some pictures of her as a young girl, and I had to say that I agreed.

My father sat up and looked into my eyes. "You do." He placed his right hand over his breast pocket and tapped it twice before reaching in. I'd seen him tap his chest like that so many times in my lifetime that I'd never even thought to ask him what he was doing. He pulled out a small piece of paper and handed it to me. "That's your mother, son. I've always kept her right next to my heart." He handed me a photo, yellowed with years. It was of a beautiful young woman.

"Holy shit," I heard Emily gasp before she passed out cold on the floor.

"She's coming to," Maggie said as I stroked Emily's face that was now resting on my lap.

Her eyes fluttered open, and she said one word: "Hi."

"Here's some water," my father offered as he came rushing back into the room. He looked at her and sighed in relief even though Maggie had insisted to both of us that Emily would be just fine.

"Hi." I bent forward and kissed her forehead. I encouraged her to slowly sit up and she took a sip of the water that I offered to her. After she passed it back, I asked her, "What happened?"

She indicated that she needed another drink of water, which Maggie swiftly handed back to her. She drank the entire glass.

"Remember when I said that your eyes look so familiar to me and Libby?" she asked slowly as if she was talking to a child. I nodded my head, and she continued. "I know that woman in that picture. That's Bailey Flemming. Bailey Flemming is Brianna Bailey." Fuck, Bailey was her last name and Flemming was Anastasia's, her grandmother's surname.

Fuck, all that time apart and Emily was the key to finding my mother the whole time.

CHAPTER
fourteen

I think my father and I both nearly fainted too when Emily said that she knew my mother—the woman in the photograph that he always keeps close to his heart. The woman whose eyes I supposedly had. I'd been looking for Brianna Bailey while she had been using the name Bailey Flemming. Both family names. Anastasia would never tell me why she never took the name Bailey, maybe my mother knew. The mother who, if I was lucky, I would meet in approximately eight hours.

Let's face it, just like with my grandmother, Lurena, calling up and saying, "Hi, Mom, it's me, the baby you gave up at birth" isn't something that can be done over the phone.

I needed to meet her in person. Maybe then I could truly understand why she gave me up. Had she really done it to help my Da and Abigail? I still had a million questions for my father. I didn't know that I would ever fully be able to understand the distance he had always kept from me, but like so many people said, we can't change the past.

I wanted to go to JFK and hop on the first plane to LAX, but then I would have had a five-hour drive ahead of me too, so Da convinced me to wait a few hours so that he could charter a private plane for us.

"Sit your arse down, mhac." My father was as nervous as I was about the trip to California; he hadn't called me son in a very long time. I had to admit, it was nice to hear. Emily hadn't seen Brie or Bailey, as she called her, since she was sixteen. Christ, I didn't even know what to call her. Anything could have happened to her in the time it had been since she last saw her. *What if we show up at her doorstep and she doesn't want anything to do with me?* My own grandmother didn't.

"Stop second guessing this." It shouldn't have surprised me that she seemed to be able to read my thoughts. She placed a chaste kiss upon my lips before adding, "What's not to love about you, Declan Hayes?"

"Thank you, Lemon Drop. Tell me again how you met her. Tell me everything you know." Emily had already told us, but I wanted to hear it all again.

"So, Libby and I went to the lake every summer to stay with our grandparents." She always had a sparkle in her eyes when she talked about them. I felt like I knew them.

"Grandma Rose and Pop Henry?" I asked, and she nodded her head in agreement.

"I miss them," Libby said as she placed her head on her twin's shoulder. It seemed our impromptu trip had become a vacation for the rest of our friends, especially since Swayed was closed for the week for annual renovations and upgrades. Matt even joked about us stopping in Nashville to pick them up before he was reminded they had a prior commitment.

"We're getting ready to go, baby, and the doctor said you should nurse her during take-off and landing." Logan kissed both his girls before handing Aria over and taking a seat next to me. Doting father looked good on Logan, and I couldn't help but hope that it would look good on me too. Crazy, right? If you asked me last November if I would ever get married or want kids, I would have given you a resounding hell no. Now, it was all I could think about. Emily's engagement ring was practically burning a hole in my pocket, but I wanted to wait for the perfect time to ask her to be mine forever. I wondered when Logan was going to ask Libby. It wouldn't have surprised me if it was soon. Logan was a carpe diem kind of guy. Libby covered Aria with a blanket to nurse her, and a few minutes later, the captain announced we were ready to depart.

"She was all upset because Pop took me on one of our special outings." Libby made a sad face at her sister.

"Those were our favorite days, as long as it was your turn. If it was the others then not so much. Gram did her best by distracting whoever was left behind, but you always knew that Pop had something special planned."

"The best," Libby agreed as we sped down the runway. I gripped the arms of my chair harder than necessary. What can I say? I'm not a fan of take-offs and landings. *Maybe Lemon Drop will let me suck her knobs when we land. It seems to be soothing to Aria.* Emily gave me a wink. *Yep, it's official, she's a mind reader.*

"Anyway, I was sitting on the front porch steps crying when Gram and Bailey came out the front door. I don't even know where she came from. She handed me a Popsicle and told Gram we'd be back. Gram just waved, said to have fun, and then went back inside the house. Bailey started walking down the road, eating a Popsicle and carrying a bucket."

"I had a great day with Pop, but I was so jealous when I came home and heard all about the adventure they had picking wild blackberries and then baking pies."

"I love your pies, M," Gabe announced from the group of chairs across the aisle where he, Nat, Suzie, and Eric sat. "I wouldn't mind getting pricked for one of your pies." He wiggled his brows up and down suggestively at my girl. "Great, now I'm thinking about my prick and warm pie which of course reminds me of a certain movie."

"Hey now." Nat slapped him playfully in the chest. I was glad for the distraction and the company of our friends. I'd missed them.

"Sometimes I was so jealous of you. You and Gram were so close, and then you met Bailey, and you loved spending time with her."

Logan mouthed, "I love you" to his girl.

Emily appeared crushed by her sister's admission. My mother lived in a cottage right next to Rose and Henry. She went on hikes and roasted marshmallows with Emily and Libby while I was shipped off to boarding school. Libby wasn't the only one who was jealous.

"I was, but then one day I realized that I had a bond with Pop that you didn't, and that Mom and I were as close as you and Gram were, maybe even more. They all loved us, and as much as we look alike, we are still different people, and that's pretty awesome if you ask me." Libby looked directly at me. "And just because Bailey wasn't in your life, doesn't mean she hasn't loved you since the moment she knew you existed." Emily got up from her seat and promptly sat in my lap.

"I love you, Declan. Dóchas." I asked her to have faith in our future and she was telling me to have it too, and Anastasia had said as much as well. "Let your faith be bigger than your fear." Hell, according to my father, being around Brianna had given him faith again. I had even asked Emily to have it when I left too. Faith, hope, trust, and love. That was all anyone could ever ask for, and I had that with Emily. Yesterday, today, and tomorrow.

"We will be at the lodge," my father told us again as we loaded into one SUV. He was riding in the other with Gabe, Nate, Suzie, and Eric. I knew he wanted to see Brianna as badly as I did, but he also knew that the trip wasn't about him. "Good luck, mhac." He looked in my eyes like he was trying to tell me more. I might have had my mother's eyes but I knew that look. Maybe I was more like him than I realized. Maybe if I wanted to hear the words, I had to say them first.

"I love you too, Da." I think he must have been in shock because he just stood there with a huge smile plastered across his face, so I closed the car door and began to drive away. When I looked up in the rearview mirror, my father had his hand on his heart, over the picture he always carried of my mother, as always he patted it twice. He loved us both, and he had been telling me that my entire life.

Emily reached across the console and squeezed my hand. The drive wasn't long to the little cottage that was right on the lake. Libby explained that my mother lived in the small guest house and used the main house as a rental property for income. Investment properties really were the family business. I guess the apple doesn't fall far from the tree.

"Just follow the path down to the water," Emily urged once we arrived. She, Libby, and the baby were going to go to the door while Logan and I waited down by the water. "It's going to be just fine," Lemon Drop assured me before rubbing noses with me and then kissing me softly.

It was pretty early to be calling on anyone, but the girls assured me that my mother was an early riser. The early morning light reflected off the lake like it was a piece of glass. Logan sank into a chair.

"Mind if I catch a few Zs?" he asked. While the rest of us were fast asleep on the long flight, he was up with Aria, but he never complained.

"Not at all, but I don't think I can just sit here. I'm going to take a walk, try and shake out these nerves."

"Need me to go with?" he asked with concern etched upon his face. Logan was a good friend. I would never have thought it would be possible with the way we first met. Hell, if things had gone the way I originally thought, he'd probably be behind bars. It's funny how things can change.

"No, I'm good. I won't go far." He put his head back and closed his eyes, and I slid my shades on and took in the beauty that surrounded me and began walking down an unmarked path until I found a spot that literally took my breath away.

"I've already claimed this spot," said a voice from behind me causing me to nearly jump out of my own skin.

"Lucky you," I replied without taking my eyes off the water. "I'm just here to see someone."

"Sounds important." A rock was tossed from beside me, and it skipped several times before sinking to the bottom of the lake.

"Impressive and yes, it's probably the most important meeting of my life." I should have felt on edge in the presence of this stranger, but instead, I felt surprisingly at ease. "Can you teach me how to do that?" I didn't know why I asked; I should have just headed back to the cottage and given her back her special place.

"Pick a rock that fits in the palm of your hand. Look for one that's pretty round and flat." I quickly found one that I thought would do the trick. "Now hold the flat side with your thumb on one side and your middle finger on the other." I did as the stranger instructed. "Good, now face the water sideways with your feet shoulder-width apart." I turned and mimicked her stance from behind her. "Squat down so you're closer to the water," she said as she did the very thing she instructed me to do. "Bend your wrist back and then snap it forward with a flick. Like cracking a whip." Her rock went skipping along the water. "Make sure to throw your arm all the way across your chest, but more importantly, just have fun. You can always toss another rock, but life is too short not to find joy in every moment." I let go of my stone, and with a smile, I watched it skip across the water.

"Thank you, that was amazing. You're a great teacher." She turned back to look at me. It was the first time I had really looked at her. She beamed with pride at me, but her smile wasn't what caught me by surprise. No, it was her eyes looking right at me—my eyes.

CHAPTER
fifteen

Few times in my life have I ever been rendered speechless. That was one of them. "You're ..." I couldn't finish my sentence, so I did the only thing I could. I took off my sunglasses.

"Declan." My name was muffled because her hands covered her mouth and tears instantly sprang from her beautiful green eyes and then her arms were around my neck. I didn't know what I was expecting. Part of me thought she would be fuming at me for disrupting her life. Part of me believed she wouldn't want anything to do with me. After all, she did give me away. I didn't know what to do, so I just held her back. Abigail Hayes never held me in her arms like that. Like a mother should.

I heard a click of a camera and then Emily's voice from behind us, "I told you. You're easy to love, Dec." I pulled slightly away from my mother to look at my lovely Lemon Drop. She was crying too.

"Emily?" Brianna asked. "How did you ...?" It seemed that I wasn't the only one who was speechless. Emily came closer and hugged us both.

"Let's go back to the cottage and talk." We all seemed to have so many unanswered questions. Just like with my father, Emily walked between us, holding both our hands. She was a bridge between my past and my future. It made me think of the photo that hung in the apartment above our bed. Before, I always saw it as going toward something or away from something, but I had it all wrong. The bridge was a link that connected it all together, just like my Lemon Drop.

Libby, Logan, and Aria were all waiting for us on the porch. Bailey fawned all over the baby, but Libby quickly excused them so that she could "go down for a nap". Obviously, we had a lot to talk about, so they took the car back to the lodge and left Emily and me alone with my mother.

"I never thought I would meet you. I mean, I hoped for it, but after all these years I just figured you didn't want to know me." *How could she possibly ever think that?*

"I've only known about you since the first of this year." That shocked her. "Abigail and my father were in a car accident. They asked me to give blood, but I wasn't a match."

"I don't understand, I ...." She was visibly upset to hear about the accident. "Are they OK?" Looking around at the cottage, it was easy to see how she didn't know about the accident. It was big news in the New York social scene, but this was a little cabin in the woods in the Eastern Sierra Nevada Mountains of California. She was undeniably concerned for my parents. Both of them.

I got up from my seat at her small kitchen table and walked over to the windows overlooking the lake.

"Abigail passed away," Emily told her, and I heard the sound of a chair moving and then I was once again surrounded by her arms. *I could get used to this.*

"I'm so sorry about your mom, Declan." Mom? Abigail Hayes was never a mother to me. Da told me that Brianna was a bit of a martyr; she was young and thought that by giving me up she was doing the right thing. I'd felt more of a connection with Brie in the last half an hour than I ever did with Abigail.

She let me go, and I missed her instantly—the only thing that had ever felt better were Emily's arms around me. She began pacing around the room, visibly upset.

"I don't understand. What do you mean you've only known about me since January? None of this makes any sense. How on Earth do you and Emily know each other? It's not that I'm not beyond happy that you are here, but I have to ask, why now?" As shocked as Brianna had been to see Emily there with me, that was really the first chance she had to ask any questions. And honestly, I felt like I had more questions now than when we arrived.

"Maybe we should start at the beginning," Emily suggested as she encouraged us both to sit down.

"That sounds like a good idea to me," my father said from the door. Actually, I was surprised he lasted as long as he did.

"You never told him?" Brie refused to sit down and her shock quickly turned into anger.

"No."

"Why?" That was the question of the day, and only one person knew the reason. It was my father's turn to pace the room.

"You know why, Brianna. We all agreed on no contact for a year. You never contacted us again. I assumed you moved on with your life."

"What are you talking about? I sent a letter on every single birthday." This couldn't be happening.

"You changed your name, you plainly didn't want to be found, and we never heard a word from you."

"I changed my name because I couldn't just go back to being Brianna Bailey like nothing happened. Like everything was the same. Nothing was the same, I made the dumbest decision of my life by giving up the man that I loved and our baby. I thought … Oh, God, I'm so sorry, Declan. You have to know." Tears flowed freely down her face. "I have loved you every minute of every day since the moment I knew you existed." She turned her attention toward my father. "Both of you." *Holy shit.*

My mother loved me, or should I say she *loves* me, and my father. Abigail truly was a desperate and broken woman. My father never knew about the birthday cards. Brie never had a chance, but we all paid the price.

"You gave up everything you ever knew because of me," I whispered as the shock wore off. Emily was by my side, holding my hand as the truth came out.

"No, son, not because of you, *for* you," my mother said as she stood before me and placed a kiss on my forehead like I had dreamed of my entire life.

"Thank you, Mom." It just felt right, so I said the words without giving it much thought. It felt good, damn good. Who knew that one word, *Mom*, could bring four adults instantly to tears.

We all still had a lifetime of questions to ask but for the moment, we sat at the table and enjoyed a glass of fresh-squeezed lemonade.

"I always imagined you two together," my mother said with a sigh as she sat down across from us after pouring the drinks. "I still can't get over the fact that she led you back to me." Emily and I had explained how we met, and my new found mother actually whacked me on the back of the head when she found out about me leaving my girl. She cried when she heard about the way her mother had treated me, and she cried again, only this time with happy tears when I told her about my time with her beloved grandmother,

Anastasia. Thankfully, she already knew about her father's death.

"What do you mean?" Emily asked.

"I guess you could say that imagining Declan and his life has become my life."

"I don't understand."

"It's probably just easier to show you. Follow me." All of us stood from the table and followed her down the small hall. She opened the first door we came to.

"Welcome to *The Adventures of Bash and June Bug*." The walls of the room were lined in drawings and a table sat in front of the window.

"Oh, my God, are these D. Mathair?" Lemon Drop plainly knew who Bash and June Bug were. She was really excited. I was just confused.

My father began to chuckle. "D. Mathair. Declan's mother. That's brilliant, Brie. How did I ever miss it?" I took a step closer toward the drawings on the wall.

"This kid kind of looks like me." The boy in the drawings had bright green eyes and disheveled brown hair.

"He is you, and this is June Bug." Emily giggled as she pointed out that the girl most definitely looked like her with eyes the color of chocolate and a smile as bright as the sun.

"I can't believe I never knew this about you." It had been hard on Emily when her grandparents passed away. Not only did she lose them but also her reason to return to the lake every summer. Bailey was important to her.

"Nobody knows my real identity, not even my publisher. Bash was the only part of you I had left, I couldn't lose him too." I looked around the room. The panels weren't an adventure; they were a wish from a mother to her son for an amazing life. Maybe now that I had her and my real life June Bug I would have it.

CHAPTER
sixteen

Both Eric and Suzie and Gabe and Nat decided to stay at the lodge, using the excuse of being newlyweds. Eric and Suzie never had a proper honeymoon and this seemed like the perfect place, and honestly sleeping in a room next to Natalie and Gabe wasn't something I would wish upon anyone. Logan, Libby, Aria, Da, Emily, and I had all agreed to stay with Brianna, I mean Bailey. Shit, I had no idea what to call the woman, my mother. Looking at her, I could definitely see a resemblance, and it wasn't just her eyes.

"Penny for your thoughts?" Emily asked as she wrapped her arms around me from behind. I was sitting on the dock with my feet in the cool lake water trying to process everything that we had learned so far. Not only did my mother love me, but she had reached out to me my entire life, and to think I was starting to feel sorry for Abigail Hayes.

"I still can't believe you knew her all this time."

Even more shocking was that we had just learned that my mother had sent me a birthday card and Christmas card from the time I was born until I was twenty-one years of age. She had also sent a signed first edition of every single *Adventures of Bash* book she ever wrote. That did explain why Abigail had always been so steadfast in her rules about her being the only one to process any correspondence that came to our residence. Not even my father was allowed to touch the mail before she did. The latest *Bash* book was probably sitting in a pile at the house this very second. It was the first one published since Abigail's death. Brianna had stopped "torturing" herself with the birthday and Christmas cards when I reached the age of twenty-one because she figured I was an adult who had no "use" for her since I had never reached out to her. Hearing her say that nearly killed me.

My father was also plagued with guilt because he hadn't yet gone through Abigail's private storage or desk. If he had, he might have found the cards and books. I was glad to know that my parents had each other. When Brianna discovered that neither my father nor I had any idea about the books and cards, she cried in relief and then she quickly soothed my father's growing anger while Emily soothed mine. This was how a woman who loved a man behaved. Not in the desperate, evil, and manipulating way that Abigail always had.

Emily kicked off her shoes and joined me at my side.

Peace.

I felt like I finally had it. Now, if she would have me, we could start our life together. I had to figure out a way to get to her father. I knew I already had the blessing of her mother, and no matter what the current state of the relationship was, I had to at least meet the man before I asked for his daughter's hand in marriage.

"Thank you for giving me this." I lifted our joined hands to my mouth and kissed her.

"Giving you what exactly?" she asked as she now pressed her lips to the back of my hand.

"The best Mother's Day ever." At least, it would be until she gave me children of our own. Most people didn't understand my need to continue making up for the things that I had missed while I was off being an arse, but my Lemon Drop did, and she was the only one that needed to understand.

"Let's go pick some blackberries and bake a pie to celebrate you reuniting with your mom." That sounded like the perfect way to commemorate the way in which the two most important women in my life had met so many years ago.

Logan was using the kitchen in the main house. It wasn't rented that weekend because Brianna was painting two of the bedrooms. It was rustic but well maintained and had beautiful lake and mountain views. My father had volunteered to actually help her. That was a sight I never thought I would see. Kian Hayes didn't do manual labor. I was kind of surprised when he rolled up his sleeves instead of calling his assistant to book a painting crew. Perhaps Emily was right and I really didn't know my father like I thought I did. It was refreshing to see him in a different light. Libby was on the back deck reading *Bash* books to Aria because Logan didn't want his little princess anywhere near the paint fumes. Aria had no idea what her mother was reading, but she didn't seem to care, and Emily and I were baking in the kitchen at the cottage.

"God, that's sexy," I muttered too loudly as I watched Emily stand at the stove while she stirred the blackberries.

"Some assistant you are; you're distracting me. I need that lemon, babe," she said with a wink as she looked back at me.

"Coming right up, Lemon Drop." I moved right behind her and wrapped my arms around her. She shimmied her delectable little arse against me as I squeezed the juice into the pot like she instructed me to. "Keep that up and the only one having dessert tonight will be me." It had been far too many hours since I had been inside of her. My lad throbbed against my zipper.

"Oh, God," she groaned as I pressed closer to her. *Yeah, baby, that's what you do to me.* She tilted her head to the side as she continued to stir the berries in the pot at a frenzied rate. I took full advantage of the bare skin of her neck with my lips. "Ouch." *What? I didn't bite her.*

I stepped away to see what was wrong. She quickly turned off the heat and turned and put her finger in her mouth. "Did you burn yourself?" I asked as she sucked the digit. That wasn't doing anything to help the current problem I had going in my pants. She nodded. Smoothly, I pulled her finger out of her mouth and placed it in mine. If she was hurt, I wanted to be the one to make her better. Always.

"Go check on your parents while I make the dough, and then we'll have thirty minutes while it chills." Thirty minutes, I could work with that, but no way could I walk up to the main house right then. I continued to suck her finger while I looked down at the giant denim bulge I was sporting with a raised brow. *What? I'm a guy, of course, I think my dick is giant; I know Emily thinks it is.* Now, I was thinking about her begging me to fuck her with my ginormous cock which was only making things harder. Pun intended.

She licked her lips and with a pout said, "You poor baby" before falling to her knees at my feet. Quickly, she undid my pants as I continued to suck her finger. She kissed the tip of my mammoth member before she swirled her tongue around once and then sucked me just like I was sucking her finger. Jesus H. Christ, she was good at that. I couldn't take my eyes off her, but just for fun, I circled my tongue around her burnt finger. She mimicked the action, so I changed to counterclockwise. She did too. Holy hell, it felt good. Then I bared my teeth to her and began to slowly drag her finger out of my mouth. She did exactly the same

173

thing. I don't know what was hotter, what she was actually doing or watching her do it.

The tension inside me was building. I tapped her head as a signal that I was about to come, but experience told me that my girl wasn't going to stop for anything. A warm tingling sensation hit me and I knew it was going to be intense. Emily took me as deep as she could, and I let out a deep groan as that first shot of fluid was expelled from my shaft. I had to take hold of the counter to keep myself up as I continued to explode in her mouth. She swallowed it like a champ. *Fuck, I'm a lucky stook.*

I helped her off of the floor once I recovered. "Better now?" she asked as she wiped her mouth with the back of her hand. *I swear she's trying to kill me.*

"Yeah, but I better go now while I still can." My colossal dick was starting to get hard again. "I'll buy the next round," I told her with a smack to her ass before leaving the kitchen.

"Make it two," she yelled as the screen door was about to close behind me. Oh, hell yeah, she'd be drunk on my love if I had anything to say about it.

I had a spring in my step as I walked up the steps that led to the back deck. All was right with the world. Libby had a smirk on her face and Aria was zonked out in her carrier.

"Is everything all right in the cottage? It sounded like you were really praying. Hard." *Oh, fuck!* Having Emily's long, sexy finger in my mouth hadn't quieted my cries of pleasure. "And I heard Nat was the loud one." Luckily, her laughter woke the baby. I ducked inside while she tended to her. Hopefully, she wouldn't say anything to embarrass her sister. *Maybe I should say something to her or bribe her with a special deposit to the trust I already set up for Aria.*

I bypassed the kitchen, not wanting to hear it from Logan too, and was surprised what I walked in on with my parents. Brianna was in my father's arms and they were both covered in paint and laughing. I said nothing as he pressed his lips to hers. I backed away as to not disrupt them. *Go, Da.*

Logan was enjoying the kitchen after his trip to the local farmer's market with "his girls" that afternoon.

"Want a beer? It's local," my friend and business partner offered. He handed me a bottle, and we both sat down at the table. It was funny to think how far we'd come from the way we first met. I guess I should have realized sooner that anything was possible. A pound of a fist had started my friendship with the man that was now sitting across from me. An obligatory stop by my parents' apartment, my relationship with Emily. The giving of blood, the truth about my parents. The sight of a photograph yellowed with years, the identity of my birth mother. Yes, it really was true that everything could change in just the blink of an eye.

Logan looked around the room. "I've been doing some thinking," he said as he toyed with the label on his beer. He wasn't the only one, but suddenly I was nervous about what he might say.

"I'm going to ask Libby to marry me. I want to legally adopt Aria." OK, I knew he was crazy about them. I checked to make sure Libby couldn't hear us through any open windows and then I began to laugh.

"What's so funny?" he asked, frustrated with my outburst. I couldn't stop, so I pulled the chain out of my pocket and held up the engagement ring. Soon, he was laughing too. "Oh, shit, that's rich, brother." I liked the sound of him calling me that, and if Libby and Emily would have us, that's exactly what we would be.

CHAPTER
seventeen

"How long have you had that?"

"I was going to ask her at the stroke of midnight on New Year's Eve." Just thinking about the stupid decisions I made that night put a frown on my face.

"No shit?" He seemed surprised. It seemed that the Barnes women surely had a way with us.

"No shit." I shook my head, trying to shake off the funk that thinking of the past always did to me.

"Stop beating yourself up." Logan knew me so well. "You can't change what happened in the past, but the future is yet to come. They call now the present because it's a gift, so live it with no regrets." No regrets was his motto, in fact, he had it inked on his arm. He was certainly right about that.

Having Emily and now my mother in my life certainly were gifts that I wanted to always treasure.

"Thanks, man, I guess it's time for a trip for us to go see Mr. Barnes." I knew he was right, but still I was worried. Hell, from what I knew, the man hadn't even attempted to call Libby when she had Aria. He could have at least sent flowers or a card. I didn't think I would ever understand how parents could just give up on their children. He was the one that let them down when he cheated on Cheryl but I couldn't help but remember the way Emily talked about him when she tied my tie for me. She loved him, no matter what, and because of that, I would ask him for his blessing to marry his daughter.

"That was wonderful, Logan." We all sat around the table on the deck stuffed from the delicious meal that Logan prepared for us.

"Thank you, Bri— Bai—" It wasn't the first time one of us had struggled with what to call my mother. To my father, she was Brianna. To Emily and Libby, she was Bailey. I honestly had no idea if I should I refer to her as my mother, my birth mother, my biological mother, or just her first name. It was confusing as shit.

"Why don't you all just call me, Mam?" It was a question that she pointed directly at me. Emily gave my thigh a squeeze underneath the table. Unable to speak, I nodded my head in approval of the idea. Even as a child, I had never been allowed to call Abigail Mom. It was always Mother.

"Mam," I tested the word, and her green eyes, that were the same color as mine, sparkled. I had a feeling that hers weren't the only ones that shone bright. My father made a strange noise, and with his napkin partially covering his face, he quickly excused himself from the table. It looked like he had tears in his eyes.

"Excuse me," my mother said as she followed my father inside the house.

"Talk about chemistry," Libby noted as soon as the two were out of earshot. I hadn't told anyone yet what I had witnessed while they were painting. I thought maybe I was seeing things that I just wanted to see. I know I'm an adult, but the thought of having my parents together, and happy, has crossed my mind more times than I will admit to.

"They are pretty cute together," Emily added as she laid her head on my shoulder with a dreamy sigh.

"You don't think it's kind of sudden?" Logan asked. He put his hands up in defense as both girls were giving him the death glare. I wanted to know Emily's thoughts on the matter. It was my biggest fear in asking her to marry me. That she would think it was too soon. Honestly, it had taken everything in my power not to ask her when she comforted me at the dock. I didn't know it at the time, but I realized that I had loved Emily from the first time I laid eyes on her. She was dancing around in my parents' kitchen in her barely-there outfit, singing off-key, and loving every minute of it. She filled the room with her personality and passion and my heart right along with it, and the second she did that bend and snap move to wipe up the egg I was a goner for sure.

"It's not exactly insta-love," Emily explained to Logan. "I think they've been in love with each other for the last twenty-nine years." She gave me another squeeze. Yes, it felt good to know that my parents not only loved me but each other too. Things could have been so different, so much better for all of us, if they hadn't let guilt and obligation guide them. But Logan was right: living in the past wouldn't lead us to the future.

"Insta-love?" I asked curiously where the term came from.

Libby snorted, yes snorted, before burying her head in Logan's chest. I didn't get what was so funny. Emily stared at her twin sister. Minutes passed without anyone saying anything. Finally, Libby composed herself and looked up to find us all waiting for an explanation.

"Are you kidding me? You two are the poster couple for insta-love."

"So what if we are?" Emily replied with a tinge of annoyance in her voice. "It's not like you and Logan are any different than us." I put my arms around her shoulder. *OK, so this was good. Right?* Lemon Drop continued, "When you know, you know." That was exactly what I needed to hear; in fact, it deserved a celebration, so I grasped her chin, tilted her face toward me, and kissed her like we were the only two people around.

"That was fun." Emily sighed contentedly as she slid into the sleeping bag next to me. After dinner, we ate Grandma Rose's delicious wild blackberry pie and played a game called Apples to Apples. It was my first ever family game night and Emily decided that we were camping when I mentioned I had never slept in a tent or sleeping bag. According to her, I'd been missing out my entire life. Seeing the excitement in my girl's eyes in sharing this new adventure was now at the top of my "Emily list". I didn't have a list of things I wanted to check off of a bucket list before I died, I had an Emily list. All the things I wanted to share with her. It was a pretty long list, but I hoped we would have a lifetime to complete it.

Swat.

"Is being eaten alive part of the fun I've been missing?" I asked sarcastically as I flicked the carcass of the little bloodsucker off my arm.

"Don't be so delicate." That was one of the green cards that was picked from the pile. As a joke, my ex-friend had said Declan for his blank card. *Fucker.* I hardly think I'm easily broken or fragile, though I might agree with him on "of intricate workmanship".

"Har har har," I said as I pulled her out of her bag. No way were we sleeping that far apart.

"What are you doing?"

"Get your luscious ass over here." That had been another green card in our game. I was the judge and my choices for the winner of the round were Homer Simpson, Larry the Cable Guy, ear wax, volcano, and Martha Washington. Ear wax? Luscious? I didn't think I'd never laughed so hard as when Libby tried to convince me that the yellow substance was delicious according to one of those wacky fetish shows on cable television.

Due to many years of house renters that left all sorts of equipment, my mother had a large collection of camping gear. Libby and Logan had a good laugh at our expense while they sat back and watched us as we attempted to erect the small tent in the near dark, but when my mother said that she could tell that we were a good team because of the way we worked together instead of bitching and moaning, it made me smile. I just met her that morning, her approval of my relationship with Emily shouldn't have mattered to me, but it did.

"Luscious? I know I should take that as a compliment, but it's a little difficult when you also said that about Martha Washington."

"D'Oh," I said in my best Homer Simpson voice while I slid my hands down her sides and promptly pulled them down. It was time to become one with nature.

"Declan? What if they still have the windows open?" Logan, Libby, and Aria were sleeping in my mother's room, which was closest to where we had set-up our tent. Dad was sleeping on the couch which shocked the hell out of me. He could have easily slept in one of the rooms that weren't being painted in the main house. I knew he wouldn't admit to it, but I'm pretty sure he wanted to be close to Mam who was sleeping on the day bed in her studio. She'd spent many late nights working in the room over the years. When we came back in the house, she showed us a drawing for a current storyline she was working on for Bash and June Bug where they were pitching a tent. Pretty ironic, right?

"I'd been meaning to ask you this. If Emily is June Bug, who am I?" Libby asked excitedly as we all looked at the drawing. My mother bit her lip and her cheeks flushed. It did make sense that Libby, who also had known my mother the same amount of time would also be featured in *The Adventures of Bash*, while Bash had an amazing older brother who was always looking after him. I had an older brother. I never knew him, but I hoped he was watching over me.

The character June Bug only had a dog. The dog was a little pug, named Fluffy. Now, with a name like Fluffy you would think that dog was this sweet little thing that everyone loved. That couldn't be any further from the truth. Fluffy was a mean little troublemaker who always wreaked havoc for June Bug and Bash. I told Mam that Fluffy reminded me of the Nellie Oleson character on that prairie show and everyone agreed with the comparison, even Libby.

"Oh, shit," Logan muttered as we all came to the same conclusion. All eyes went to my Lemon Drop's twin.

"I'm sorry, Libby." It looked like both my mother and Libby were about to cry. My father put a protective arm

183

around her. "I swear I didn't mean to—" Libby cut in before she could finish.

"It's fine, Bailey." Minutes before, she had called her Mam, and now she was back to being Bailey. She could have just slapped her—it might have hurt less, but Libby was hurt too. Fluffy was a little shite. "I need to give Aria a bath before bed, if you'll excuse me." Libby quickly left the room with Logan hot on her tail.

"She'll be fine," Lemon Drop assured her before we said our goodnights.

"It'll get her mind off the Fluffy bits if they hear us."

"A'ye now get your fluffy bits up here over my mouth. You heard me, mo eala," I said as I lifted her shirt, or should I say *my* shirt, and positioned her so that she was straddling my face. "God, you're beautiful." We left the fly off the top of the tent, so the light of the moon shone through the mesh roof that covered us.

First, I kissed her left thigh and then I repeated the action on her right thigh. She mewled in delight and I groaned. "Play with those beautiful diddies," I encouraged before I licked her pussy which was already gleaming with wetness. Nothing tasted as sweet as my Lemon Drop. I don't know what it is about her, but if you told me I could only eat one thing for the rest of my life, it would be her.

She'd sat on my face before. She was a little reluctant the first time, but now she knew how good it was. I gave her a long lick and she ground her pussy against me, and once again, I felt blessed to have been given the gene that allowed me to roll my tongue. While I was giving her pleasure in this position, she held so much of the power, she rolled her hips against my face. God, yes. We established a rhythm that I knew was driving her crazy. Lick, lick, tongue roll, poke, repeat.

"Oh, God, yes. Jesus, fuck!" she yelled and her legs began to tremble.

If I didn't know any better, I might have thought we were having an earthquake. *Fuck me, I have to get inside of her.* I pulled her off my face and sat up to kiss her. I loved that she let me kiss her when I still had her all over my face. I'm not wiping it off. That would be like spilling a glass of Henri Jayer Vosne-Romanee. Tragic. My bod mor was hard as a rock. I almost lost my load when she came. I lifted her hips, but she needed no further instruction as she practically impaled herself on my cock.

"Fuck yes!" I yelled before she covered my mouth with hers. I wedged my arms between us and plucked at her nipples which were still hard from when she was playing with them. She was close again, and I was already on the brink before I even got inside of her. I thrust up at the same time that she ground down, and this time, I wasn't so sure we really weren't in an earthquake because it felt like the earth was actually moving beneath us. We were both breathing hard and covered in sweat. That was one hell of a workout, and after several minutes of us both trying to catch our breath, I decided that I'd been slacking on my exercise regimen because not only could I not breathe, but all of my muscles were starting to ache. I felt her entire body shaking before I heard her laughter.

She was still in my lap, so I had to lean back a little so that I could see her face. There I was thinking we just rocked the entire world and she was laughing. Before I could ask her what was so funny, she told me, "We popped the air mattress."

"I guess we won't be sleeping here tonight." Well, that explained the sore muscles and the seismic activity. "Let's get out of here." I already wanted my Lemon Drop again. I climbed out of the tent, naked as the day I was born, and grabbed her foot and yanked her out and into my waiting arms. I loved the sound of her giggling. It was as beautiful as this place. She snuggled into me as I took a moment to take in our surroundings. That was when I decided it was time to do something else on the list. I took off running with her in my arms before she could object.

When we emerged, she wiped the water from her face before splashing more in mine. She was still in my arms, so I tossed her high in the air and I knew she was laughing by the time she hit the water.

I swear, she was the most beautiful thing I'd ever seen when she came out of the water and pushed her hair back. My breath hitched again and it was not because of the elevation or from exertion. It was her. She took my breath away.

I pulled her into my arms. She wrapped her legs around me; my hardness nestled between us. "Declan Hayes skinny dipping," she mocked with a raised brow as if she was one of the society snobs Mother would have pretended were her "friends".

"Abso-fucking-lutely," I said before kissing her. She shivered in my arms. While I loved it when she trembled in my arms, I didn't like this. I didn't want her to get sick, so I backed out of the water and stopped at the tent only for a moment so that I could grab my shirt for her. Carefully, I put it on her before lifting her in my arms again. I never liked cuddly women before, but I loved it when my Lemon Drop practically burrowed into me like she couldn't get close enough. Hell, I felt the same exact way.

When we reached the top of the stairs, I could smell the familiar scent of the cigar my father enjoyed from time to time. He was sitting in a chair that was facing the water when we were up there earlier. He must have turned it to give us some privacy. I'm just glad I took that moment to cover Emily. I couldn't care less if he saw me naked, but I'm the only one who got to see her. Without a single word, he acknowledged me. I responded with a slight nod. Once again grateful that he didn't say anything and was not seen by Emily, who would have been mortified. Maybe it wasn't just a new beginning for me and my mam. Maybe it was a new beginning for all of us.

CHAPTER

eighteen

It was early in the morning, and I should have been curled up beside Emily, but I couldn't sleep and I didn't want to wake her. She giggled when I tossed her on the bed the night before, and what can I say, the sound got me every single time but unlike our hot and quick romp in the tent, that time, we made slow passionate love. I covered every single inch of her body with my lips and tongue. I worshipped her.

Luckily, we stored our overnight bags in the room we ended up in. I couldn't help but smirk as I remembered being caught in my birthday suit by my father. At least Lemon Drop was covered up with my shirt and didn't notice her new BFF sitting on the deck. She would have been so embarrassed. I'd hate to run into Mam or Libby this morning with me sporting nothing but wood.

Mam? Who would have ever thought twenty-four hours before that things would be where they stood now? Not me. Not only had I met my birth mother, but she was an amazing woman, who was genuine, and really wanted to get to know me.

I heard him before I saw him, actually—I was a little surprised he was there because everyone else was in the cottage. He probably just came up there the night before so that he wouldn't get caught smoking his stogie. The sound stopped me in my tracks. Not because it was unpleasant, it just caught me off-guard. It was the same tune I hummed to Aria. Could he have been the one that taught it to me? I'd never heard my father whistle. Ever, and it was such a happy tune. Quietly, I rounded the corner and was taken back again. My father was in the kitchen, and he was cooking. I didn't think he knew how to boil water. He stopped briefly before he poured a cup of coffee and motioned me toward it before he resumed what I now saw was baking, not cooking, and began whistling again. I watch in awed silence while I enjoyed my drink. The man was so far removed from the man that I thought was my father.

"I was thinking ..." he started after closing the oven where he just placed a muffin tin to bake.

"Are those Emily's?" I asked brusquely before he could finish his sentence.

"Yes, she taught me how to make them. We've become quite close in the time you were gone." I already knew that, but hearing him say it stung, and knowing that she taught him how to bake her muffins really pissed me off. Sure, I'd helped her put things in the oven and taken them out before, but she'd never taught me her recipes. *I'm jealous of my fucking father.*

"Don't," he said as he slammed down the coffee cup he had picked up. The action so hard that hot liquid sloshed over the top and onto his hand. "Son-of-a—" he stopped himself and turned toward the sink and held his burnt hand under water. I watch in stunned silence as he turned off the water and placed his hands on the counter. He lowered his head and began to shake it back and forth before speaking. "She didn't do it for me." His head raised and he looked out the window before turning to face me. "She did it for you." He smiled, and in that moment, I knew she was behind me. "Because she loves you." He placed his hand on my shoulder before walking past me and kissing my girl on her temple. He told her that the timer was set before walking out the back door.

She put her arms around me from behind and placed her lips at the base of my neck.

"Is he right?" I asked. She knew that I knew she loved me, but I'd never really understood why she befriended my father in my absence. It wasn't like we had a good relationship before, and when the truth came out, I couldn't imagine a scenario where we ever would. He lied to me my entire life. Now, of course, that had changed. I'm not sure if he'd changed or just my view of him had changed. Seeing him broken at Finn's grave site, and then remembering all the times in my life where he had patted at the photo of my mother he always carried next to his heart just before pulling away from me did change things. What if he had known that Mam had sent those letters? Would he have left Abigail? *I guess we will never know.*

"Maybe." Her lips brushed against my skin. "I know you probably don't want to hear this, but he was so alone, and so was I. He lost his wife and his son in one day. At first, I thought he needed me. I helped him make arrangements. I sat beside him at the funeral. I held his hand when they buried Abigail, and I watched him fall apart at your brother's grave. He cried for both of the sons he had lost. He's not you, but being with him helped me to remember all of the reasons why I fell in love with you in the first place, and when I cried for you, he was the one that held me. He was the one that reminded me you loved me. He was the one that told me not to give up on us. So maybe, I did it for us."

She pressed her lips against me again before I turned in her arms and kissed her, but it wasn't just a kiss. It was a promise. A promise that I was there now and that I wasn't going anywhere. A commitment that from then on, I would be the one to kiss away her tears.

"Thank you. I love you, Lemon Drop."

"I love you too, Dec. Now go and talk to your father." The timer went off on the oven. She moved past me, and I couldn't help myself when I swatted her beautiful arse in a pair of sleep shorts that caused my body to react just like it did when I heard her laugh. OK, that was a lie—everything she did got me hard.

"I'm glad you had each other." Before talking to my father, I grabbed my camera and took some pictures. Something about seeing things through the lens gave me a different perspective, helped me see things in focus. At a time when I couldn't be there for her, he was, and I couldn't help but think it was because he loved me too.

He was sitting in the very spot I met my mother for the first time and I couldn't help but notice the smooth rock he was holding in his hand and smile.

"Me too. She's pretty special." The fact that she didn't think so made her even more so.

"Kind of like Mam."

"Exactly." My father agreed, and then I taught him to skip rocks too.

Eric, Suzie, Gabe, and Nat joined us for brunch. We were all heading back to New York that day. The trip wasn't planned and honestly we didn't even know if we would find Brianna Bailey or Bailey Flemming. She didn't believe in social media and her number was unlisted. Eric probably could have gotten it if I had given him more time, but what would I have done with her number anyway? No, coming out to California was the right choice—the only choice. I wasn't ready to say goodbye to this remarkable woman I just met, hell I didn't know if I ever would be. As happy as Mam was to have us all here, something was off, and she looked exhausted.

I gave Emily a squeeze of her hand to let her know that things were good with me and Da, and when I motioned toward my mother with my head, she hunched her shoulders in response. I could tell she noticed it too but had no idea what was bothering her.

"Good morning, Nellie," I offered to Libby because even I knew better than to call a woman Fluffy. Besides, her boyfriend could kick my ass. This I know from first-hand experience. *Hell, he still might beat me for calling her Nellie.*

"Declan Kieran Hayes!" My mother used my full name, and I have to say it made me feel like I was five years old. I knew I probably would have hated it at that time, but now, I revel in it. And she was giving me the "Mom" look.

"Oh, you're in trouble," Eric teased before Suzie smacked him in the chest.

My mother looked nervous, as if she crossed some line, but it was a line I wanted her to cross. She was my mother. "Sorry, Mam," I offered contritely and she smiled before snapping back into "Mom" mode and motioning toward Libby whose feelings were already hurt about being compared to the evil pug. "I'm sorry, Libby." I looked toward my mother who was looking at me proudly. *Yep, I'm five.*

"I have something for you, Libby." My mother interjected as she held out what looked like a sketch pad.

Emily took Aria, and I couldn't help but think again how great she looked holding a baby. Libby then took the fore offered pad and began to flip through the pages.

"Oh, my God, is this really what I think it is?" she asked as a tear fell down her face. Logan was instantly at her side. He began to look at the pad and Libby raced into my mother's arms.

"This must have taken you all night." Logan seemed as affected as Libby.

"It did," my mother confirmed. *Well, at least that explains why she looks like she didn't get any sleep last night. She didn't.*

"I thought you said you would never do anything but *The Adventures of Bash.*" Libby was a bit of a fan of my mother's work. When I asked why the boy in the book, me, was named Bash, Libby answered the question for her. According to an interview she read about my mother, Bash was the nickname she gave me when I wouldn't cooperate during her ultrasound. She shorted Bashful to just Bash, and it had stuck.

"That's not exactly what I said," my mother corrected. The sketchbook was now being passed around the room. "I said that I would draw Bash until I didn't need him anymore."

"You don't need him anymore?" It was almost a whisper, and I almost said me instead of him. Emily began to move closer to me but stopped when my mother looked at me with tears in her eyes.

She placed her hand on my jaw and shook her head. "No, I don't need Bash anymore because now I have you." I'm pretty sure it was both Emily and Da who gulped loudly. Me, I just tilted my head into my mother's hand and let her love me. It felt perfect.

"Come with us," I requested. I just met her, and I couldn't leave her now, but our life was in New York. "I need you. Da needs you." I'm not sure when I realized it, but deep down I knew she was the reason my father was whistling. I knew I was an adult, with a life of my own, but I was also that kid who wanted his parents together. We'd all lost enough. We couldn't change what happened, but maybe, just maybe, we could have a chance at what could have been.

"I don't understand why you didn't mention this before." Emily and Libby weren't exactly happy that Logan and I decided to "take a meeting" in Los Angeles while we were both there in California. It wasn't exactly a spoof—a restaurant group had been bugging us about opening a Swayed LA location, and they didn't need to know that we were really going to talk to their father. We were going to meet with a local property rental company for Mam and finish up the painting while they all left on the private jet for home. It didn't take much to convince my mother to come with us. She said she needed to be near Aria since she was the star of what she hoped would be her new book series. With the success she had had with Bash, I had no doubt that it would be a great accomplishment too, but we all also know she didn't need to see Aria to draw her, but I didn't care. She was coming home with us to New York. I was also being honest when I said Da needed her; I was worried about what other secrets Abigail was keeping. I didn't even want to think about what he would find besides my mother's letters and books when he went through her things. If anyone could help him with that, it was her.

"Stop fidgeting!" Logan was nervous, and I wasn't exactly helping. We talked a lot while we were finishing the painting. While he knew he wanted a lifetime with Libby and Aria, he was not quite ready to pop the question yet, but he did want to find out why Grant hadn't even acknowledged the birth of his first grandchild. Logan agreed to let me go first in case things didn't go well with him. Logan had come a long way from when I first met him. He had no problem mincing garlic, but wouldn't do it with words. If he didn't like what Mr. Barnes had to say, he'd let him know it.

Cheryl gave us the address to Grant's office. She said that he normally worked late. We were hoping that night was no exception. The office was empty, in fact, it kind of looked unoccupied by the layer of dust that covered the desk of what I could only assume belonged to his secretary.

"I don't like this." Logan was on guard and I couldn't say that I blamed him. I didn't like it, either.

"Hello?" I called out. Minutes later, the door to his office flew open.

"You know the goddamn drill," he bellowed before he realized that two men he'd never seen before were standing in his otherwise empty office. His defenses went up immediately. "You're not the delivery kid. Who the hell are you?" Normally, I would have dressed to impressed, but when we packed for our trip to California, Emily teased me that where we were going meant clean socks and underwear, so I made do with jeans and a plain white t-shirt. Logan wore his usual—black.

Just then, a kid walked in with a bag. By the smell, I would say it was Chinese. He must have gone there on a regular basis because he did know the drill. Without a single word, he set the bag down, opened the top drawer of the empty desk, took out a bill, and left with just a shrug.

"We're closed," he said as he reached down for his bag. He wasn't dressed for the office at all. I had always envisioned him with a tie perfectly tied around his neck by his amazing daughter like she did when she was a girl. Instead, he was wearing a pair of ill-fitting track pants and a wife beater. Yeah, totally not what I was expecting, but it was definitely Grant Barnes. Emily and Libby were a perfect blend of Cheryl and Grant.

"We're here about your daughters," Logan grunted out as Grant was turning away from us because he was more interested in his dinner than he was us. I knew that the recession had been hard on independent auditors like Grant Barnes, but according to Emily, her father was the best of the best. Nothing about the broken man in front of me screamed cream of the crop.

His shoulders tensed. "Are you guys cops? What's Libby done? Last time I heard, she got herself knocked-up. Did she involve Emily in one of her schemes?" Wheeler balled his fists. "I don't have any money to bail them out." At that point, I was probably the only one that could keep Logan from needing bail money himself.

"He's Aria's grandfather," I whispered, which caused my buddy to take a deep breath before nodding his head.

"Not cops."

"Then like I said, we're closed." OK, wow. That wasn't what I was expecting. From the way Emily talked, it was like she had this perfect family until her father cheated on his wife and pretty much ditched his teenage daughters. Hell, she even believed Cheryl stayed close because she was still in love with the man. She thought that her mother was holding out hope. This man didn't deserve that. Not for a second.

"Really? This is a bunch of bullshit." Logan grumbled as he stepped closer toward Grant. "We came here out of respect for both you and your daughters and this is the way you react. Fuck!" Logan was at the end of his rope so, I did the only thing I could and put myself between him and the man I hoped would be my future father-in-law.

"I'm Declan Hayes. You may have heard of Hayes Investment Properties." I put out my hand to shake his. As soon as he heard my name, everything about him changed.

If I had been wearing the Armani, I never would have seen this side of Grant Barnes. The true side of Grant Barnes. The side he never showed his ex-wife or daughters. Some monsters live under the bed or in the closet, this one is in plain sight, but now that I knew what I was dealing with, I had the upper-hand.

I could tell by Logan's reaction that he was pissed that I played the money card, but it was a game I'd played before, and I didn't intend to lose.

"Mr. Hayes, what's this about my daughters?" Cue doting father.

"Let me introduce you to my associate, Logan Wheeler. You may have heard of him. He's a James Beard award winner and his restaurant, Swayed, has three Michelin stars." *It's our restaurant, but he doesn't need to know that.*

"It's a pleasure to meet you, Mr. Wheeler." Logan hated being called Mr. "I'm sorry I don't have anything Michelin-worthy to offer you." He actually held up his to-go bag of cheap Chinese. A quick glance around the room confirmed my suspicions that Grant seemed to be sleeping in his office. As a guy who threw everything away six months ago because he didn't know who he was, I felt kind of sorry for this guy. This was a man who had it all, and now he's sleeping on a cheap leather couch in his office. He was probably showering at his gym and living off take-out food. The question was, what did I do about it? I was certainly in a position to be able to help him, but did I want to?

"We ate," Logan offered, which was nowhere near true. Both of us were too nervous to eat before coming and neither of us said it, but I know it crossed my mind that breaking bread could have gone a long way with the man. Logan was waiting for me since I was the one that started this game.

"Let me cut to the chase, Mr. Barnes, or should we call you Grant?"

"Sure, sure have a seat, and by all means, call me Grant. Can I at least get you a drink?"

"Do you have any Voss or Pellegrino?" Logan asked, and I had to cover my laugh with a cough. Wheeler couldn't stand food snobs.

"Oh, shit. No, I'm sorry." What's even funnier was that I swear if we had been cops he was going to tell us to get the hell out and if we didn't he was going to call the cops and now he's practically kissing our asses. I hated brown-nosers.

"As I said, Grant, let's get down to business." I hadn't decided what to do with this guy yet but his daughter, my Lemon Drop, loved him. "We are involved with Libby and Emily." I motioned toward Logan and myself so that he knew which girl we were attached to.

The fucker laughed. "Like I didn't know which one of you belonged to which of my daughters." I guess you could say that Logan with his tattoos and lack of color looked more bad boy where I with my jeans and T looked more? What? Average Joe Monthly?

"You're pushing it, sir." Logan grit through his teeth. *Hell, at this rate someone might need to bail us both out.*

"Cool your jets, Turbo. My girls have a type, that's all. Brooding biker has Libby written all over it and boardroom boring is my Emily." *I'm not boring. What the fuck? I don't even know what to say to that.*

"This isn't getting us anywhere, Sparky," Logan retorted. "Let's just go, Dec. I don't even need to ask him what I was going to, my girls are better off without this guy."

"She had a girl?" Grant asked like he had no idea Libby had the baby. She was born two weeks before. I swear to God, when I became a father, not a day would go by that I didn't know what was going on in my child's life. Not a day would go by that they didn't know I loved them more than anything.

"For Pete's sake." Logan produced his phone from his pocket. I swear he had hundreds of pictures already. "She said she called you."

"She's beautiful." *Now I'm right back to not being sure what to do with this guy.* "What's her name?"

"Well, right now it's Aria Jane Barnes, but I want to marry your daughter and adopt Aria."

"… and I was hoping for your blessing to ask Emily to marry me." Logan seems pleased with our one, two combination. I've got to say it kind of knocked the wind right out of his sails.

"Does Cheryl approve?" he asked, and I had to admit that I was warming up to the guy.

"She gave me Grandma Rose's ring." Saying that would never get old. He nodded in understanding.

"And you think you can handle my pistol and some other guy's baby?" he asked my friend and soon-to-be brother.

"She handles me, sir, and that little girl is mine." You could say that Aria had Logan wrapped around her little finger. Hell, you could call us both pussy whipped. Who cares? We got the girls, and as far as I was concerned, that was all that mattered.

CHAPTER
nineteen

"Should we tell them?" Wheeler and I were sitting at a bar at LAX, waiting to hop on the red-eye back to New York. I'd been asking myself the same question since we left Grant Barnes' office. I'd seen firsthand what damage could be done by lies, and trust me, not telling her was the same thing. *I'm damned if I do, damned if I don't.*

"What do we really know?" I asked after taking a long pull from my beer.

"That Daddy Dearest is a real piece of work. As soon as he knew who you were, everything about him changed, and when you shoved my stars in his face he looked like he had won the Publishers Clearing House Sweepstakes or something." Logan's drink was poised at his lips, but he lowered it before he took a sip and looked at me. "But when he found out about Aria and saw her pictures it was like he changed again. I don't get it." He shook his head and then polished off the rest of his pint.

"True, and when he asked about Cheryl it happened again." He respected her even though he didn't show it when he cheated on her. He trusted her judgment when it came to Emily and Libby. Maybe the guy was smarter than he looked. That and Emily loved him. I had no choice.

"What I can't understand is why Lib didn't at least tell him about the baby. She told me she did. Why would she lie to me about it?" He shrugged before adding, "I could care less if Daddy'o is in the picture. Who needs him?" Logan may say that, but I knew it bothered him that his family was no longer a part of his life. At one point, they were his entire life. A life he almost lost because of them.

"I'll tell her after I ask her and in the meantime, I'll have Eric see what he can find on Grant." I'd help him in any way that I could, but what I wouldn't let him do was hurt any of the Barnes women again.

"You think he'll be a problem?" That was when I ordered two shots for each of us. Grant was a ticking time bomb, and we both knew it. The question was when, not if, he was going to go off. The man was visibly down on his luck. A messy divorce, a downturn in the economy at the same time, a much-younger new wife to impress, two daughters who no longer believed he could do no wrong. I would say it all added up. That was fine, as long as it didn't cost me Emily.

"Not if I can help it."

She leaped into my arms the moment she saw me and began peppering kisses all over my face. "I missed you," she said between pecks.

"I missed you too." It was ridiculous seeing as how we were apart less than twelve hours, but I felt exactly the same way. I thought about her the whole flight home.

"Are you two about done?" Eric asked as he and Logan moved from the trunk of the car where they just placed our bags toward their doors. Not by a longshot, but the TSA guy was blowing his whistle and motioning at Eric to move along.

Emily and Eric told us about the flight home before we dropped Logan off at Swayed so that he could check on the progress being made on the renovations before he dropped us at the apartment. I was so happy she was back with me, where she belonged.

"Do you want to take a shower while I make breakfast?" She was always taking care of me and everyone else around her. I wanted to do that for her.

"I'd rather take a shower with you. I'll make us breakfast." I think I'd just stunned her. "What? I can cook a couple of eggs and I won't burn your toast." I began to chuckle at myself. "Well, not too badly, anyway."

"I'll take my chances."

She was sitting at the counter watching me. It was a good thing I wasn't using any sharp instruments or I'd probably cut a finger off. "You're making me nervous."

"Do you want me to go?" she asked after she was finished giggling like a schoolgirl.

"Never." I was sure she knew I wasn't just talking about right then. The bacon in the microwave dinged, and I was pretty impressed with myself when the perfectly-toasted bread popped up at almost the same time. The eggs I scrambled were fluffy and the bacon crisp. Not bad, if I do say so myself. I passed Emily her plate of food. She seemed impressed.

"I think you've been holding out on me, Mr. Hayes."

"Just waiting for the right time to reveal myself, Mrs. Hayes." *Shit.* I guess I wasn't the only one that couldn't believe I just said that out loud because Emily was practically choking on her eggs. I don't know why it surprised us both so much, I had already told her I planned to take her to Ireland on our honeymoon. Not that I didn't want it more than anything, I just couldn't believe I let it slip out like that. It was so natural. Maybe because it was what she was destined to be—Mrs. Emily Hayes. I watched her carefully as she took a sip of her water, trying to gauge her reaction. Was she opposed to the idea of being my wife? We'd never really talked about marriage, but I'd made it very clear that I planned on being around. Forever, if she'd have me. She resumed eating like it wasn't a big deal. Maybe I needed to start wearing my glasses for more than just reading because she was sure not giving me much to go by.

We finished our breakfast in silence. It wasn't awkward. Just quiet. I cleared the dishes before sitting back down at the table across from her.

"What's on your mind?" I could tell the wheels were turning in that beautiful brain of hers. She seemed surprised that I knew something was going on. "Those beautiful eyes of yours, they are so expressive. It's one of the million things that I love about you." I couldn't believe I ever hesitated to say those words to her. Now I didn't think I could ever say them enough. With my words, her smile widened and some of the concern she was just showing in those chocolate windows to her soul just melted away.

"This is going to sound crazy," she said, and I took her hands in mine, lifting them to my lips and kissing them both

"I seriously doubt that." Emily was the smartest person I knew, and while she was often humorous, she was rarely crazy.

She was hesitant, so I squeezed her hands gently to encourage her that I was there and I wasn't going anywhere. "I'm kind of glad you left." Fuck, it was a good thing I was already sitting down because those were the last words I ever expected to hear from her. She must have sensed the hurt in my eyes, because in a flash, she was around the table and sitting in my lap. Her soft hands cupped my face and she kissed me once softly on the lips before looking me straight in the eye. "It's not like that, Declan. I missed you every second that you were gone."

I think I breathed for the first time since she shocked me with her admission. She placed a kiss on the end of my

207

nose, but instead of returning her gaze to mine, she put her forehead against mine and closed her eyes. That was hard for her. "I did a lot of thinking after you left, and I didn't really like some of the things I did when we were together."

"What are you talking about? You were perfect." Her eyes were still closed and she was shaking her head in disagreement. She needed to hear what I was about to say loud and clear, so I clinched her chin and tipped her head up. "Look at me, Lemon Drop," I begged, and she finally looked at me. "You were perfect," I said again, because she was. I never felt more alive or loved than in the time that we spent together. She made me feel things I didn't even know I was capable of feeling.

"No, I was petty, jealous, and immature." She was dead serious. Didn't we already clear all this shit up? *How could she think she was any of those things?* Now I shook my head in disbelief, but she stood and walked toward the windows, frustrated. "On our first date, I was so possessive that I publicly humiliated the hostess at Swayed." I couldn't help but laugh out loud because she was so cute. "It's not funny," she snapped with her hands on her hips.

"I love it when you're feisty." I loved her all the time.

"I'm serious, Declan. I made assumptions so many times. First about you and Marissa and then again with Brit. I saw you with this beautiful blonde bombshell and I just assumed you were together. I made a complete ass of myself. Here everyone thinks I'm this strong independent woman yet I was so insecure. Anytime something happened that I couldn't deal with I just took off. I don't know why you even bothered coming after me. I was a hot mess." She was serious, and I couldn't stand the space between us any longer, but she held out her hand to stop me. "Don't, I need to finish and you can't touch me or I won't be able to." I didn't like it, but if that was what she needed, I'd give it to her, for now. Hell, I would give her the world if I could, but before she was done, she was going to understand without a doubt exactly how wrong she was.

She began to pace in front of the windows that overlooked the river and the city. "I didn't even think I needed or wanted a man in my life." *Ouch.* "But then I met you and you changed everything, you challenged me, you made me want more, and you gave me my bakery." *Are we really back to this?*

I put my hands in my hair in frustration. She moved toward me like she couldn't stand the distance she wanted between us just moments before. "That's not what I meant, Dec." She traced her thumb against my stubbled jawline and left her hand on my face, stroking me softly. "You didn't do it because you could. I know that now. You did it because you wanted to. You made my dreams come true. Even the ones I didn't know I had. It wasn't a man that I needed in my life. It was you that I needed. Just you. I don't think I saw it clearly until you were gone. What we had, have, it might have been insta, but that doesn't make it any less real. I don't think I ever would have been sure of that if you hadn't left like you did." I couldn't stand it any longer; I needed to get my hands on her. I kissed the palm of her hand that was resting on my cheek before scooping her up in my arms and carrying her in my arms to our bed.

I laid her down on the bed and removed her sandals one at a time, kissing her toes on each foot. She tried to squirm away from me, but I tightened my hold on her as I continued to kiss my way up her body. "You weren't a hot mess, Lemon Drop." As much as I wanted nothing more than to ravish her right then, she needed to understand how she made me feel. "You gave me a home, and I don't mean a roof over my head." I placed a kiss on the inside of both of her wrists before placing her hands over her head. "You welcomed me to your family, the one you created." Pressing against her collar bone with my lips, I kissed her from one side to the other. "They accepted me without question because you mean that much to them." I kissed back to the other side. I couldn't help but smirk at the memory of Nat, Gabe, and Matty all threatening me with bodily harm if I hurt her. "OK, well, they did threaten to kick my ass if I hurt you, but then they let me in. I've never felt so surrounded by people that cared about me before."

"Oh, Declan." Tears begin to fill her eyes. I didn't want to make her cry; I just wanted her to know exactly how I felt.

"No, now you let me finish." I kissed her lips chastely. "You being jealous was hot, not a hot mess. It just proved to me how much you cared about me. Like you wanted me to be yours and because you always made such a fuss whenever I spent any of my money or resources on you, everyone knew it wasn't about that for you. Making your dreams come true was as much for me as it was for you. Being with you made me realize that as alone as I always felt before, I wasn't. I was surrounded by people that cared about me, but I never recognized their love." I kissed her again, this time more deeply before I continued, "But you showed me what it looked like, what it felt like. You called me out on my bullshit and stood up to Abigail. Fuck, I think they are still talking about you at the Pembroke, and I could give two shits if people think we what we have isn't real because we fell in love instantly. It doesn't feel instant to me; I've been waiting my whole life for you, Emily Barnes." I kissed her forehead once then dragged my lips down her nose before placing a kiss on the tip. "If it took for me to go for you to realize that too, then I'm glad too." I never thought I would say those words, but maybe she was right. Maybe our time apart was exactly what we needed. "Now I'm going to make love to you, Lemon Drop."

"OK," she said breathlessly as her unshed tears finally began to fall, having received my message loud and clear.

"OK." We were a far cry from just OK—we were exactly where we were supposed to be, and as I made love to the woman of my dreams it finally felt like both of our bodies, hearts, and minds were in sync. All the pieces were in place—it was time for us to make our new dreams come true, but first we had to deal with Grant.

CHAPTER
twenty

"Thanks for coming over."

"It's what you pay me for. Where's Emily?" Eric took a look around the apartment for her.

"She's downstairs working on a recipe for some hipster's birthday party. I guess he's on one of those reality television shows." Eric rolled his eyes because his wife had one of those shows. He hated it. So far, he'd been able to stay off camera, but from what he'd told me, the producers wanted him and they were starting to be pretty insistent. I guess you could say that Eric was a good looking guy and the fans would "eat him up". I didn't get it, but I'm a dude.

"Good." That sounded ominous. I text Eric from Los Angeles and told him to get my everything he could on Grant Barnes, and I was anxious to hear what he learned.

A knock on the door interrupted us. "That will be Logan." I opened the door for my friend and business partner. After our meeting with the girls' father, he was concerned as I was to know what we were dealing with so I cut right to the chase. "What did you find out?"

"Let's sit." Eric stopped at the fridge and produced three beers before joining us at the table. He handed us each a bottle and a folder. Eric was the best at what he did. With the exception of finding my mother, he had always been able to get me any information that I needed. It wasn't his style to drink while he was on the job, so I watched him cautiously before lifting my bottle to my lips. He wasn't giving anything away. Either he didn't find anything of concern or he was trying to get us to relax before he delivered us news we didn't want to hear.

"It's not good, guys." He took a long drink before he opened his file. "You were right, Declan; it seems that Barnes is living at this office. Wife number two filed for divorce six weeks ago. Right about the same time the IRS showed up." So much for in good times and in bad.

"Fuck!" Logan slammed his fist on the table.

"When the going gets tough," I muttered, but they both heard me.

"The good news is that I don't think he'll be coming around anytime soon since he'll be going away for five to ten."

"Son-of-a-bitch." Despite the strained relationship they had, Emily loved her father. She looked up to him until he cheated on Cheryl and turned her in for a younger model. It served him right that he was alone now. I didn't know about Libby, but I was pretty sure Cheryl and Emily would have stood by his side through just about anything. Hell, he might not even be in that situation if he hadn't strayed in the first place.

"I knew I saw dollar signs flashing in his eyes when you told him who we were. He's probably trying to figure out how he can get us to pay to get him out of this mess right now." Logan was out of his seat pacing the floor and clenching his fists. He'd come a long away—not so long ago he would already have a hole punched through my sheetrock. While people may think that an award-winning, Michelin star chef had more money than they knew what to do with, that just wasn't true in Logan's case. Don't get me wrong, he was doing well. Better than I could have ever imagined when we first met, but money to spare wasn't a luxury Logan had yet.

Eric flipped to the second page in his file. "According to my sources, they've frozen all his accounts, business and personal. My guy at the Department of Justice tells me the U.S. Attorney's office is prepared to go to trial. If the douchebag was smart, he'd plead out. It's his first offense and white collar, so they'll probably just send him off to some country club lock-up."

"We need to tell the girls." That wasn't the kind of thing I could just put on the back burner. Cheryl knew we were going to see Grant. If Emily and Libby found out we withheld information like that about their father, they could choose to never forgive us. I wouldn't let something Grant did come between me and Lemon Drop, and I was sure Logan felt the same way about Libby. If the girls wanted to help him after they knew the truth, I would support them. I knew that was what Emily would do for me.

"This is going to be so much fun, but I don't understand why you didn't want to invite your mom and dad." After Eric and Logan left, I called Emily—who had finished at the bakery and was delivering muffins to The Bowery before meeting with Willow to talk about expanding Hugs for Home—to ask her if it was all right if we had Libby, Logan, Aria, Maggie, and Billy over for dinner. Maggie was for all purposes an aunt to the girls and would know how to best tell Cheryl the truth about her ex-husband.

"Because they need some time alone to finish going through Abigail's things. Besides, I thought you would be thrilled to finally see Maggie and Billy together." I always knew the two were a couple, but they felt it would be better if they kept their private life, private. Especially from the busybody gossips that lived in the building. It wasn't that they purposely tried to hide it from Emily, it was just what they were used to.

"Do you think they are going to be all right?" Mam and Da had spent the day in the storage locker that Abigail kept in the basement of the building. They asked me if I wanted to see it, but I just couldn't do it. It was enough for me to know that not only had my birth mother sent me a card on every birthday that she missed up until my twenty-first year, but also a signed first edition of each book she ever published. I couldn't begin to imagine why Abigail had not only hidden the truth from both me and my father, but she had kept every single one of those books and cards. Not only that, but she had written back. Every single year, a letter, including photos chronicling my life had been written in return. None of them were sent. I didn't know when they would be all right, but I did know that they had each other and that together they could get through anything.

"Da says he's never seen someone cry so many tears." He tried to convince Mam that reading the letters would serve no purpose now, but she said she had wondered what her son was like for twenty-nine years and that this was her chance to know me. She didn't need the letters of a broken woman to know me. Depending on how things went at dinner, I was hoping that we could spend some quality time together over the long holiday weekend.

"I'm sorry, Dec." Emily's arms wrapped around me from behind and she squeezed me tight. It was amazing how just a touch from her could make me feel so much better. The door announced the arrival of either our guests or our food, but before Emily could leave me, I turned and took her in my arms. Returning the hug and placing a kiss on the top of her head while asking God to protect the woman I loved from being hurt. She'd already been hurt enough by men who claimed to love her. First her father and then by me. I didn't care if she thought that my leaving ended up being a good thing for us; I hurt her, and I'd never stop feeling bad about it. I was prepared to spend the rest of my life making it up to her.

"I love you," I whispered against her head before I let her go to open the door.

She looked at me before opening the door. She knew something was wrong. All of our guests were standing in the hall. Maggie and Billy were busy showering Aria with attention, but I saw a look pass between Libby and Lemon Drop. Something told me they knew this was more than just a friendly family dinner.

"Come in, come in." Logan looked like he was about to walk to plank. His jaw was clenched and his hand that wasn't holding Libby's was clenched in a fist. Normally, that is where my girl would turn on her hostess-with-the-mostest charm and offer everyone a drink, but she wasn't having any of it. She took the baby from a questioning Maggie. "If we had two babies, I'd hand you each one." She looked at both me and Logan. "Looks like you need her more than he does." She handed Logan his daughter and his entire demeanor changed instantly. God, my girl was good. Then she turned her attention back to me. "Now you sit down."

I put my hands up in surrender as I backed up toward the couch and sat. She immediately sat in my lap and placed my hands around her midsection before covering them with her own. I couldn't help but wonder if I was holding my baby, our baby, at that very moment too. I wasn't sure if it was conscious on Emily's part. It was possible but highly unlikely that she was already pregnant. I Googled it. A woman was only fertile for forty-eight hours a month, and I had no idea where she was in her cycle. It's not like I could just say, "Hey, baby, when is your Aunt Flow coming for a visit?" That's a good way to end up in the doghouse for sure. I figured it would happen when it happened.

Maggie and Billy seemed to understand that something was up. "Unless you want me to start calling you Dicklan again, you better start talking now." *Note to self: Emily and Libby together are a dangerous tag team.*

I decided to rip it off like a Band-Aid. "We have news about your father."

I couldn't see Emily's face, but I could see Libby's and she didn't seem surprised that something was going on with Grant. Logan seemed to pick-up on it as well.

So did Maggie because she was first to ask the question, "What's he done now?"

A knock at the door startled us all, but when nobody moved to answer it, Billy got up to take care of it. I already paid for our meal, but Billy gave the delivery guy a generous tip before moving to the kitchen with the bags.

"He's under criminal investigation with the IRS and his second wife filed for divorce." Emily snorted, yes snorted, before breaking into a fit of laughter, followed by both her sister and aunt. Did Logan and I miss the punch line? We both must have that look on our face. You know, the one that says, "What the fuck?"

"Lemon Drop, your dad is going to go to jail." Are we being Punked? We were prepared for tears, anger, devastation, but not uncontrollable fits of laughter. Emily had managed to squirm off my lap and was now practically rolling on the floor.

"This is crazy." I couldn't agree with my friend more. "Could one of you please explain this to me?" Logan tried since my statement only garnered more laughter from the three women who were now in tears from laughing so hard.

"Do you boys want to eat while it's hot?" Billy asked from the kitchen where he had arranged all the food and removed all the lids. *Eat? Is he crazy now too? This is fucking nuts.*

"I'm starved," Emily finally said when she came to her senses.

"Me too," Libby added before getting up and walking toward the kitchen.

"Freeze," Logan said firmly but not loudly since he was still holding Aria. "Declan and I have been freaking out since we got this news. You girls act like a bunch of loons and then just expect us to eat like nothing just happened. That's not going to work for me, Libby."

"You're right." Emily put her arm around me and gave me a squeeze but let her twin continue. "Grandma Rose always used to tell Daddy that without Mom he would end up in the clink."

Damn, Grandma Rose was one smart lady, and fuck if I wasn't tempted to get down on one knee and ask Emily to put her ring on right that very minute.

CHAPTER
twenty-one

"Are you sure you're all right?" I asked as I placed the last of my things in my bag. The night before, after everyone sat down at the table, we talked about the Grant situation. It was obvious that Libby and Emily loved their father but that the relationship had been strained since he left Cheryl. Their main worry was her and not the fact that he was more than likely facing jail time. Luckily nobody asked how we became aware of the current events. It was decided that Maggie would fly out to California that morning and break the news to her best friend in person. If everything went like we hoped, Maggie wouldn't be coming home alone.

"I think so." I knew she was sad, but at the same time, I think she saw it as a chance at a new beginning for her mother. Her family, our family was there in New York. That was where she needed to be. Despite being worried about her mom, I knew she was excited about going back to the Hamptons. I was even surprising her by inviting Willow and Fay to come along. I was sure Willow could use a break from being a single parent since her husband was deployed and with my Mam and Da also joining us, there would be no shortage of people who could give her the rest she needed. "I couldn't wait to see Hund." The friendly Bernese left a lasting impression on both of us. "And Alva and Theo, too, of course." I didn't think Emily had ever met a person who wasn't instantly a friend, well, except for Abigail Hayes, but if you were a person, you were human, and the more I thought about Abigail, the less likely I believed that to be true.

"About that." She looked beautiful in a dress that I wasn't so sure she should have been wearing. Not because she didn't look great—she did. Her wearing that dress while I was driving was a road hazard. It was short, and fuck, her legs looked gorgeous. She had these wedge sandals on that made them look even longer than normal. I swear, the only thing that would be better was if they were up on my shoulders with my face buried in her pussy. Believe me, I was tempted.

"About what?" She looked up from her packing. "Oh, my God, would you please stop looking at me like you haven't eaten in weeks, Declan Hayes?" She tossed a pair of panties at me.

"That's not helping," I told her as I held the scrap of lace up and tried to think of anything besides her and her sexy as hell knickers. *Taxes. Bad wine. American chocolate. Chips in a fry.*

Her giggle caused me to lose track of things I hated. It was a good thing we were interrupted by a knock at the door. "I'll get it." Although, I did have to adjust my shorts before I moved which just made Lemon Drop laugh again. "I'll get you for this." The threat was weak, but she could bet her sweet as that as soon as I had the opportunity, I'd have the panties she was currently wearing off and would be buried deep inside of her.

"Declan." Fay bowled into me as she entered the apartment, and I swear the blow almost brought me to the floor. I didn't know if my clackers would ever recover.

"My plums," I hissed out as I doubled over.

"Oh, my God, I'm so sorry," Willow offered as I tried to right myself.

"Plums? I love plums. Can I have one?" Fay asked innocently as she began to look around for the purple fruit. No doubt my angry balls might have been the right color.

"I bet Emily already ate them," Willow said with a smirk that she tried to cover with her hand. "Let's see if we can find you something else in the kitchen." With Fay's back to me, she turned and mouthed, "I'm sorry" again to me before noting from the freezer that we had bags of peas. Emily walked out of our room and I was reminded again how gorgeous she looked. *Fuck, the peas might not be a bad idea.*

"Surprise," Fay said as she rushed Emily with a banana in her hand. Willow saw me eye the fruit and gave me an exaggerated wink. *Oh, she's a gas.*

"What are you two doing here?" Emily asked as she caught the girl and brought her up to her hip.

Fay could hardly contain herself. "We're going with you."

Lemon Drop looked at me and I could tell that this surprise was a good one. I knew that she worried about Willow and Fay. I'm sure it wasn't easy having your husband and father so far away for so long. At this point, I can hardly imagine a day without Emily, let alone months at a time.

"Well, let's get on the road." Eric already texted me that the car was downstairs and my Mam and Da drove out to the house the night before. After reading all those letters, Da said he had to get her out of there. Emily said he was acting just like me, and for once in my life, I didn't mind the comparison. I liked the way he was trying to protect Brianna; it meant he still cared, and what kid didn't want to see his parents together? I hadn't been to this house in ages. Hanging out with my parents wasn't exactly on my list of things to do before. Now, I look forward to spending the long weekend with them.

I still hadn't told Emily where we were staying. "Where are we going?" she asked as we drove by the inn.

"We have a house out here."

"Of course you do," she said with a roll of her eyes before turning to look out the window.

I placed my hand on her knee and gave it a pat and she looked back at me. "We close it for the winter and Suzie and Eric invited us to the inn, to be with them for their special day." She smiled, and I knew I was forgiven.

"Are we there yet?" Fay asked again from the backseat. I'd just turned onto the street, so this time, I could happily say yes to the cutie whose patience had just about run out.

I slowed the car and Emily let out a gasp when the house finally came into view. It was hidden from the road by trees and because of the size of the lot. "Wow." Willow whistled as she leaned forward between the seats to see what Emily was staring at in awe of. "We're not in Kansas anymore," she added as I stopped the car and turned off the engine.

It'd been so long since I'd been there that I almost had to ask my father for the address. My parents came out the door like they had been waiting for our arrival. As soon as Fay was free from her booster seat, she was out the door running excitedly toward my father. I almost warned him to protect himself but figured he should hurt like I did. The look on his face was priceless as he too suffered her innocent yet painful attack.

"She should come with a warning sign," Willow said, embarrassed by her daughter's quest to ensure the Hayes family name stopped with me. She left the vehicle apologizing to my father, leaving me alone with Lemon Drop.

"I hope you're not too disappointed about the inn. I promise we'll still see Alva, Theo, and of course Hund. I'm sure Fay would love to meet him." Before I can finish apologizing for not telling her about the house, she had her arms around me with her face buried in my chest. I felt wetness on my shirt so I pulled her back so that I could see her face. Shit, if she was that upset, we'd stay at the inn. Before I could even ask her, she pressed her soft lips to mine and kissed me tenderly.

"You're a good man, Declan Hayes." She brushed the side of my face before leaning in to kiss me again.

"Are you going to get out of the car or are you going to kiss all day?" Fay asked from the front steps. It was a good thing she was so cute. Emily started to giggle which did nothing to help me or my plums at all.

"This place is amazing." The women all oohed and aahed while Da showed them around. Fay went crazy the second she saw the pool, but for Emily, it was the view of the water. She was drawn to it. I'd seen the way she looked at it from the windows in the apartment and while we were in California, she seemed mesmerized by the cool lake water. That was something I would definitely keep in mind while planning for our future.

"You and Emily take the master bedroom, son." I wasn't going to argue with the man over the sleeping arrangements. Honestly, I couldn't wait to get Lemon Drop in the giant tub with me.

We'd spent the day soaking up the sun and playing in the water. Fay wouldn't get out of the pool for anything; she even ate her ice cream on the steps. Emily had been distracted by worry for her mother, and although she hadn't said it, I knew she was also thinking of her father. My mother seemed to be struggling with something too. True, I hadn't known her very long, but at the same time, I felt like I'd known her my entire life. Maybe it was because she just seemed to fit so well. I couldn't explain it. It may sound cliché, but it seemed like all the pieces of the puzzle that were my life were finally starting to come together.

"What's troubling you, Mam?"

We were alone in the kitchen freshening the drinks. She crossed the room to the kitchen table that sat in a nook with floor to ceiling windows that overlooked the crystal-blue water. She was such a vibrant woman that it was obvious something was bothering her. Like my Emily, she too wore her heart on her sleeve. On the table lay a piece of driftwood. Not that the piece was out of place, but Abigail would have happily bragged about how much she paid for the piece of wood that someone once found washed up on the beach and then sold as a piece of custom art at one of the trendy boutiques in town. The center was somewhat hollowed out like a bowl. I didn't notice before, but a white envelope rest inside of it. Mam took it in her hand before continuing toward the windows.

"None of them were addressed." It took me a moment to realize she was talking about the envelopes that were left by Abigail. I couldn't for the life of me understand why she wrote them if she never meant to send them. I had no desire to know what the woman had to say, especially since they seemed to do nothing but hurt the woman who gave birth to me, the woman who thought she was doing right by me and my father when she gave me up. I knew without a doubt that she would have come to rescue us both if she had known we were so unhappy. I couldn't stand the distance between us, so I crossed the room and took my mother in my arms. She didn't hesitate to put her arms around me, and although I towered over her, I felt like a young boy being held in my mother's arms, and it was one of the best feelings I've ever had. I didn't know how much time passed before she took a deep breath and pulled away from me.

"Until this one. It's dated the day of the accident. I think you should read it." A tear rolled down her cheek as she handed me the envelope. I wasn't so sure I could take any more of Abigail's abuse. She was dead, and I was a grown ass man, but I knew her cruel words had the power to destroy me, even from the great beyond, but I also knew that my mother would not ask this of me unless it meant something to her. I couldn't deny her.

"OK." Funny how those two simple letters could hold so much. What, I didn't know. Hurt? Hope? Faith? It was hard to tell, but whatever it was, I knew it was important.

"Thank you, son. I'll give you some privacy." She hugged me once more before leaving me with Abigail's final words.

The walls of the massive house seemed to be closing in around me, so I took the envelope and headed outside. Beyond the deck and grass area steps led down to the private beach and dock. I walked the weathered wooden planks like a dead man. How was it possible that a dead woman could have this much power to hurt me?

I sat at the end of the dock with my feet hanging over the water watching boats adorned with red, white, and blue sail by. I was lost in thought when I was joined by Emily. She sat behind me with her legs on either side of me. She wrapped her arms around me, and I immediately felt the strength of her love. How did I even believe for one second that I had to do this by myself? Her soft words on the back of my neck confirmed what I already knew.

"I'm here for you, Declan." She kissed me and tightened her hold. "And I love you." Her simple words gave me exactly what I needed. Faith that anything was possible as long as we are together. Hope that even when things seemed like they were falling apart, they were actually falling into place, and that the biggest way she had shown me she loved me was by trusting me even though I had given her reason not to.

"I love you too, Lemon Drop." And with that, I opened the envelope, pulled out the familiar personalized stationary, and began to read out loud.

Dear Brianna -

Twenty-eight years ago, you gave me
something that most people rarely have,
a second chance. Unfortunately, I wasn't
able to see this gift for what it truly was.
Instead of rejoicing in being a mother, to a
beautiful, healthy child, I wallowed in
the loss of my son, Finnigan. I couldn't
blame Kian for ending up with you, you
were there for him in a time of need. You
shined a light on a very dark period of his
life. I couldn't forgive him for having even
a second of happiness, and every single time
he looked at Declan, I was jealous of the
love I knew he had for you and the child

you shared. He felt guilty, and I fed off
that guilt, so much so that he distanced
himself from his own flesh and blood.
I know now that I should not have
delighted in it, but I did. I could never be
happy; knowing that someone else was able
to give him what I couldn't and every time
I saw you in Declan's eyes I was reminded
of that fact. I should have let him go, but
I couldn't. He was the only part of Finn
that I still had. I hope that you can
understand. I know that you didn't lose a
child, you gave him and the man that you
loved up because you believed you were doing
the right thing. Now that I think about it,
I probably fed off of your guilt too. You're
probably wondering why I'm telling you all
this now. Well, I'll tell you. Recently

Declan met a woman. I've seen something new in his eyes since the first time I saw them together, and I know what it is because I recognize it as something that has shined in his father's eyes. It's love, and Declan feels it possibly the first time ever in his life. Kian used to look at me that way, he looked at Finnigan that way, and at you. He would have looked at Declan like that too had it not been for me. He doesn't know that I know this, but he has held a picture of you on the day you had Declan in his breast pocket since that day. I'm not sure if he even realizes it, but every time your son does something that makes him proud he puts his hand over his heart, where the picture and his love for you and his son lives. So again, why am I telling you this now? I don't know, maybe seeing

Declan so alive, so in love, has finally made me feel guilty for not giving him what he always should have had. Love. Declan looks at this girl, Emily, like she is his everything, and she loves him fiercely. This she proved beyond a doubt when she not only stood up to me but then welcomed me into her home because I am the mother of the man she loves. Only, I'm not. Declan deserves a mother like you, a woman that loves him so much that she would give up everything just to make him happy. Kian deserves that too. I hope that it's not too late for either of them. Forgive me. I'm counting on you to love them the way I couldn't.

Sincerely,
Abigail Hayes

Holy shit. The paper was stained with tears. I wasn't sure if they were mine, my mother's, or Abigail's. It was then that I noticed the back of my shirt was wet too. The words "I love you" repeated between kisses over and over again as Emily continued to hold me from behind.

"Do you think?" I never really asked any questions about the accident. I never even really knew what happened, or why Abigail was driving. I was so hurt by the lies they kept from me my entire life that I never bothered to ask.

"I don't know," Emily whispered before placing another kiss on the back of my neck.

I was so angry and hurt when I left the hospital that I never knew the circumstances behind the accident. Was this my fault? Had I set this in motion the minute I called her about the fundraiser? Did she? Was it possible that the woman who as far as I was concerned only cared about herself, had done this for me? I couldn't think. I turned when I heard the sound of my mother crying. She was in my father's arms. Where she always should have been. It was too much. I handed Emily the letter before pushing myself off the end of the dock. I don't why but when you're under water, everything seems to go in slow motion. I thought back to my phone call. I was so cold to her.

"I need you to plan a fundraiser. Yes. As soon as possible. For The Bowery, I'll send you the contact information."

That was all I said before I hung up on her. I then told Emily that she was good at two things, "Spending my father's money and getting her so-called friends into spending money on her latest cause." That afternoon, Gabe delivered a plant to my office from my lovely Lemon Drop. The quote she had referenced was perfect. No, deep roots are not reached by the frost, and although Abigail Hayes was the ice queen, I wouldn't let her get to me anymore. I finally had something I wanted all my life in the form of a smart, sexy, and giving baker—love. After e-mailing Abigail The Bowery details, I did something that I knew would prevent her from backing out of the fundraiser. I told my personal assistant, Monica Bristol, about it. I knew when I told her that it wouldn't take long for her mother-in-law, Belinda Bristol to know all about it, and if Belinda knew about it, that meant everyone in the who's who of New York City would soon know too.

Her arms came around me, and I opened my eyes. She was a vision of beauty in the water in her white sundress. She looked like an angel. She placed her lips to mine before kicking us to the surface.

"Oh, thank God," my mother cried as we made our way back to the dock. My eyes stung, and I'm not sure if was from the salt water or the tears that threatened my eyes. For someone who once felt like he had no one who cared about him, it was more than a little overwhelming sometimes to feel so surrounded by so much love. My father helped Emily out of the water first and then he pulled me out. He put his arms around me, not seeming to care one bit that he was drenched too.

"Don't be a plonker, son. Let's get changed so that we can chat."

I was grateful that Fay and Willow had gone to town for ice cream. My little dip in the ocean had scared my parents and my girl. Honestly, that hadn't been my intention. I just couldn't help it.

Mam threw her arms around both of us, squeezing us tightly. When she finally released us she said I was lucky I was so much bigger than her, because she had a mind to put me over her knee and spank me. Yeah, that wasn't going to happen, but the thought of having a mother that cared enough about me to want to do it warmed me right up. Emily, on the other hand, looked like her bits were about to freeze off, so I put my arm around her and told my parents we needed an hour to shower and change.

As tempting as the bath looked, I knew I needed to get my girl stripped and in the hot water quick, so I turned on the water in the shower before I started shucking off her soaking-wet clothes. She stood with her arms wrapped around her now beautifully bare body but made no move toward the hot shower, so I lifted her and placed her in the soothing water before stripping off my clothes and joining her.

"You frightened me," she said once I pulled her tight against my body. I kissed the top of her head.

"I'm sorry, mo eala." She smiled against my skin before pressing her lips against my chest. I knew she liked it when I called her my swan, but to me, she would also always be my Lemon Drop.

"Just because you didn't leave the country, this time, it doesn't mean that it did feel like you left me again when you shut down on me like that. As much as said that I think your leaving was what we both needed before, I don't think I would survive it again." I understood what she was saying because a life without her wouldn't be a life worth living to me. It was never my intention to make her feel that way.

"I wasn't trying to shut you out," I said as I tipped her head up so that she would have to look me in the eyes. "I just ..."

It was overwhelming. I tried to look away from her now, but she clutched my chin. "This wasn't your fault." How did she always seem to know what I was thinking? I was so lucky to have her. I was once again filled with a desire to show her just how much I needed her. To show her that shutting her out was the last thing on my mind.

"I need you, Lemon Drop." It was a plea.

"You have me, Declan." She wrapped her legs around me as I lifted her against the shower wall. I slipped inside of her and couldn't help the moan that escaped my lips. Every single time that we were together, it was better than the last, and this was no exception. Water rained down from above us as I thrust deeply inside of her. She pulled at my hair as I sucked at the base of her neck. She wasn't wearing my ring yet, but I could still mark her as mine. I bit down when the walls of her pussy clamped down on me, and the screaming of my name as she came pushed me over the edge of sheer bliss. Maybe, just maybe, I marked her in more ways than one with our lovemaking. Her legs were still trembling when she lowered them to the ground, so I held her firmly between the wall and my body until she was once again steady. We took turns washing each other. It's an intimacy I'd happily never shared with anyone else.

"I love you, Emily, go deo na ndeor." We had been in there so long the water was starting to go cold. She shivered, and I knew it was time to get her dry and dressed so that we could talk to my parents.

After turning off the water, I wrapped her up in the oversized bath towel before placing one around my waist. I placed another towel over her head and began to dry her off. I loved taking care of her—she always did so much for everyone else, especially me. She smiled brightly after I wrapped the towel around her head like a genie.

"What does that mean?"

"Forever," I simply said before I began to dry myself.

"Forever," she agreed before turning toward the mirror and realizing in horror that she now had one hell of a love bite on her neck.

"I'm so mad at you," Lemon Drop said as I pulled her away from the vanity mirror she sat at trying to cover the mark I left on her neck with what little make-up she had. My girl didn't need crap on her face; she was beautiful without it. "They are going to know we were in here having crazy monkey against the wall shower sex." I couldn't help but laugh. Is that what we had had? I guess I was a bit of a wild animal. On second thought, maybe she was the monkey and I was the tree she climbed. My thoughts had me doubled over laughing. "It's not funny, Declan, they are your parents. And what will Fay and Willow think?"

"I could care less." I knew instantly that was the wrong thing to say. It's a good thing I'm pretty fast on my feet, because I quickly changed tactics. "Would you like to bite me?" I offered while pulling down the collar of my fresh t-shirt.

"You would let me?" she asked hopefully, and I was starting to think I didn't know this woman as well as I thought.

"Of course," I lied as I moved closer toward her. The last thing I wanted was a hickey on my neck, but if it made her happy, I would certainly let her do it.

"You should see your face right now." She laughed, and I pulled her into my arms. I placed a soft kiss upon her mark.

"I truly am sorry; you make me go a little crazy."

"A little?" she teased as we began to walk out of our room ahead of me. She stopped abruptly, causing me to run right into her. "Shhh," she chastised before I could ask her what the hell was going on. With the finger that she had placed over her lips, she pointed to whatever had caused her to stop so abruptly. I followed her digit and was shocked by what I saw. Jungle fever was definitely in the air because Emily and I weren't the only wild animals in the house. My mother and father were afflicted by it too. *Holy shit!*

Quickly, I pulled Emily back into our room.

"I knew it," Emily boasted as soon as we were safely behind closed doors.

"Knew what?" I asked like an eejit.

She looked at me like she couldn't believe I had missed it. "That they were into each other." Her "duh" at the end of her sentence was implied.

"Are you OK, Declan?" she asked seriously as I thought about it. My thoughts from earlier resurfaced. I really needed to talk to my father.

"I think so, but it's past time Da and I had that chat. What do we do?" I motioned toward the door where my parents were snogging on the other side. At least they were both still fully dressed.

She giggled at my clear discomfort—maybe they wouldn't even notice we were missing.

"Nope," Emily said as she once again read my thoughts. "You said it yourself, it's time." She opened the door and began yelling, "I can't believe you, Declan." She waited several minutes, gave me a wink, and then proceeded toward the living room. Both of them were flushed when we entered the room, but my mother was no longer in my father's lap. I almost died when he pulled one of the decorative pillows into his lap. The poor Hayes plums were not having a good day. It took everything in me not to laugh as my mother tried to smooth down her out-of-place hair.

Emily flopped down on the sofa near my mother and feigned anger. After looking over Emily, my mother covered her mouth with an, "Oh, my." I found myself examining her neck, maybe biting was a symptom of the fever we were all suffering from. My mother was fine, but when I looked at my father I couldn't help but notice the small purple bruise that was forming behind his ear. I nearly lost my shite. I quickly turned to pour us all drinks. As tempting as the aged Tullamore Dew was, I didn't want Emily drinking it if she was with child, so instead, I poured us each a tall glass of cold water with a twist of lime and handed them out before taking my seat next to Emily.

I asked the first of many questions I had. "Where was the letter?"

"On her desk. If only I had looked through her things." I could see the guilt eating at my father. He couldn't have known. Abigail had hidden all of my mother's correspondence over the years. He had no reason to think that Abigail would be the key to finding Mam.

She must have sensed that it was killing him because she moved to his side and took his hand in hers. "Kian, you can't blame yourself for this."

"She's right," I added, and he nodded. I was quickly learning that guilt is like a cancer that will kill you if you let it. It had already killed Abigail. It was time to cut it out of our lives. For good.

"What happened the night of the fundraiser?" Abigail knew that I wanted the event done before the end of the year. The Bowery needed the money. Dragging it out wouldn't make it any more successful and most of her "friends" were looking for year-end tax deductions anyway. That left very little time, but like I said, once Belinda Bristol

241

was aware of the event, everyone else was too, and nobody ever missed an Abigail Hayes party.

That being said, Emily and I were unable to attend the event that was held at one of the few spaces that were available that were also acceptable to Abigail, because of the rehearsal dinner for Nat and Gabe. We were devastated. *Not.* Actually, the one bad thing about us not attending was that Joe and the board of directors of The Bowery decided to create a new award. It would be given annually to a volunteer that would be selected by the people who actually used the services of the facility. Emily was honored that not only had she been selected by a landslide but that the name of the award was in her honor too.

My father finished his water and put down the glass. "The night was going exceptionally well. Abigail was completely in her element; she raised a hell of a lot of money." I couldn't disagree with that. I knew the funds raised would be substantial. His eyes went to Emily. Somehow, I knew what he was going to say next had something to do with her, so I pulled her close and put my arm around her. Even in death, Abigail had the power to hurt us. "The damn golden muffin award video really set her off." The video was something that Matty and I had put together. It was a combination of still photos that I had taken and clips that he recorded of people at The Bowery conveying stories of Emily's generosity. I still had yet to see the completed montage. We were going to watch it at a lunch that was going to be given in her honor at The Bowery after the first of the year. That meant more to her than getting it in front of a bunch of fake people she didn't know.

"I'm sorry I missed it," I said before kissing her temple. Guilt wouldn't bring back the months we lost. Besides, she thought it made us stronger.

"I know," she said with a squeeze of my hand.

"We were supposed to stay at the hotel, but for some reason, she decided she just had to get back to the apartment."

"The letter?" Emily asked.

"I guess we will never know." My father shrugged before continuing. "I had spent my night at the bar. I was in no condition to drive." He shook his head. "I don't think she meant to get herself killed if that's what you're thinking." That was exactly what I was thinking. A tear rolled down my mother's face. I didn't think it was for Abigail. I think it was for my father. It was clear it wasn't easy for him to talk about the events of that evening. "I shouldn't have let her drive, she hadn't in years. The roads were icy." I couldn't remember a time in my life that I had ever seen Abigail drive. I didn't even know she knew how. "She only ever allowed herself two cocktails at events." This everyone knew about the woman who raised me—she always said that good manners and alcohol didn't mix.

"But she asked for forgiveness in her letter," Emily pointed out.

"She did. Obviously, she was planning on mailing the letter. She booked a single one-way ticket to Prague too. She was leaving on the first. If only she had worn her damn seat belt." I never knew that. Apparently, she was just planning on leaving. Is it possible what she wrote in her letter was the truth, she just wanted us to be happy and the icy roads, a lack of driving experience, and poor decision making had led to her death?

CHAPTER
twenty-two

The morning was my favorite time of day. The only thing that would have made it better was if Lemon Drop were awake, but she needed her rest. The previous night, she held me in her arms as I came to terms with the letter that Abigail left behind and then she made love to me. It was sweet, tender, and beautiful. Before her, I never felt loved or cherished. Now I felt that way all the time, and although her love meant the most to me, I knew that I was loved by many, and maybe, just maybe, Abigail loved me the only way she could. It was ironic that Emily was the one that finally made her see the error of her ways. Emily seemed to bring out the best in everyone. Even the woman I used to believe was my mother.

The cool morning weather reminded me of Ireland. I couldn't wait to show my country to Lemon Drop; I knew she would love it.

I'd been waiting for this day, but now that it was finally here, I didn't think I could go through with my original plan. Her chestnut hair was fanned out behind her and her left hand was on my pillow. Her mood ring was dark blue, almost indigo which told me she was deeply relaxed and happy. I couldn't believe we were both still wearing the cheap novelty rings, but I knew I would only ever replace mine with one other ring. I hoped she felt the same. It was amazing how often they were the same color, but right then, mine was green because I was the most nervous I had ever been in my life. Maybe it was because I'd changed my mind.

After leaving our room, I moved the bistro table to the end of the dock before heading to the kitchen.

"I'm hungry," Fay said as she stretched with both hands behind her head. We were the first ones up for the day. I hid my amused laugh with my coffee cup as I looked at her outfit. Sparkly purple cowboy boots were on her feet, correct that, cow*girl* boots. Her shorts were black and covered with bright geometric patterns, and her patriotic shirt was one or two sizes too small. This little firecracker was ready to start her day. I had to take a picture of her before her mother helped her change; luckily, my camera was never far out of reach.

"Aoibh gháire," I said as I held up my Canon. The irritated look she gave me instead of the smile I had asked for made it even more perfect. Then the little cailín actually stomped her booted foot at me.

"What does that mean?" she asked when I peered over the top of my camera.

"Smile." And so she did. After showing her the pictures, I poured her a cup of juice from the refrigerator.

"What were you doing?" I scratched my head because I wasn't exactly sure. I had no idea when Emily was going to wake up and I had left her instructions.

"I was going to make Lemon Drop some breakfast, but she's still sleeping, and I don't want it to get cold." If my Da was awake, I might have asked him to whip up some of her muffins.

"I know what we can make," she said happily as her tummy growled loudly. Fay and I alone in the kitchen probably wasn't a great idea. Part of me wished Willow or Mam would appear, but then I knew they both needed the rest. The last few days had been an emotional roller coaster for my parents, and Emily mentioned Willow was expecting a late night video conference with her husband. The wink she gave me told me everything else I needed to know about what Dillon and Willow would be chatting about. I couldn't even imagine how difficult it would be to be so far away from your wife and child. I could barely make it an hour without touching Lemon Drop—they go months on end. Yes, technology is great, but nothing compares to skin to skin.

"Maybe we should wait for your mommy," I tried to convince her, and once again I got the impatient boot tap. It was cute the first time, not so much the second.

"I make breakfast all the time by myself at home." The look on my face must have said that I wasn't sure. "Cross my heart. I'm just not allowed to use things with plugs," she said as she did just that and then took charge. "Do we have bread?" she asked as she slid a chair up to the counter. I nodded and she grinned. "What about peanut butter?" I opened the large fully-stocked pantry as she reached for the fruit bowl and took a banana. As I pulled the jar off the shelf, I noticed something—my ring was the same indigo as Emily's. Spending time with Fay made me happy.

I placed the jar next to her and tugged lightly at her messy hair which was still in a braid from the day before. She giggled at the action before asking for her next ingredient. "Raisins." She said it much in the way a doctor says "scalpel" to a nurse on television or the movies. I returned to the pantry and began my search. I was beginning to worry what would happen if I returned empty handed when I finally found a box of the petrified fruit.

Fay had spread peanut butter carefully on three pieces of bread and without assistance cut slices of banana. I guess she *had* done it before. Luckily, she had used a butter knife to cut the fruit while I was inside the bottomless pantry. A single slice of banana was carefully placed in the center of each piece of bread before she then placed another piece on the upper right side of each piece followed by the upper left. I opened the box of raisins and poured some into my hand.

She put one raisin on the slice in the center before putting two more just above said slice.

"Beary cute," I beamed as she finished the other two bear creations. She giggled at my joke. Her stomach rumbled again, and without hesitation, she began to eat one of her masterpieces. I couldn't even think about eating, but while I was inside the pantry, I saw something that would go perfectly with Fay's creation. She was tickled pink when I showed her.

Fay "helped" me carry things out to the table, and as luck would have it, Willow was up and in the kitchen when we returned. As tired as she looked, I couldn't help but notice the look on her face when she caught a glimpse of her daughter's outfit.

"I made a special breakfast for Miss Emily," she announced a little louder than she should have since we still had yet to see my parents or Lemon Drop. Willow scolded her to be quiet, but honestly, I was ready for M to wake up, so that I could get it over with.

With Fay back in her mother's charge, I excused myself to go wait on the dock where the note and pale-blue satin robe I left on our bed instructed Emily to meet me. I decided not to give her the matching nightgown yet because I thought what she slipped into before we fell asleep last night was perfect for the occasion.

I don't know how long I waited. It felt like hours, but it was probably only minutes.

Not for the first time, she took my breath away when I saw her. The robe was tied loosely with the sash, but underneath was the same outfit she was wearing the first time I ever laid eyes on her. Her fun bags looked fantastic. Huge, in fact. Had they looked that way when she was singing out of tune and dancing around my parents' kitchen? She smiled and swung her hips a little more than usual when she saw me standing open mouthed while she made her way toward me. My girl was workin' it.

"You'll catch more flies with honey," she teased, and I closed my mouth and smiled. She may have wobbled a little bit.

"I hope I'll catch something other than flies." I winked as she came closer. It took everything in me not to move toward her. I pulled her seat out for her and motioned for her to sit.

"Good morning, beautiful," I said after kissing the top of her head and stepping away. I was tempted to smell her hair; it always smelled like grapefruit, vanilla, and maybe gardenia. Like everything about her, it was intoxicating.

"Are you OK?" I'd negotiated deals worth millions without ever breaking a sweat and right then I felt the need to wipe my brow. *Maybe I should jump off the dock again. She rescued me yesterday.* Hell, she rescued me the day we met. The thought dropped me to my knees, or should I say knee. The polished silver domes covering the toast that looked like bear faces remained untouched as I took her hand in mine.

"I'm more than OK; I'm perfect because I'm with you." She raised the hand that I wasn't holding to the side of my face and I closed my eyes and pressed my head firmly into her palm before turning and pressing my lips to her wrist. I wanted to remember the moment forever. It was more than I could have ever imagined. She was perfect.

"Mo chroí." She moved her free hand to cover my rapidly beating heart. "My heart is in your hands." She knew that. "Is breá liom tú, Emily Grace Barnes." It was so easy to say I love you to her then. Why did I ever struggle with those words? I didn't know if I should say the next part in English or Gaelic, but ultimately, I decided it didn't matter what language I used because she would know what I was asking without any words at all. That morning I had put her ring back around my neck since I didn't have any pockets. "An bpósfaidh tú mé?" I pulled the chain out from underneath my shirt. Her tears flowed freely, and she gasped when I held up her grandmother's ring. I knew she would recognize it instantly; it was one of a kind. Grandpa Henry had good taste in both women and in jewelry.

"Oh, my God."

"You're killing me, Lemon Drop. Is that a yes?" It was a good thing the ring was still on a chain around my neck because she launched herself at me. If it had been loose it might be at the bottom of the Atlantic. She knocked me right on my ass. It was fitting since that was what she did to me that very first day in the kitchen.

"OK," was all I heard as she peppered me with kisses all over my face. I reluctantly pulled her away.

"OK?" I knew it would be, but I still wanted to hear a different word.

"Tá. Sí. Aye. Oui. Hai. In a hundred different languages, my answer will always me the same." She kissed me firmly on the lips. "Yes, I will marry you, Declan Kieran Hayes." She began to giggle in my lap, and as usual, I got hard. Thank God we had a private entry to our room off the back of the house because as tempted as I was to make love to my fiancé right then, I didn't for two reasons. One, splinters, and two, windows. Fay, Willow, and my parents didn't need to see us consummate our engagement. Although, I did want to tell the world this beautiful swan was mine. Forever.

While our lovemaking had filled one hunger, it hadn't satisfied another and now my stomach rumbled as loudly as Fay's had earlier.

"Happy Fourth of July." After playing with the chain that still hung around my neck, she traced a familiar infinity symbol over my heart.

"Happy Fourth of July, my fiancée." I didn't plan on her being that for very long.

"Let's go eat. I'm starving." I was too, but we still had some business to attend to. I sprang from the bed, nearly shifting my bride-to-be to the floor. Her laughter would not deter me this time. I settled her back into the middle of the mattress.

From my knees, beside her, I playfully scolded, "This is serious, Lemon Drop." I took the chain from around my neck and kissed the ring before undoing the clasp and placing the heirloom diamond on her delicate finger. It was a perfect fit. Just like her.

"Very serious," she said as she held her hand up to the light and smiled happily.

"I don't want to wait."

She responded with my favorite two-letter word, "OK".

We showered and got dressed quickly. She started to pull her hair up into a ponytail but decided otherwise when she noticed the purple mark at the base of her next that I left the day before. I wrapped my arms around her from behind and kissed the spot.

"I really am sorry. You're gorgeous, and have I ever told you how grateful I am that you don't take hours to get ready?" Her dress was white eyelet and she added a thin red leather belt and blue canvas shoes. She was a true American beauty.

She blushed at the compliment and openly checked me out. I was wearing a pair of navy shorts and a plain white tee, but she seemed pleased, and if it weren't for needing to eat, I would have taken her back to bed. If only eating her could sustain me.

I took her by the hand and led her out of our room. The large open room roared to life when we entered. Balloons and a banner that read "congratulations" had been hastily hung and corks were heard popping. I invited just about everyone we knew to join us today. It was nice to see so many familiar faces. It looked like almost everyone was already there. Both sides of Gabe and Nat's families and the entire Medina family, including Matty and Hope, had arrived. I mean Kenzie. I didn't know if I'd ever think of her as anything other than Hope.

I always knew that girl was hiding something. Eric knew it still pissed me off that he hadn't told me the truth about her true identity as soon as he learned it. Luckily for him, everything seemed to work out for the best. Eric lifted up his glass to me before going back to his conversation with his wife, Suzie and our friends Alva and Theo.

"Irish Car Bomb!" Matty greeted me with a firm slap to the back. Fortunately, it seemed that I wasn't going to have to endure the same speech about hurting Emily again. He seemed genuinely happy for us. I'd missed Matt. I really need to catch up on what had been going on with him. I'd been so wrapped up in getting my Lemon Drop back that I really hadn't been focusing on anything else.

The front door burst open, and Cheryl, Maggie, Billy, Libby, and Logan, who carried a sleeping Aria in her car seat, entered the room, followed by a reluctant Tank. *Who the hell invited him?* I guess it doesn't really matter. Emily cared for the guy, so I'd be cool, but he needed to get over it. *She's mine.*

All the women surrounded Emily. They all went bananas over her ring as my father and mother passed out champagne glasses for a toast. Cheryl gave me a warm hug and told me how happy Grandma Rose would be.

"They almost missed the champagne," Nat scolded me as she handed glasses to the late arrivals. "Thank God you guys are like rabbits." Lemon Drop turned beet red and buried her face in my chest as I wrapped a protective arm around her. *Don't worry, baby, I'll protect you from your loud-mouth friend.*

The room erupted in laughter when Fay asked Willow loudly, "How are they like rabbits, Mommy?" Gone were her colorful shorts and the too tight t-shirt. They had been replaced by a very patriotic summer dress that fit her perfectly. Her mother must have lost the battle on the boots because she was still wearing them.

The room went silent in anticipation of Willow's answer. "They talk a lot, baby girl." We collectively held our breath to see if that answer would satisfy the curious young girl.

Now it was Fay's turn to laugh. "Rabbits don't talk, Mommy." But before she could ask any more questions, Hund, Theo, and Alva's friendly Bernese came up and licked her squarely on the face, and with that, the girl and her new best friend were off to see what kind of trouble they could find elsewhere.

After we all stopped laughing, several toasts were made. We were surrounded by all the people we cared about. Tank chatted with my parents and Logan, but whenever he could, he gave me that "don't fuck this up or she's mine" look he had perfected. I held her a little tighter every time that he did. I was pretty sure Emily was on to me, but she never complained or said anything.

"When are you getting married?" Natalie asked innocently.

"How long does it take to get a marriage license?" That was the only thing I needed to know.

CHAPTER
twenty-three

"Twenty-four hours and thirty-five bucks. You'll both need to go and take your passport and birth certificate." That was the kind of helpful information I paid Eric for.

"How do you know all that?" Tank asked, surprised by his wealth of knowledge when it came to getting married. Eric simply lifted his hand and showed his ring in reply. Although Suzie and Eric had been the topic of a lot of tabloid speculation when news first hit of them getting married so abruptly, it quickly became old news. That's not to say "Suzic" rumors didn't circulate, because they did. Suzie and Eric just chose to ignore them. They had enough drama without the addition of the tabloids. The network wanted more from them. Eric wasn't about to let them exploit him or his wife.

"I brought you your birth certificate, sweetie," Cheryl told her daughter. Cheryl winked at me after admiring her mother's ring on her daughter's finger. "Yours too, Libby." The party had moved outside to the pool and deck. Libby blushed a color I had seen many times on her twin sister. Libby liked to act like a badass, but really she was just as sweet as her sister beneath the thick make-up, dark clothes, and tattoos. Looking at her, I couldn't believe for a few minutes the first time I ever saw her I thought she was my Lemon Drop. To my defense, she was in a hospital bed having a baby.

"The city clerk's office is open tomorrow," Eric confirmed before putting his phone back in his pocket.

"Great, we can get married on Wednesday and spend your birthday in Dublin." Emily spat out the iced tea that was in her mouth and began to cough. All eyes were on us as I patted her back.

"It's Monday, Declan," she said to me as if I didn't know what day it was.

"And?" I asked as she looked at me like I was growing a second head.

"We can't plan a wedding by Wednesday." It was my turn to look at her like she had lost her mind.

"You said you wanted to get married as soon as possible." She nodded her head in agreement that she had said that. "Wednesday is the soonest we can do that."

Suzie must have felt the need to come to her rescue. "It takes longer than that to plan a proper wedding, Declan."

"It took Nat a year and a half. I nearly killed her at least twice, and she threatened to kill me at least once a month." Natalie gave him a seething look. "But for the record, it was the greatest wedding ever. I had the most beautiful bride in the world." Gabe blew a kiss to his wife before adding, "Worth every minute of hell those eighteen months cost me."

"Easy for you to say, I'm still paying for it," Seth Chapman added before getting an elbow to the gut from Nat's mother, Marion.

It was past time to squash the conversation. I wasn't waiting to marry Emily. Hell, if it was legal, I would have asked Theo and Alva to marry us right then. "Suzie, would you change one thing about your wedding day?"

"Not a thing," she answered without hesitation. If Suzie and Eric could put together their wedding so quickly, we could too. It would be everything my Lemon Drop ever dreamed of.

"Are you all right with Theo and Alva performing the ceremony?" I knew she would be, but we never talked about weddings. Maybe my girl was one of those women who had her entire wedding already planned. I said a silent prayer that she didn't have one of those dream board things made up.

"I'd love that." I could tell by her smile that she meant it.

"Logan, can you put together a meal to remember for—" I took a moment to count everyone that surrounded us now and did some mental math "—seventy-five on Wednesday?" I knew he could, easily.

"They'll be talking about it for years." Yeah, my buddy had Michelin stars and a kick ass staff at his disposal.

"But …"

"I've got a great flower lady," I added before she could come up with another excuse. "And, Nat, didn't you say that those crazy women at the place you got your dress already have a dress picked out for Emily?" I knew they did; she mentioned it after her last fitting for Nat and Gabe's wedding. I'd thought of her in a beautiful white dress walking toward me more times than I should probably admit. I'd probably risk losing my man card if the guys ever knew how many times I'd imagined marrying Emily. They would probably accuse me of having a uterus.

"It's not that simple, Declan," she said with a sad look on her face but I could tell she was struggling to see my way of thinking.

"Why can't it be? I love you. You love me. Just because we do it quickly doesn't mean it can't be everything you have ever dreamed of." Like she had done to me earlier, I put my hand on her cheek. She closed her eyes and placed a kiss on my wrist. "Tell me your wedding dreams, mo eala, and I'll make every single one of them come true." I kneeled before her and placed my other hand on her other cheek. She opened her beautiful brown eyes before she answered me.

"You are everything I ever dreamed of. You are everything I never knew I wanted and so much more." She leaned forward and placed her lips on mine. "You are my yesterday." *Kiss.* "You are my today." *Kiss.* "You are my tomorrow, and I'm going to be your wife but we need a prenup and we can't get one that fast." I should have anticipated this. Lemon Drop was a sharp businesswoman.

"We don't need one."

"Declan." She was cute when she was mad. Her hands were on her hips, and I swear she stomped her foot at me like Fay did. Maybe if I got her some cowgirl boots like Fay's she'd do it again with nothing more on than said boots. "Hello?" She snapped her finger at me with a knowing look on her face

"It's all in a trust, Lemon Drop." I'm not saying I don't have any cash in the bank, but the majority of it was held in our family trust. It was protected. Not that it mattered, because without her it would all be pointless. It wasn't my first rodeo. *And I'm back to thinking about the damn boots again. Fuck.*

Emily paced back and forth several times in front of me. She was thinking. Thinking was good. Finally, she stopped and looked at my father. He gave her a nod, his confirmation that what I told her was accurate. I knew she believed me, but she wanted his blessing. She had it.

"OK." She beamed at me. It was more than OK; it was perfect.

"We're getting married on Wednesday!" I shouted. It was ridiculous because everyone's attention was already centered squarely on us. "You're all invited." I kissed her this time. "You just need to show up in a white dress. I'll do everything else. You won't regret this, Lemon Drop. I promise."

Famous last words. Maybe they'll put them on my headstone.

"Are you all right?" We had retreated to our room to change into our swimsuits. It was funny how different this Fourth of July was from the others this house has hosted. Even with our door closed, I could hear our friends and family, laughing and having a good time. Abigail would have had the day catered and all her "friends" would have been dressed to impress, sitting inside in the air conditioning, perfectly poised on the overpriced sofas, while the men drank my father's best scotch in the wood-paneled den overlooking the pool. Not that I would have come. I probably would have been in my office relishing in being able to get so much done because of the lack of interruptions. I might have watched the fireworks from my window.

It feels like my first family holiday. True, I got a glimpse of it at Christmas when we spent time with the Medina,

Sutherland, and Chapman clans, but today my family is here as well. *My family*. You would think I would have felt overwhelmed, but I didn't. Hell, I didn't even really mind Tank being there. After all, she was marrying me. I didn't know his story yet, but I did know that everyone deserved to feel like they belonged.

Logan needed it too. I never really knew what I was missing, but he did, and I was glad he had it back with Libby, Aria, and the rest of this group. Brit and Sadie were the only two we were missing. I swear when Emily sent a text with her holding up her ring finger surrounded by my arms we heard the screams from Ashbury. Brit had promised to be home first thing in the morning so that she could help me plan my wedding. I reminded her that I had Suzie, the number one wedding planner in the city, at my disposal, but that did not deter her. This was Brit we were talking about. I was so lost in thought I didn't even realize Emily was back.

"You look so happy." *Jesus H. Christ.*

Emily slipped into the bathroom to change while I was still daydreaming about our happy family. Now she was leaning against the wall with one knee bent back against it wearing an all-black bikini.

"Fuck, Lemon Drop, are you trying to kill me before we're even married?" Of course, my trunks were tight now. They were fine when I put them on.

Before she could even reply, Tyler, Gabe's four-year-old nephew, was at our glass sliding door yelling loudly, "Hurry up, Auntie M." I turned to the impatient child who miraculously scaled the private staircase to our room unattended without thinking and the next thing we heard was, "Declan has a giant peanut, Mommy."

"Oh, my God." Emily lifted her hand to her mouth in an attempt to hide her laughter.

"Shit, we're never going to hear the end of this." Usually, the sound of her giggles would just get me harder, but somehow, the idea of all of our friends and family blatantly aware of the current state of my cock had tamed him.

"I seriously doubt it, but we better get down there before they all assume we are up here, you know …" I was so tempted to tease her because of the pink blush in her cheeks, but that would most have certainly led to more "you know".

"Let's go." I grabbed her hand and led her out of our room to go face to music.

"Well, if it isn't the happy couple." Gabe began clapping as we descended the stairs to the pool.

"Where's wee wonder willy?" Nat asked with a wink. *Wee? Nothing about my willy is wee. Even Tyler said it was "giant".*

"Did you holster your nut pistol?" Matt asked as he slapped me on the back and handed me a beer before yelling, "Torpedoes under" and diving in the pool.

"Dear, is that a woodpecker?" Gwen asked her husband who was standing at the massive grill with my father. Great, even the parents were going to join in the festivities.

"Babe, maybe you could have some kind of meat sick or a wiener on the menu Wednesday for the reception. Emily loves eating meat." Libby beamed before returning her attention to her daughter.

"Careful, Libby, you made your mom choke on her *cock*tail." *Good lord, Maggie too.*

"Let's talk about something else." Emily directed the group as I tightened my grip on her hand.

"How about fireworks?" my mother asked. "I love morning glory." *Fuck my life. That was one image I wanted to be burned from my head.*

"I've always been a huge fan of tall Tommy," Marion added while fanning herself.

"Maybe the big George for the finale." *For the love of God, Cheryl.*

"I wonder if Declan is going to have a problem launching his rocket?" Innocent Hope asked. Matt was rubbing off on her, all their time together changed her. She wasn't sweet little Hope anymore, now she was Kenzie. I invited Hope. Failure to launch certainly wasn't a problem.

"Look! You've all had your fun but that's enough," Emily scolded them all. "Besides, the cobra is in its cage." The next thing I knew, I was covered in water that was a result of her perfect cannonball into the pool.

"You have a snake?" a jubilant Tyler asked before I followed her into the water. *Damn right I do, but it's not a cobra, it's a python.*

The rest of the day was a blur. We ate burgers, corn on the cob, and watermelon. Emily and I played in the pool with Fay and Tyler. She even brought eight-month-old Reese in—she looked like she was made to hold a baby. We were joined in the pool with the "big kids" when the munchkins were taken inside for some much-needed naps when I heard two words that put me instantly on edge: "chicken fight." No way in hell was Emily, the mother of my children, being put at risk. She could be, couldn't she? We did fuck like rabbits as Nat pointed out. She told me once that she and Libby always wanted kids close in age. Aria needs playmates.

"Not going to happen." Nat was already on Gabe's shoulders. I put my arms around Lemon Drop.

"I'll just play with Zeke or Matty," she stated like I simply didn't want to play. My hands went instantly to her hair and I licked her lips to distract her. She groaned in my mouth as I pulled at her scalp more firmly than I should have in our mixed company.

"Man, we all know that she's yours," Tank complained. "What's next, are you going to lift your leg and pee on her?" And there I was being nice to the prick for Willow and Emily's sake. Fuck that. Gabe placed himself and Natalie between us.

Right. This wasn't the time or place for this. "Let's go." I led Emily to the stairs to get out of the pool.

"He'd probably knock her up before he peed on her," Nat said as we walked away. *Damn straight.* Emily never said a word.

I grabbed us each a bottled water and led us to the far side of the house.

"I didn't even know this was here." The large hammock was private. I sunk into it and cautiously helped her down beside me. She fit perfectly at my side. We were both quiet for a long time. Maybe she was waiting for me to explain why I didn't want her to chicken fight or maybe she knew why and an explanation wasn't necessary. Maybe we should have talked about the fact that she had never gone back on her smarties, that she never went to the chemist, and that I never wrapped up, but we didn't.

I couldn't tell you how much time passed as we rocked gently in the hammock.

"Are we really doing this?" she asked nervously. She could have been asking about anything. I took a guess.

"Getting married?"

She looked up at me and her smile eclipsed the sun, "No, that I can believe, but are we really doing it the day after tomorrow? What about my dad?" I knew that would be the one downfall to my plan to marry Lemon Drop as soon as possible.

"He's been told not to leave the state of California." She already knew that. "We could take everyone to California, get married up at the lake," I offered. It would probably make my plan to be married before her birthday near impossible, but if it made her happy, I would do it in a heartbeat.

"No, New York is our home, it's where our story began."

The idea of saying it made me ill, but I would do anything for this woman. "We can wait for your dad to clear up his legal issues." *Please say no, please say no, please say no,* I began to chant over and over again in my head.

"What were you just thinking?" She put her hands on my shoulders and pushed me back and carefully straddled me before bending forward and kissing my forehead. Were the words I was silently pleading running across it like a ticker tape? "We're going to be husband and wife, Dec, you can tell me anything."

"Wife," I tried the new title out. I liked it. Mrs. Declan Hayes.

"Yes, now tell me, husband." I liked the sound of that too. Yeah, Mr. and Mrs. Declan Hayes. *She better not plan on fucking hyphenating anything.*

"Do you have any idea how much you mean to me? You changed my life. I don't want to go another day without you being my wife," and because I didn't ever want her to feel like by marrying me she was giving herself up I added, "without me being your husband."

"I don't want to wait, either."

"Thank fuck." She raised her brow at me.

"You're probably going to have to start working on cleaning up that mouth of yours." Holy shit. Did she know something I didn't know? Was she just talking about the future? Nothing more was said. She would tell me when the time was right, hopefully soon.

"Holy shit, there's a sick sixty-five Shelby GT 350 in your driveway. Who does it belong to?" I had no idea Gabe was such a gearhead, but he had a glow about him when he rejoined us on the deck. If he was a girl, I would think he just had the best orgasm of his life.

"No way! Are you sure it's a sixty-five? Seeing that on the road is like seeing a unicorn." Tank moved faster than I thought possible. That day was the first time I'd seen his injuries. I knew he had a limp, but I never realized he lost his left leg below his knee due to a roadside bomb while on tour in Afghanistan. He's always worn pants at the bakery. I felt like a bastard because I hadn't taken the time to learn anything about him or his story but since he was important to my soon-to-be-bride I would.

He pulled himself out of the pool and yelled at Fay that he needed his leg. She and Tyler were fascinated with it and had been "playing" with it much to the dismay of their mothers. If they had been allowed they would have played fetch with Hund with it.

I looked around and realized my parents were nowhere to be found. Maybe they were inside talking to the owner of the vehicle in question. I got out of the pool too. Fine whiskey or wine I could appreciate and tell you most anything about. Cars, not so much. Don't get me wrong, I liked driving them. That was about as far as my appreciation for them went. Tank grilled Gabe about the car as he put his prosthetic on, and soon, the two car junkies were headed out to drool over the "thing of beauty".

"Who are you looking for?" Marion asked when I arrived in the kitchen.

"My Mam and Da." I couldn't help but smile.

"I think they are still talking to that lovely young lady in the study," Gwen answered. What young lady? From the way Gabe talked about the car, it sounded like something a guy would drive.

"Thanks," I said with a wave of my hand as I headed in that direction. Emily, who had been changing in our bedroom, came down the stairs, looking as beautiful as ever.

"What's going on?" she asked as she joined me at my side and laced our fingers together.

"That's what I'm trying to find out." Knowing our luck, it wasn't good. The study door was closed so I knocked and waited impatiently for permission to enter.

"Come in," my father offered from behind the closed door. My mother and a young woman were on the sofa, embracing each other. From the sniffles we heard it was obvious they were both crying. I tightened my grip on my fiancé's hand. I didn't like seeing my Mam upset.

Concern must have flashed in my eyes. "It's all right mhac, they are happy tears." My father offered before I could ask, and I relaxed my grip on my poor Lemon Drop's hand. The women's attention turned to us.

"Declan, come here, son." It felt really good to hear her call me that. "Let me introduce you to my sister, your aunt. Shelby, this is Declan and my daughter-in-law to be, Emily." She looked like a younger version of my mother.

After introductions were made, my mother asked her half-sister to stay and enjoy the rest of the day with us. After the way Lurena treated me, I wasn't so sure this was a great idea, but it was what my mother wanted, so, for now, I would reserve judgment on my newest relative. My mother deserved to be surrounded by family and friends. She gave up everyone and everything she ever knew when she had me. She was eighteen and alone. What she'd done with her life was remarkable, but now that we are reunited, I hoped she could have what I now had in abundance. Love.

"You might want to go out and rescue your car," I offered as we left the study.

"Let me guess, someone's a wrench." She didn't seem surprised that her vehicle was causing a commotion. "Sometimes I think I should just trade it in for a bat mobile or the wiener mobile. I'd probably get less attention that way." I couldn't help but laugh. This car must be something really special if it gets more attention than a giant hot dog.

"See for yourself." It appeared that every male was now in the driveway ogling her vehicle. My father whistled in appreciation and all eyes turned to us.

"Everybody this is Shelby, my aintín." She was younger than me, but that's what she was. Sure, maybe only by half, but any way you sliced it, if my mam wanted her around, she was family. Emily chuckled at my side.

"You drive a Shelby and your name is Shelby," Gabe pointed out.

"Just like Hund. Dog, the dog." Lemon Drop laughed, and I couldn't help but join her.

Tank stood staring open-mouthed. "Does anyone want a ride?" Shelby asked. If Grandma Rose were there, she would tell him that he would catch more flies with honey, and that's what Shelby was, a honey. I only had eyes for one woman, but I'm a guy. She's a very attractive girl. Some might even say she's sexy, but she's my aunt, so it won't be me.

I guess I was wrong, Tank *could* move faster.

CHAPTER
twenty-four

"What's this?"

I came straight to Suzie's loft from the city clerk's office where Emily and I secured our marriage license. On the way back to the city, we talked about how I got her grandmother's ring and my proposal. Brit was anxiously waiting for my arrival. She hugged me tight and told me she was happy for us.

"I still can't believe my mom sent this to you right after she met you at Christmas."

"What can I say? I'm a total stud." I knew I wouldn't get any arguments from my girl. Let's just say that the fireworks in the sky last night were nothing compared to the ones we let off in the bedroom.

"Mmhmm, my stud muffin." She placed her hand on my lap.

"Careful, fiancée, or we will never make it back to the city." As much as I liked where she was going with her hand, we didn't have time for an accident, so I laced our hands together.

"And you really wore it around your neck the entire time you were gone?"

"You weren't only inside of my heart, you surrounded it." I lifted our joined hands to my lips and kissed her.

"Were you really going to ask me to marry you on New Year's Eve? We hadn't even said I love you. Well, not sober, anyway

"Such a smartass. Yes. I had it all planned. I was going to drop to my knees and profess my love at the stroke of midnight and beg you to be my wife." I'm not sure that I'll ever stop feeling guilty about leaving her the way I did. Even if she thinks it ended up making us better in the long run.

"Don't do that." How does she always seem to know what I'm thinking? *"Because I know you, future husband of mine."* Dang, she's good. *"So why did you change your mind yesterday?"* Yesterday, I planned the same proposal. I was going to do it at the end of the fireworks display, surrounded by our friends and family.

"Because I couldn't wait another minute."

"Good answer and I might be a little biased, but I think what you did was very or should I say beary romantic." God, I love this woman. *"I can't wait to marry you tomorrow."*

Suzie held her own giant folder in her hand. "That's your wedding checklist. You might think this is going to be a piece of cake, but it's not." Suzie was all business.

"Speaking of cake." Brit hopped up and down in her seat beside me excited; Suzie shot her a warning glare.

"We do this by the list." Maybe I was wrong about who wore the pants in Suzie and Eric's relationship.

Thank goodness we had already decided the night before that Fay would be a flower girl, Libby would be Emily's maid of honor, and Logan would be my best man. We didn't need a big wedding party or have time for one.

"So you've already told everyone about tomorrow, but still, need to give them the specifics." A vague e-mail was sent to everyone we wanted to invite that wasn't already at the house. We didn't want our wedding to become a media circus.

"Emily wants to get married outside," Brit added, like I didn't already know. I knew the perfect place.

"Central Park."

"Not going to happen." Suzie didn't hesitate. "You need a permit and that takes twenty to thirty days." *What the hell? It's a public park.* "I'm serious, Declan. You won't be able to get one. Don't waste our time."

Fuck that shit. We are getting married in Central Park. I got out of my chair and made a few phone calls.

"I told you." Suzie wasn't being smug but it still pissed me off. While I had spent the last forty-five minutes on the phone, Brit had called Jasmine at the flower shop and Suzie had secured a small cake. I had other plans for dessert, but I also wanted to follow tradition. We're only doing this once.

"You look so defeated, my friend," Matt said when he walked in the door with Hope, I mean Kenzie, and Eric.

"Yeah, well, who would have thought it would be such a pain in the ass to get married in a public place. It's got to be Central Park." Now that I had it in my head, I was certain it was exactly where we were supposed to become man and wife.

"You're Declan Hayes; can't you call the mayor or some shit like that?" I already had. I shook my head and tried to think of some other way to make it happen. I was drawing a complete blank.

"Maybe if you made a trade," Kenzie offered before lifting her phone and walking out of the room. We tried to brainstorm other locations while Kenzie was on the phone but Matt compelled us to hold tight. Suzie grew more and more flustered as time ticked by.

"Done." Kenzie smiled and we all looked at her like she had lost her mind. "What, I know a few people." Everyone began to laugh, yeah, she definitely knew a few people.

As soon as Suzie talked to a few more of her contacts, another e-mail was sent out to all our guests asking them to meet us at Swayed for cocktail hour at noon.

"You've got another problem, Declan." Suzie pointed at the large map of the park. We had already arranged transportation and thanks to Kenzie, the city coughed up the permit we needed. "This area is going to be really crowded especially because of what Kenzie has planned. You're going to need people to get to the area early to stake it out and everyone you know is going to be at the wedding ceremony."

Well, shit. She was right. Where could I get a lot of people who would drop just about anything they had going on to help Lemon Drop? I could ask my staff at Hayes Investment Properties, but it probably would make me look like a complete dick. *Hey, can you come early to my wedding and as soon as we arrive leave?* Yeah, that would not be good. I thought about it some more and then it hit. Everyone loved The Muffin Lady.

"She's a lovely girl, son." The apartment was quiet. I'd been sitting there trying to write my vows. All the ladies were already at the hotel being pampered and my best man was at the restaurant preparing our feast.

I missed Lemon Drop the night before. Instead of a rehearsal dinner, we had a family birthday dinner at my father's apartment. It was nice. Cheryl and my mam cooked all of the girls' favorites and we had two small cakes. One for each of them, but at the end of the night, Emily, Libby, her mother, and mine all left for an impromptu hen night. The guys all came over and we played poker. Well, some of us played poker; Matt was on the phone most of the night. I knew what Kenzie did was a big deal, but until I heard him make arrangements, I had no idea how big. Matt had come a long way from his t-shirt days for Emily. I was impressed. I slept in my bed at my father's place alone. Slept being the farthest thing from what I actually did. No, I spent most of the night with Suzie's damn binder, making sure I had every I dotted and every T crossed for my bride's special day.

"She is." My future wife was truly amazing. "Thank you for your help yesterday." The day wouldn't have been possible without my parents, or maybe I should say the night. While I planned our wedding and Emily shopped for her dress and made arrangements for Mama M's in her absence, my parents planned our honeymoon. I didn't know everything they had planned, but I did know that my wife and I would be spending her birthday in Dublin, just as I promised.

"I'm proud of you, son." I'd waited my whole life to hear my father say those words.

"Thank you, Da, that means a lot to me." It really did. He looked down at my blank piece of paper.

"Just tell her what's in here. It will never lead you wrong." He placed his hand on my chest and tapped twice, just like he had always done to the photo he carried in his pocket of my mother and then he left me to my thoughts. Like I said before, it's funny how much can change so fast.

"Thank you for coming," I greeted our guests at the restaurant. I got a lot of strange looks, but I didn't care. This was our day. Cam, Suzie's intern who was also an aspiring photographer, took photos. He was also the kid that I kept sending across the hall with gifts for Emily when I royally pissed her off. Suzie said he was good and I trusted her. Photographing our wedding could have been just the break he needed.

"You look ridiculous," my best friend said in greeting, which was amusing since he was the one with a baby strapped to his chest. As Cam took our photos, we helped each other pin boutonnieres of English lavender to our lapels. Like all the flowers I had given her before, those too represent something on our special day. Love and devotion.

"So do you, and I wouldn't change it for the world. Would you?"

"Me either." I didn't know what happened to the tatted bad boy I met all those years ago because he was nowhere in sight. At one point in time, I would have laughed at you if you ever told me that Logan and I would ever be friends and now today he's going to stand by my side as I marry the love of my life, and if everything goes according to plan, one day soon I'd be able to call him my brother.

"Let's do this."

"Ready." Logan was to my left and Theo and Alva to my right. A small group of our invited guests stood nearby along with a few park visitors who had stopped to watch, including Tank and my aunt. They seemed to hit it off on the Fourth and he asked her to be his date. *He better not be messing with her just to fuck with me.* Our best friends and family lined the bridge. Yes, the bridge that was in the picture above our bed. This image before me was so much better, and I would remember it for the rest of my life.

She arrived in the same horse and carriage she rode in last December. She told me it was magical the first time, and that the white horse was meant to bring good luck. I hoped she was right. I'm not superstitious, but couldn't we all use a little magic and luck sometimes?

Fay led the way. We may have gotten a permit, but we're still not allowed to toss anything, so she was blowing bubbles as she made her way across the bridge and having a blast. We couldn't toss petals, and assholes toss trash constantly, but I wasn't going to let anything ruin our day.

Libby was next.

"I thought you were supposed to be keeping me calm." Because his hand was on my shoulder, I felt him falter when he saw his girl. She looked beautiful, but I couldn't wait to see her sister.

"I'm going to marry that girl." My best friend was whipped, take it from a guy that knew firsthand.

"Yeah, well, wait your turn. Today belongs to me and Emily." As Fay and Libby got closer, the bells began to chime. A lot more people have stopped to watch, but I didn't care. As she passed them on the bridge, they began to ring their bells and follow behind her. Her hair was braided, as a symbol of luck and power, and she wore a wreath of wildflowers similar to Fay's in her hair instead of a veil. In her hands, she carried Bells of Ireland. Her dress was simple yet elegant, just like my bride. She looked absolutely stunning. I could no longer stand the distance between us and strode toward her. She stopped when I reached her, as did all the bells. New York city was silent, and I swear we were the only two people in the park.

"Waiting for me?" she asked before handing her bouquet to her mother who was at her side. I was speechless as she tied my tie—the Tartan tie she gave me for Christmas that was hanging loosely around my neck. I thought this would remind her of her father. He'd made a mess of his life, but I knew she still wished he was there for her big day. This is something they shared, and now my wife would share it with me.

"Thank you," she said with a pat after finishing and I knew that my gesture had served its purpose. I had been asked several times why my tie wasn't knotted, and Cam even suggested my mother tie it for some photos, but I just said I had it covered, and laughed off questions. Nobody else might get it, but we did, and that was all that mattered to me.

"Always," I was finally able to answer as I took her hand in mine so that we could stand before our friends and family and vow our love to each other. The single harp began to play softly as Theo and Alva welcomed our guests.

"Welcome friends and family to the union for Emily and Declan. We're not going to ask if anyone here feels that they should not be joined together because even someone blind could see that these two belong together." The crowd laughed. "Who supports this woman in her marriage to this man?"

"We do," everyone answered together. Theo and Alva spent the next few minutes talking about the foundation for a solid marriage. I'm sure it was meaningful, but honestly, I couldn't tell you a word they said. I was transfixed by my beautiful bride.

"Declan, today you will be joined to Emily forever. The promises and vows that you make this day will guide you in your future," Alva prompted me to begin.

I had so many things I wanted to say to her. The words I wrote could not express what I feel. "Somebody important told me to just tell you what's in my heart." I took a moment to tap my chest and look at my parents. They were holding hands, and my mother was trying not to cry.

"I love you, son," my father mouthed. *Wow.* I didn't know if I'd ever get used to him telling me that. Emily squeezed the hand she was still holding as I took her other one in mine.

"Lemon Drop, I love who you were yesterday, who you are today, and who you will become tomorrow. You make me a better man, a better person, and I promise to spend my life making you proud to be my wife. I know I won't always be perfect, but I also know that you will stand by my side no matter what. You give me hope that anything is possible. You give me faith that big things can grow from small. You give me trust in a world where it's so much easier to see the bad instead of the good. But most importantly, you give me your unyielding love. You don't just have mo chorí you are mo chorí. Is breá liom tú, Emily Grace. I gcónaí agus go deo. I love you. Always and forever." I don't know when everyone, including me, started crying.

Theo repeated his wife's earlier words, "Emily, today you will be joined to Declan forever. The promises and vows that you make this day will guide you in your future."

"You're a tough act to follow, Declan Hayes." Everyone laughed and my swan took a graceful moment to collect herself before continuing. She let go of our joined left hands and placed her hand on my chest. "I know you didn't always think so, but I knew from the very beginning that you have the biggest heart of anyone I have ever known in my life." I shook my head in disbelief. *No, that's her, not me.* "Let me finish. I know your heart, Declan, because you gave it to me. You are patient and kind. You would do anything for someone you care about. You always trust. Always hope. Always protect. Because of you, I know that our love will never fail. Mo chorí, my heart. It is yours to have faith in, to trust in, to hope for, and to protect. I give it to you again on this day, because without yours I'm just Emily, and the only thing I want to be in this life and the next is mise go deo agus I gcónaí. Yours. Always and forever. Is breá liom tú, I love you, Declan Kieran Hayes."

"May we have the rings?" Alva and Theo asked in tandem. Libby and Logan both stepped forward. Theo began, "Emily and Declan, these rings are a symbol of your love and commitment to each other." Alva continued, "Imperfect metal has been formed to create something striking, a symbol of perfection, completion, and eternity."

"It is worn on your ring finger because of the vein that runs directly to the heart. Wear these as a visible, outward

283

sign of the promises you have just made to each other," Theo finished before handing me Emily's ring.

"I give you this ring, as a symbol of our love. For today, tomorrow, and all of eternity." Her eyes never left mine as I slipped the simple band on her finger.

Alva handed my ring to Emily and she repeated the same words as she slipped my band on my finger. It was then that she looked down at the Ammolite bands. When I told the jeweler about the mood rings we wore, he told me he had the perfect thing. Gone were the dime store trinkets. They were replaced by white gold bands inset with the multi-color gemstone. I was glad that the predominate colors were blue and purple. The color of love and happiness, but I knew that sometimes red, yellow, and green would be present in our marriage. Good times and bad were inevitable, but I knew that together we were strong. Emily giggled when she looked at the rings. Yeah, they were perfect.

"Emily and Declan will now be bound together." My mother handed Alva the cord that was sent from Ireland by my Great Grandmother, Anastasia, and arrived just that morning. We held hands as Alva began to weave the cord around our hands before tying a knot.

"These are the hands of your best friend. These are the hands that will work alongside you as together you build your future. These are the hands that will passionately love you and cherish you through the years. These are the hands that will comfort you like no other. When fear and grief fill you, these are the hands that will hold you up and make you strong. These are the hands that will wipe away your tears, happy or sad. These are the hands that will hold your children. They will be what holds your family together as one. When you are wrinkled with age, these will be the hands that still give you the same unspoken tenderness with just one touch as you share today."

Alva wiped away a tear from her eye and cleared her throat. "You have professed your love by exchanging vows and rings, but we have one more question for you." Theo took her hand and they continued together, "Do you promise to love each other, comfort each other, honor and keep each other in sickness and in health, forsaking all others, to be faithful to each other for as long as you both shall live?"

Without hesitation, together we answered, "I do."

The crowd began cheering and ringing the bells. I'm pretty sure Alva and Theo said something about pronouncing us husband and wife, and they might have given me permission to kiss my wife, I'm really not sure because all I could focus on was getting my lips on my Lemon Drop.

"Will someone please untie us?" Emily grinned as Theo began working at the knots. Somebody was either a heck of a sailor or liked to play with rope. As soon as we were free, we were in each other's arms.

"This is simply amazing, husband, thank you." Her happy smile was all the thanks I needed. "I love you."

"I love you too."

A line of pedicabs arrived to whisk our guests away while we remained on the bridge for photos before I lifted her into the ornate carriage she had arrived in earlier.

"The boats?" she asked when we arrived at Conservatory Water.

"Yeah. For the journey we're about to start together." I helped her down and my father handed us our vessel. I had asked him a million times when I was a kid to do this. We never did. I didn't ask him that day. I think it was his way of saying again how sorry he was. He didn't have to apologize. He was already forgiven.

"Thanks, Da, I love you too." That was all I said. It was everything.

We placed our boat in the water and the crowd cheered as champagne in plastic flutes for the toast were handed out.

Logan and Libby stood before us. "As the best man and maid of honor, we were asked to give a toast," Logan began as Libby fetched what looked like a white wire cage from the bottom of the pram our niece was sleeping in.

My niece. It dawned on me that Aria was officially my niece.

"Do you know what they are doing?"

"No idea." I shrugged before kissing my wife.

"We thought about reading one of those Irish blessings," Libby continued. "You know, may the road rise up and all that blah, blah, blah. But instead, we decided that today was about celebrating a new beginning." That it was.

"So, lift your glass for Emily and Declan as they release these butterflies as a symbol of luck, love, and blessings for their union." Emily held up the cage and together we lifted the lid as hundreds of little yellow butterflies filled the air around us and our guests raised their glasses in agreement. I took my bride in my arms and kissed her. Surely, she was the greatest blessing I had ever received.

"Are we going to the restaurant now?" Emily asked as we boarded the antique trolley that would take us all to our next location. She had no idea what I had planned. I avoided answering her by kissing her. It's amazing how accommodating the city became once Kenzie called them. She looked pretty ridiculous in her floppy brim hat and too large for her face sunglasses, but I was glad she and Matt were still able to share the day with us instead of worrying about the night. We'd never be able to thank her for what she did to make the most important day of our lives possible.

Just as Suzie had predicted, the park was abuzz but thanks to a call the day before to The Bowery; we had just what we needed when we arrived at the Sheep's Meadow for our picnic reception.

The Tartan blankets we spread out and surrounded by a large group of people all wearing Mama M's #bestmuffintopsinnyc t-shirts. They all cheered for the muffin lady when we got off the trolley.

"I can't believe they did this for us." Didn't she know by now how many people would do anything for her? She was overcome by the number of volunteers who were there to save our spots in the well-known picnic area.

"You're kidding, right?" All I had to do was say the words "favor for Emily" and Joe was all in. He assured me that anyone at The Bowery would do anything for the muffin lady and the stocking man. I didn't know I had been given a nickname, but it was one I would always treasure.

Based on the smile on my wife's face, I would say she was pretty happy with the day so far. We'd finally just made it to our sweetheart picnic blanket surrounded by our guests who were then surrounded by our friends from The Bowery. Greta had supplied all of the volunteers with her delicious box lunches. I was sure it was a special treat, but I knew they would have helped regardless of the offer to feed them. You know the old saying, you reap what you sew? Well, my bride sewed love and a giving heart and it was coming full circle.

"I can't believe you pulled all of this together so fast. It must have cost a fortune, Declan." Frankly, I couldn't care less how much it cost. I would have spent my entire fortune to make her mine, and by comparison to other weddings I'd attended in the past, I knew I'd gotten off pretty cheap. All that mattered was that Lemon Drop was now officially my wife.

"I'm just glad you're happy." I pressed my lips to hers and our guests all began to cheer. It was probably a good thing, because if it weren't for them, I didn't know if I would have been able to stop myself. Getting arrested for public indecency wasn't on my list of things to do that day. Or any day, for that matter.

"Blissfully. How do you say husband in Gaelic?"

"Fear céile."

"Fear céile," she repeated after me and the words were both sweet and sexy coming from her lips.

I distracted myself with our basket. "Shall we eat, bean chéile?"

"Your wife?" she asked with a smile, and I nodded as I held up a skewered piece of watermelon and cheese with some sort of drizzle. I put my hand below the food as to not get anything on her beautiful dress just like I did when we ate fondue.

We continue feeding each other from our basket. Logan created an amazing meal. One that we would never forget. Guests had come over to wish us congratulations and we'd kissed every single time a bell began to chime. Since we didn't have crystal and silverware to clang for us to kiss, it had been replaced by the bells.

"I'm stuffed." We'd finished our meal and somehow I ended up with my head in her lap. One hand ran through my hair as she leaned back against the throw pillows that also adorned our blanket. Other than her sitting in my lap, I think that was my favorite position. *Maybe we should consider getting rid of our couch.* "This has been the best day ever."

"It's far from over, Lemon Drop." Although I could have laid like that forever, I got up and helped my bride up.

289

I took her hand in mine and we began our walk toward our next destination. It was just across the meadow. I knew Nat and Libby weren't happy when I told them I wanted Emily in flat, comfortable shoes, but I knew my bride, and I knew at the end of the day, she wouldn't be the one complaining about her sore feet.

"Are we doing what I think we are doing?" I could hear the excitement in her voice,

"That depends on what you're thinking," I said with a suggestive wink. Most of our friends and family were now walking behind us. I couldn't help but laugh when she realized that we weren't exactly alone on our walk.

"I've always wanted to ride." I'd ridden before, but like the boats at the conservatory, I always wanted my parents to bring me; not a nanny or a school event. I was no longer a child. I was a successful businessman, with a wife, and hopefully soon a family of my own, but it seemed like the day to really put those things I had always longed for in the past. The photos that I took there in Central Park would no longer be things that I had always wished for because I had sailed model boats, shared a picnic with my family in the park, watched my wife walk across a span of water so that we might be joined together, and now ridden off together.

I tried to rent out the entire carousel but wasn't successful. That idiot Trump held the lease from the city, and according to my people, he was still pissed about the deal we stole right from under him, thanks largely in part to my bride. Something incredible happened when we took our place at the end of the line. It was like when Heston parted the Red Sea. Everyone in line let our entire party go ahead. *And they say New Yorkers are rude?*

I helped my wife mount a white stallion and I took the one at her side. We probably looked ridiculous, but I didn't give a rat's ass. It was our day. Emily hadn't mentioned the pictures, but I knew she was thinking the same thing as I was. I couldn't wait to get our wedding photos back. It was time the old pictures were replaced for good.

"We'll see you guys later," Matt said with a quick bro hug to me while Kenzie and Emily hugged like they were never going to see each other again. *Women.* Matt snuck away to check on things after the ceremony. Kenzie stayed tucked between his brothers, Mark and Mike. It could have been a big problem if she had been recognized. I guess nobody thought she would be out in plain sight. Sometimes, that was the best place to hide.

"Where will we see you later?" I could tell Emily was confused by that. She still had no idea what Kenzie did for us so that the day would be possible, and I was sure she was thinking that our festivities would soon be over. Yes, I loved our friends, but no way in hell was our honeymoon going to be a group trip.

The old Matt would have jumped all over this. Instead, he just kissed my girl on the cheek and told her, "It's a surprise."

"Wow, he's not the same guy." I didn't really mean to say my thought out loud.

"Love is a powerful thing." Truer words had never been said.

"That's for sure. It's time to cut the cake."

Suzie said the cake was "small". I guess by her "fabglam" standards it was small. It was probably a good thing Suzie didn't do half-assed because I knew my Lemon Drop would want everyone to have cake, even though the lunch boxes Greta made The Bowery volunteers included a giant cookie.

"Oh, Declan." I couldn't tell you much about the cake, but I can tell you that my wife liked it, and I would bet you a million bucks based on the yellow color of the frosting and the slices of fruit that decorated the side that the flavor was, you guessed it, lemon. A lemon cake for my lovely Lemon Drop. Suzie totally nailed it.

"Thank you," I mouthed to the woman that helped me make our day so wonderful. My friend was lucky to have, like me, married up.

"Be nice," she pleaded as I raised a small piece of cakes to her lips and she raised one to mine. She opened, and I just did that. Now Lemon Drop wasn't so sweet. She had dipped her finger in frosting, and when she placed her piece in my mouth she sneakily dabbed the end of my nose. "Oh, my, dear husband. Look what I've done." And before I could wipe away the sweet spread, she leaned forward and licked it off my nose. Just like she did with my birthday cake.

"You'll pay for the later," I whispered in her ear and goose bumps rose on her arms and my pants got uncomfortable again. *Damn, the things this woman does to me.*

"I hope so." *Fuck me.*

"Emily," I warned.

"Fine, I'll be good. We've cut the cake. What else do we need to do?" It seemed to me that I wasn't the only one anxious to begin the honeymoon.

"You still have a few more surprises." Before she could complain, I pointed one out.

"Have I told you today how amazing you are? How blessed I am to be your wife?" I'm the lucky one.

"I'd give you the world, bean chéile."

"I know you would, but I don't need the world, I just need you, fear céile."

I hired the cart with the crème brûlée we shared on our first date as one of her surprises. Like that day, I took only one of the perfectly torched treats and cracked the topping with the side of our spoon.

"Open up," I commanded, just like she did that first night. I already knew she was different from any woman I had ever met before, but I think that night maybe she saw something in me. She called me "hoity-toity" and then I told her I had to kiss her. I think that kiss sealed our fate, and when she welcomed me to her world, I prayed that I would never have to leave.

"Now it's our world," she said with a grin as if she was remembering that night too before she held up the spoon to my mouth. Yes, it was, and it was as sweet as the crème brûlée.

We held hands and handed out small white boxes containing pieces of the famous Sutherland fruitcake to our guests.

"I have one more surprise for you." The trolley car returned to the meadow to take us to our next location.

"Where are we going?" Emily was the one person I knew who didn't live or die by social media. If it weren't for Nat, she probably wouldn't even have any pages, so I knew she wouldn't learn the news that way. I was just surprised nobody had mentioned it. She had talked to every single guest and all The Bowery volunteers.

"You'll see, but not yet. In fact, it's time for you to put these on." First, I covered her eyes and then her ears. I loved the fact that she trusted me so completely. No complaints or arguments, just total faith in me. Once she was unaware of her surroundings, Suzie and Nat worked to hand out credentials. According to Matt, it was about to get crazy. I wasn't so sure it was a good idea.

"It's going to be fine." Eric must have sensed my concern. Mark and Mike had volunteered their services as well. They nodded in agreement. They were trained professionals, but she was the most valuable thing I have ever had in my life. I wouldn't put her in jeopardy. Ever.

I don't think I'd ever seen so many people at Rumsey, and to think the first announcement was just made the day before. I could only imagine what a zoo it would be if more advance notice had been given. Somehow, we were ushered to our spot without incident. Lemon Drop was cradled in my arms because it was simpler than trying to direct her through the mass of people and equipment without the aid of sight or sound.

Showtime. I stood in front of her. I wanted her to know that I was there with her. I knew she could feel my presence. First, I removed her mask and she blinked several times before taking in our surroundings. Once she figured out where we were, I took off the headphones. The noise was almost deafening. Excitement crackled in the air all around us. Seconds later, the crowd erupted when Kenzie took the stage. I could hardly believe it was the same girl who called herself Hope while she hid that she was country music royalty from us. She was the princess of Nashville. This was Music City's little darling and she was putting on this free concert in the park for us so that we could have the wedding of our dreams.

"Thank you, New York." I was wrong, it could get louder. Amongst the screaming fans was my wife, who stood beside me at the edge of the stage while our guests were in a VIP section at the front of the stage. "I love you too," Kenzie responded to the numerous I love yous that were screamed.

"I know you came to hear me, but today I have a very special treat." The crowd quieted slightly as she talked to them. "Today, a very good friend of mine got married." That had them cheering again. "She gave me hope when I had lost it." Emily took my hand and dropped her head on my shoulder. "And because of her, I met a very special guy." Not that I paid attention, but from what I'd heard, the tabloids were always all over Matt and Kenzie. They seemed good together. They were happy and that made my wife happy, so even though she lied about who she was, I'd let it go. I wasn't around when the truth came out. It wasn't pretty, but they seemed to have gotten past it. "He happens to be crazy about the bride too—" she tossed a wink our way "—so he's agreed to sing this little song we've been working on together while they share their first dance." Matt joined her on stage with a guitar around his neck.

"I can't believe it." I tightened my hold on her hand. Believe it, baby.

"Please join us in welcoming to the stage for the first time as man and wife, Mr. and Mrs. Declan Hayes." All the lights went out and one spotlight followed us out to the center of the stage. It was all surreal. Kenzie played the piano while Matt strummed the guitar. I took her in my arms as Matt asked God to give him a lifetime. Or in our case, us. The crowd swayed back and forth to the song holding glowing yellow sticks and a huge screen above us flashed images of Emily and me together. I didn't even want to know how they put it all together. In this lifetime, I didn't know that another moment would ever be more perfect.

I wiped my wife's tears as the song came to an end. "I love you, Lemon Drop."

"And I love you, my Irish Car Bomb." Impossibly, we were the only two people on the field. I had no doubt that I was loved. By her, and by many others.

"Was our wedding everything you wanted?" I hoped I had made all her dreams come true.

"Almost." I didn't know what I missed, but I would do anything to make it right.

"What'd I miss?" *I'm serious. I'll do anything for this woman.*

"I still haven't made love to my husband." My wife broke her serious poker face and smiled shyly at me.

"Your wish is my command." And with that, I swept her off her feet and carried her off stage; the crowd went crazy and our friends and family waved their goodbyes. I had a promise to keep to my wife, and I fully intended to keep it. Over and over again, if I had anything to say about it.

EPILOGUE

Emily

One Year Later

I stretched and couldn't help the grin on my face when I caught a glimpse of my husband sitting in the chair across the room near the window. This is my favorite time of day. I knew it was his too. Sometimes, I had to pinch myself just to be sure this is real and not a wonderful dream. For our first wedding anniversary, my husband presented me with tickets back to Ireland. I almost fell as deeply in love with the Emerald Isle as I was with the beautiful man that had eyes the very color our honeymoon spot was known for. A soft knock on the door interrupted the awe in which I stared at the man that I loved so much, or should I say, *men*. In his strong arms, he holds our Carrick, our rock. We didn't call him that because of his size, no we called him that because of the strength he showed even before he left my womb. Declan rose smoothly from his seat and smiled brightly at me when he realized that I was already awake.

"We're you watching us again?" he asked with a hint of amusement in his voice. I sat up further in the bed and brought the covers up to cover myself, although I was wearing a nightgown, it could have been anyone at the door. Our happy little man kicked his feet in delight at the sound of our voices.

"I'm sorry, but your little raven couldn't wait any longer." Brianna, or Mam as Declan and I now affectionately called her, held a very unhappy Branna in her arms. She was swaddled in a beautiful pink blanket that Anastasia knitted for her before she passed away just after the first of the year, but because of the twins, it was the first time we had been back there. It saddened me greatly that she never got to meet them in person. Her shock of dark hair that inspired her name and nickname were all that I could glimpse as her grandmother tried unsuccessfully to soothe her. As to not be outdone by his sister, Carrick decided to join in on her displeasure. Hearing the cries of both my babies caused my milk to let down. I lifted my arms as a sign that I was ready and was first handed Branna. While I didn't really care if Mam stayed in our room while I fed our babies, she quickly excused herself. Declan had shared with her on more than one occasion how much he loved his day to start with just the four of us.

Once our daughter was settled, Declan joined me on the bed and positioned Carrick for me. With my husband at my side and our children grunting as they greedily sucked down their morning fill, I was blissfully happy. I tried to make Declan come before Anastasia passed away, but to say my pregnancy had been an easy one would be the lie of the century. He could do nothing to save his failing great grandmother, who had lived a long and wonderful life, but seeing the agony his father suffered at Finn's grave had left its mark on Dec. If he only had minutes with one or more of our unborn children he never would have forgiven himself if he had missed a single second. Luckily for us, Carrick saved us from that fate. Besides, Anastasia didn't die alone, her long lost granddaughter was right at her side, with Kian, the man that she loved right beside her.

"Do you ever think about that morning?" Declan asked while stroking the top of Carrick's head. I knew instantly what he was talking about. We were staying in this very room. Most women might find staying with your new husband's great grandmother on your honeymoon as a turn off, but not me. I couldn't imagine us going anywhere else to celebrate our union, and I loved Anastasia instantly. Much like she had Declan, she welcomed me. I would have loved to name our daughter after her, but I knew that it would be hard on him. I didn't want him to be reminded of all that he missed every time he heard our daughter's name, so instead, Anastasia was her middle name. My mother liked to tease that she wanted the entire alphabet of grandchildren now that she had an A, a B, and a C. For now, I'm happy to leave that up to Libby and Logan.

"All the time," I said as I looked down at our daughter who had her father's eyes.

"I knew you were pregnant." Most men would have been freaking out at just the thought, but not my husband. I could tell by the way he looked at Logan with Aria that he was thinking about having children of his own. *Is there anything sexier than a hot man holding a baby? Talk about melting panties, and I'm not talking about Logan.* I mean yes, he's hot, but he belongs to Libby. I'm talking about my man. I wanted to see him holding our baby, and if he was shirtless that was all the better. Like he was now. *Hello, baby daddy. Come to mama.*

"You did?" I mean, it couldn't have been that big of a surprise; we were constantly going at it and although I had said more than once that I was going to go back on the pill and that Declan needed to wear a Johnny, I never stopped him. Truth be told, I didn't want to. Libby and I always dreamed of having kids close in age. Aria needed a cousin— she ended up getting a two for one deal.

"I did." He moved closer and kissed my temple. "I knew it was twins too."

"Maybe you should have warned me before it happened," I teased. Yes, having two at one time was somewhat overwhelming, but he knew I wouldn't ever change anything about having Branna and Carrick. Twins never crossed my mind; I always thought they skipped a generation. What I didn't know then that I do know was that they ran on his side of the family as well. His grandfather, Conor, was a twin—his brother sadly passed away in infancy. Declan had come across this information while he was researching his family genealogy. They say that it only depends on the mother's genes, but I'd say that's a bunch of Blarney and I was holding the proof in my arms.

"And miss this?" He grinned before kissing me again. Yes, having a man so obviously in love with his children was H-O-T. "You're just upset that you didn't get to celebrate Sunderland's' big win." Yes, I had been looking forward to celebrating my team in a real Irish pub, but somehow seeing the plus sign on the home test I secretly picked up the day before changed everything instantly. I wasn't even sure the test would work. I wasn't that late, but the plus sign showed up long before the test said it might take.

I was in shock that morning when I left our room. Anastasia was sitting at the kitchen table enjoying a cuppa tea. I joined her at the table, still in a state of shock. "Declan reáchtáil." She moved her arms back and forth in a running action which was adorable. Although she didn't speak very much English and my Gaelic was mostly limited to terms of endearment and curses, we were still able to communicate rather well, surprisingly. She looked at me curiously before rising from her chair and going to her room. Minutes later, she returned, she kissed me on the forehead, before slipping a chain around my neck, and saying the words "leanbh". I looked down at the pendant that hung from the chain, it was a religious medallion of a saint. I'm not sure which one. I was still trying to figure out what leanbh meant. "Saint Brigid," she stated as if to explain, "for leanbh". This time, she cradled her arms and began to rock them back and forth. Holy shit, she knew. How?

Declan came in the door, interrupting us. He was sweating from his run and if we had been alone in the room, I probably would have begged him to fuck me then and there. He kissed me chastely and then did the same to his great grandmother. She began speaking to him. She was talking quickly and all I could understand were my name and a few other words sporadically mixed in. Was she telling him? I watched his face, looking for a reaction. The only thing he showed was amusement.

"It appears that we're going into the city today. She wants me to show you Ha'penny bridge and the cathedral." Anastasia winked at me. For an old woman, she was sharp as a tack. We had shown her many pictures of our wedding, Bow bridge was an important part of it.

The grunts of our children brought me back to the present. "How did you know anyway and how did you know it was twins?

"I just did and I knew for sure once I saw Saint Brigid hanging around your neck. I think she protected the three of you." Even though our children were safe and healthy now, we both would forever be grateful that they were. Whether it was to the doctors who provided my prenatal care, the team of doctors and nurses in the neonatal unit, Saint Brigid, or God himself, doesn't matter.

"This is beautiful." Declan was holding my hand as we walked across the pedestrian bridge that spanned the River Liffey.

"It is," he agreed but he was looking at me, not the bridge. We stopped at a group of locks that had been placed on the railing. "I didn't bring a lock. They cut them off every night. Not a great symbol of undying love if you ask me." I almost blurt out that I was pregnant, because to me that seemed like a perfect symbol of our love, but I didn't. Not yet.

"Come, let's go ring the bells at the Cathedral." We continued our walk hand in hand. I couldn't help but giggle at the sign painted on the street that said, "look right". Thankfully, I had my husband as my guide or I would probably find myself looking left, right, left, as I was taught as a girl.

"This is where my grandparents were married," Declan told me as I took in the beautiful church with its gorgeous stained glass windows.

"It's so pretty," I said in awe as I squeezed his hand. "I'd like to have our children baptized here," I said without thinking.

"Are you saying what I think you're saying, Mrs. Hayes?" Declan asked in awe as I finally dared to look at him. Tears sprang to my eyes, unable to speak, I nodded my head as affirmation. Without hesitation, he pulled me into his strong arms, kissed my forehead, trailed his lips down my nose, kissed the tip, and then kissed my lips before falling to his knees and kissing my stomach.

"I think you knew too. You said children that day in the church."

"Maybe you're right."

"We really should get going." I now held Carrick and tried to coax a belch out of him while Declan did the same to Branna. She loudly burped while her brother refused to give his up. I reminded myself often, that if he wasn't so stubborn we might have lost both him and his sister.

"Is everything OK?" I nervously asked as Dr. Jordan whom the technician fetched while performing our twenty-week ultrasound examined the screen. My excitement at seeing our babies had instantly changed to sheer fear. Declan's hold on my hand tightened before he lifted it to his mouth and kissed the back of it.

"I don't believe in sugar coating things with my patients, Emily. I'm not happy with what I'm seeing, but I'm going to have to refer you to a specialist for further testing." Dr. Jordan repositioned the screen so that we once again could see our babies. *"This is your son and this is your daughter."* He moved with the pointer to show us. *"This is what concerns me."* He circled a spot on the screen that was beating rapidly, over our daughter's heart. *"This halo is concerning and I'm sorry but survival this early is rare, most likely for both."* Not only was our daughter's heart broken, but so were both of ours as we left Dr. Jordan's office. I couldn't deal with all of the calls and texts from our family and friends. They were just excited to find out what we were having. What could we say? I could feel them kicking. We had a son and a daughter. This was supposed to be a happy day. I should have been baking two cakes. One pink and one blue to reveal our happy news to our friends and family. This couldn't be happening. Declan turned off both of our phones and held both me and our babies as we wept. A knock at the door startled us both awake.

"I'll get rid of whoever it is," Declan said as he kissed the top of my head.

"We need to tell them something," I croaked out. He nodded and opened the door. My sister rushed in, not giving him a chance to send her away.

"Something's wrong I can feel it." Libby's eyes were red from crying.

She knew. Of course, she knew. It's a power that only a twin can understand. It was one our little rock, Carrick, certainly knew. Two days after our appointment with Dr. Jordan, I started to bleed; the specialist confirmed that my placenta had ruptured and that worse, amniotic fluid was leaking. I was admitted to the hospital and told to prepare for an inevitable miscarriage. That's must have been when Carrick's twin-tuition kicked in, because he positioned himself underneath Branna, and that's exactly where he stayed. Four weeks later, we breathed a sigh of relief. They had a chance to survive. Somehow, our tiny son seemed to know that the future of our family rested solely on his shoulders and he stayed in that place. At thirty weeks, I went into labor and had an emergency C-section. Our children were born on January tenth. Carrick was first at three pounds seven ounces. Branna followed him at three pounds two ounces. Other than being premature, they were perfect. Nothing could be found wrong with Branna's heart. I liked to believe she had an angel named Anastasia watching over her.

We returned to the cathedral. We celebrated the life of Anastasia Flemming, and we baptized our children, Carrick Conor Hayes, and Branna Anastasia Hayes with our friends and our family by our side.

It seemed so long ago that Declan gave me that slightly crooked heart-shaped necklace filled with the Celtic knot. The points of the knot represented faith, hope, and trust. It had no beginning and no end, like the heart, our love. It was not perfect—nothing ever is—but it was ours, and I wouldn't change it for anything.

What's next?

Thank you for reading Sifted, the conclusion of Declan and Emily's story. Next, I'll be writing Mixed; Logan and Libby's story. Mixed will be standalone but of course you'll get more of Declan and Emily and the entire A Recipe for Love gang. As someone who started writing on Fanfiction, I'm used to getting reader feedback. It fuels me, so please consider leaving a review wherever you bought your copy of Sifted and/or on Goodreads.

You can also connect with me online.

Facebook:

www.facebook.com/Lane-Martin-Romance-1507950139449626/

Twitter: @bylanemartin

Website: www.lanemartin.com

If you're interested in sending a box to a soldier like Hugs from Home

visit the site www.anysoldier.com

Acknowledgements

First and foremost, thank you, my readers. I wouldn't be doing this without you. I never in a million years dreamed that I would write a book, let alone two. Secondly, I'd like to thank my husband and kids. Your support means the world to me. Abby, please forgive me for naming my villain after you. You are an incredible young woman and I'm so proud to be your momo. Never forget how proud I am of you! Justin, I can't wait for you to stop acting like a teenager! You're a pain in the ass, but I love you more that you will ever know. Gerald, you're a pain in the ass too but you're my pain in the ass and I wouldn't trade you for the world.

Danielle Wright and Jacqui Melville thank you for loving Declan and for always encouraging me. I'm so lucky to call you my friends. You are both so talented. Yes, this is a shameless plug for my amazing friends. Go read their books!

https://www.amazon.com/Danielle-Wright/e/B00QSF7ZQ8/ref=sr_ntt_srch_lnk_3?qid=1470966782&sr=8-3-spell

Rebecca and Adrien thank you for reassuring me when I doubted myself. You are so much more than a co-worker Rebecca! No matter where life takes us, I know you will always be a part of my life. Adrien, I look forward to every six weeks. Not just because I know I'll walk out of the salon with a great new look, but because I'll get to talk about books! Why did it take us so long?

Wendi Temporado thank you for putting up with my hate of the dreaded em dash and my overuse of the word that. I can see that I have a problem that I need to address. Thank you for making me look good. Vodka is on the way! Oh, and one more thing – Giblets!

To my Dutch Princess, Rebecca Pau thanks for your patience. I know I made you crazy over this cover, but I'm so glad we stuck it out. It's perfect. I love it! It's fabglam!

Micheal, I asked you to draw me Bash and June Bug. You never looked at me like I was nuts. You are one-of-a-kind. I am in awe of your perseverance. Many people would have given up when faced with the challenges that you have. You should be proud of yourself, I know I am.

Thank you to all my Controlled sisters. I can ask you, girls, anything and I always get the best responses. I couldn't be part of a better group! I know you've got my back. I hope you know that I've got yours too.

Made in the USA
Monee, IL
31 May 2021

69195474R00177